THE
REBEL
OF CLAN
KINCAID

Also by Lily Blackwood

The Beast of Clan Kincaid

THE
REBEL
OF CLAN
KINCAID

LILY BLACKWOOD

St. Martin's Paperbacks

This is a work of fiction. All of the characters, organizations, and events portrayed in this novel are either products of the author's imagination or are used fictitiously.

THE REBEL OF CLAN KINCAID

Copyright © 2016 by Lily Blackwood.

All rights reserved.

For information address St. Martin's Press, 175 Fifth Avenue, New York, NY 10010.

ISBN: 978-1-250-08475-0

Our books may be purchased in bulk for promotional, educational, or business use. Please contact your local bookseller or the Macmillan Corporate and Premium Sales Department at 1-800-221-7945, ext. 5442, or by e-mail at MacmillanSpecialMarkets@macmillan.com.

Printed in the United States of America

St. Martin's Paperbacks edition / December 2016

St. Martin's Paperbacks are published by St. Martin's Press, 175 Fifth Avenue, New York, NY 10010.

10 9 8 7 6 5 4 3 2 1

For Richard and Deanne.

Thank you for raising a hero!

prologue

Magnus stared back into the face of the man, who until this moment he had considered to be the most arrogant, most self-important, son-of-a-sow he had ever had the misfortune to encounter.

His scalp tightened and the night around him seemed to convulse as he tried to make sense of the words he had just heard.

"Did you hear what I said?" murmured Niall Brae-wick, stepping closer, his features blackened by shad-ows, the bonfire blazing behind him. "That mark on your arm proves you are not the Alwyn's bastard, as you have been led for all these years to believe . . . but that like me you are a son of the murdered Laird Kincaid."

Magnus's pulse ramped again, hearing the words repeated.

He lifted a hand to the back of his neck . . . to his mouth . . . and shifted his stance, rendered unsteady by the tangled snarl of emotions blasting up from his soul, and the crashing thunder of the words repeating in his ears.

The Laird Kincaid. A legendary Highlander who years before had voiced opposition to the crown—and afterward died violently, under the most mysterious of circumstances, along with his wife, his warriors . . .

And his three young sons.

He had heard the ghost stories. The songs the bards sang. All were believed dead. Slain. Buried in some secret haunted grove in the forest known only to those Kincaids who had survived the slaughter that fateful night, and who afterward had taken to the hills beyond Inverhaven, living life like savages rather than submit to another clan or laird.

Lairds such as his father, the Alwyn. *Not his father?* Along with their neighbor, the MacClaren. Men to whom the Crown had granted the "forfeited" Kincaid lands in the aftermath of the massacre.

And yet in recent days the Kincaids had come down from those hills. All around him, in this very moment, those "savages" celebrated their victory against the defeated MacClaren, in the orange glow of the bonfire and the shadow of Inverhaven's castle walls, which in a single day, they had shockingly reclaimed with the backing of Niall's mercenary army.

And they promised vengeance against the Alwyn next.

"We are not enemies, you and I." Niall—now installed at Inverhaven as the laird of Kincaid—grasped his shoulders, hard. "*You are my brother.*"

Magnus's childhood friend, Elspeth MacClaren, who only two days before had been tricked into marrying the Kincaid and who now claimed to love the warrior with all of her heart, moved to stand at her husband's side, her eyes wide.

"The mark on Magnus's arm matches yours?" she asked in hushed amazement.

The secret mark, located on the underside of his arm,

tucked high under his shoulder, seemed to burn on Magnus's skin. He stood rigid and silent, almost wishing he could take the moment that he had revealed it back. He had only come to see if Elspeth was safe and well after her father's defeat. Instead, in a blink, the world had turned upside down.

Him, a son of the Kincaid?

A birthmark, his mother—or the woman who had called herself his mother for all these years, a one-time mistress of the Alwyn—had whispered when, as a boy, he'd discovered the anomaly. *A devil's mark* that he must never show to anyone. He'd been ashamed to bear it . . . had lain awake at night, tormented by its presence on his skin and done his best to forget it.

But later, when he was older, he'd realized Robina's explanation wasn't true.

The mark—the one he could barely see himself for its peculiar location—had been etched there not by the Devil or even by God, but by man with ink and tool, a tattoo in the shape of a wolf's head, no bigger than a thumbprint.

And yet whenever he questioned Robina about its origins, she had steadfastly refused to speak of it, pretending as if she had not heard him. If pressed, she responded with annoyance or sometimes tears, the latter of which never failed to send him into retreat, for what man with any heart or conscience could inflict pain upon his mother?

Her silence on the matter had troubled him. Raised curious questions in his mind. He could only believe she thought to protect him from something, in some way. But instead of insisting she answer, and dwelling on his clouded past, he had centered himself on becoming the man he wished to become.

Now, in the present, the warriors who surrounded him in the darkness moved close, their faces wavering in the light of the bonfire. Old men, young men. All Kincaids, all enemies of his clan.

Not his clan? Not . . . his enemies?

"The secret mark!" exclaimed a one-eyed old man, his bushy gray eyebrows going up in amazement.

"Is it true?" demanded another, pressing close, shoulder to shoulder with others doing the same.

Magnus broke free of the Kincaid's hold and stepped back, turning away from the smothering weight of their collective curiosity and expectations, away from the light of the fire and into deeper shadows where they would not see the bewilderment on his face.

"Aye, it is true," Niall said behind him. "Look for yourselves, if you must. He is my brother—the Kincaid's second son, if I judge correctly, and his name is *not* Magnus." He spat the name, as if it were an offense. "But Faelan." Boots crunched on the earth, as he came near. "Faelan, my brother. Do you remember nothing of our childhood?"

Faelan . . . it was an ancient Irish name, meaning little wolf. A saint's name, given to Highland boys to honor a brave missionary who had traveled from across the sea.

My little wolf, the man in his dreams had said with warmth and affection. A man whose face he could never recall upon awakening, but whose spirit even in waking times seemed to reside in his soul.

"None of this makes sense," Magnus uttered beneath his breath.

All of it made sense.

He rubbed his palm between his eyes because suddenly he *hurt* there from thinking so hard, from trying to understand how his life, just like that, could fall away and be replaced by another.

A life. A family. A proud ancient legacy.

Now, his?

Having lived all his days as he could recall them, as the unrecognized and unwelcome bastard son of the Alwyn, should he not feel satisfaction that he was no bastard at all, but held claim to something meaningful? That he was the son of a once powerful and respected lord and his lady? And brother to the fearsome warrior standing behind him? Should he not feel a sense of belonging, at long last?

He did not.

Because it was a *stolen* life. An *unfamiliar* family and clan. An ancient legacy *lost* to violence, treachery, and blood. All, cruelly taken from him. A lifetime of love and kinship and memories, stolen. And by whom?

Those whom he had lived among, for as long as he could remember.

Why?

A gentle hand touched his shoulder, and he flinched.

Elspeth said, "Magnus . . . Faelan? Oh, I don't know what to call you! I can only imagine how you must feel."

He turned, glancing down into her pale face before looking beyond and higher, directly toward her husband, who remained fixed to the same spot, arms crossed over his chest, his mouth tight, looking at him guardedly, perhaps even with suspicion, as if he did not understand his response or lack thereof.

"I have questions," Magnus answered, in a guttural growl. "And I would ask that you give me time, so that I might have answers."

Elspeth nodded, her eyes soft with sympathy. "But it makes sense, don't you see? You must have suffered some injury, whether to your body or your mind, that night or soon after, and that is why you remained mute for all that time, for years after, not speaking. That is why you don't remember."

Yes, that. There had always been missing time. Missing memories from his earliest days. A blurry, indistinct blot at the center of his existence. A blot that even now remained.

"I do remember . . . some things," he murmured.

Drums beating. Fear. The flash of swords. And blood. When he'd awakened in a terror, and tried to communicate the pictures in his mind to Robina, she had told him they weren't memories at all, just nightmares that he must forget. He'd been a child, and he'd believed her.

"The memories never made sense before," he said. "Now they do."

The Kincaid, his . . . *brother*—approached, his blue eyes vibrant with emotion.

"Then stay and join me against the Alwyn. He bears responsibility for the deaths of our parents and our clansmen. Our father was no traitor against the king, and 'twas no honorable battle in which he and the others were slain. The MacClaren confessed his part, and in doing so, confessed the Alwyn's as well. It was murder, plain and clear, inspired by greed to take our clan's land and power."

Eyes wide with sadness, Elspeth whispered, "It is true."

The Kincaid clenched his fist between them. "There were others also, warriors with unseen faces and unknown loyalties, who came down that night from the hills—belonging neither to the MacClaren nor the Alwyn—who carried out the massacre. We must learn who they served." His tone became more urgent. "Faelan, the Alwyn knows who sent them."

It was too much, the thoughts crowding his mind. He needed time to think, to be alone, and decide what to do.

He speared his fingers through his hair, and backed away, muttering, "I must go. I . . . I will . . . return when I can."

His boots crunched upon the path, as he stalked away from them, delving further into darkness.

"That's it?" the Kincaid called after him, his voice hollow with dismay and accusation. "You're just going to leave?"

Magnus stopped, and looked down at the earth. At the stones and dirt and grass beneath his leather boot. Kincaid land.

His land. *His legacy.*

Turning, he found them all gathered in a line, shoulder to shoulder, looking at him.

He took several steps toward them, until he was close enough to look into his brother's eyes.

"I *dinnae* know you." His gaze swept across the faces of the others. "I *dinnae* know any of you. Ye are strangers to me—and aye, I'm angry about that."

Anger. Yes. That was what he felt. He wanted to rage. He wanted to punch a stone wall. He wanted to bellow until he was hoarse from it.

"Then stay," said the Kincaid, stepping forward out of the line. "Take your place here."

"Yes, stay," Elspeth pleaded.

He shook his head and exhaled through his nose, commanding self-control as a fury such as he had never known reverberated through his veins.

"Brothers. A mother and father. A clan." He lifted his hands, as the fire in his soul burned hotter. "It is all I ever wanted."

He paused, and clenched his hands into fists.

"But it was taken from me." His heart thundered in his chest. "I have been *grievously* deceived. Because of that deceit, all these years I have lived at that lecher's feet, a cast off. His bastard. His second best." He again met Niall's gaze, and slowly nodded. "Aye, there is revenge to be had against the Alwyn, brother—but know this. It is I who will take it."

Chapter 1

Near about the same time.

"Awaken, child," said a woman's voice, low with urgency. The dim light of a lantern washed over the stone walls of Tara Iverach's small chamber. "Your guardian sends word that he travels near and wishes an audience."

Tara pushed up on the narrow bed. The drab blanket fell away, exposing her skin to the chill. She shivered and seized the wool back against her neck and shoulders. Sister Agnes's words echoed in her ears.

Her guardian . . . Alexander Stewart, the powerful Earl of Buchan . . . *here*, in this humble place?

To see her?

"You must be mistaken," she said, her voice thick with sleep.

She had never even met him. Her "guardian" had shown no interest in her in the five years since her parents' deaths, when he had become responsible for her and her older sister, Arabel. Almost immediately he had summoned Arabel to be presented at court, while Tara had been delivered to Duncroft Priory where she had remained ever since, with only a rare letter from Arabel—once, perhaps twice a year—to remind her she had not been completely forgotten.

"I wish that I were mistaken," Sister Agnes replied with a peevish lift of her brows. "I would much rather be sleeping than tending to you. Now hurry. You must be ready before sixth hour prayers."

Tara's heart jumped, beating faster. At long last, she would meet Buchan . . . the man who controlled her destiny. But what did his visit mean? Would she be taken away from Duncroft? Would her life change somehow, from this day on? Or did the earl simply pass by in his travels, and seek to lay eyes on her for a brief moment before continuing on?

Sister Agnes took hold of her braid. Deftly unfastening it, she combed out Tara's hair with quick, brusque strokes.

Tara gasped, wincing, and rubbing at her temple.

Others entered then, two sleepy-eyed sisters carrying a small hip tub and novices with steaming buckets of water. Oh . . . a *real* bath—a rare luxury here. Most certainly she would be rushed through, and not allowed to enjoy it. Tara had learned early on that the sisters of Duncroft were not ones to waste time on indulgent pleasures, and she very much doubted her early-morning, harried bath would be the exception. After five years of living among them, each day very much a mirror of the day before, she'd learned not to expect special attention or coddling of any sort.

In less than an hour, she stood in the chapel along with the other inhabitants of the priory reciting prayers, her skin scrubbed pink and her hair tightly braided—and covered, as it was *always* covered with a veil. She dutifully murmured the words, but her thoughts wandered elsewhere.

She could not subdue her feelings of optimism. Might

this be the last time she stood here? The last time she would wear this shapeless gray gown? It was almost too much to hope for. After years of the cloister's quiet, uneventful existence, she had come to believe she would be confined here forevermore, forgotten by all, her life unlived—her heart never having loved.

Not that the other women who resided at the priory served an unimportant or unfulfilled purpose. They had chosen to devote themselves to the Lord, striving each day to center their thoughts and energies on Him.

Well, *most* of them had chosen to be here. Some were here, not precisely by choice. There was Lady Gavina, a lively and intriguing gentlewoman who had been deposited here around the same time as Tara, but by a husband who claimed she was mad in order to repudiate her so that he could marry her prettier and much younger cousin.

Lady Gavina was not the only "mad" wife at Duncroft Priory. Indeed, there was a row of rooms, just beside Tara's, each one occupied by a raving lunatic who never raved, never lunaticked. Scattered among them were a few accused adulteresses.

Some of the sequestered ladies seemed completely content to exist in the peace and quiet, away from the turmoil that had committed them here. Indeed, some only left their chambers for prayers.

Others ached to return to at least some aspects of the life they had left behind—as did Tara. She remembered happy scenes of life as it had been when her parents were alive. Now, no longer a child, she wanted to attend festivals and tournaments, as her sister described in her letters. She wanted to gossip with friends, and dance and laugh, and be introduced to—and flirt—with young men, the sort of creature she'd not caught a single glimpse of in her five long years here. Her chest tightened with wistful hope.

She wanted to *live*.

And now Buchan was coming. Perhaps now that she was twenty, he would present her at court, as he had Arabel, and she and her sister could spend their days together in happy coexistence, as they had when they were younger. Maybe not every day, because Arabel would be married soon, if she was not already, as the last letter she'd written several months before had shared the news the earl had betrothed her to the eldest son of a powerful ally.

Alwyn. It was a name she had never heard, but she heard very little within these quiet walls. Unfortunately, Arabel had always been a disappointing writer of letters and as usual, her letter was maddeningly devoid of the details Tara craved. Was Buchan a kind and considerate guardian who acted with Arabel's happiness in mind? Was she pleased with his choice of husband for her? Would she have a new gown for the occasion. If yes, was it threaded with glass beads or pearls—or both? Instead, Tara was left knowing very little about the earl's temperament, and what she might expect from him as a guardian, and whether Arabel was even happy . . .

Just as the prayers came to an end, from behind Tara there came a sudden, excited whispering of female voices. Glancing over her shoulder, she saw two dark-haired, angular-jawed young men in the doorway wearing fine leather hauberks belted with silver-studded scabbards, their boots splattered with mud. They peered inside, their cheeks ruddy, their hair ruffled as if from travel, smiling arrogantly, at least to her unpracticed eye, though she could not claim to be an expert on male expressions. Several of the younger ladies from the Mad and Adulterous Wives corridor smiled back at them.

An older man with a close-trimmed dark beard and imperious bearing joined them, shouldering between them, his features drawn with impatience. All three men had similar prominent noses and dark eyes that identified them as kin to one another. Tara's pulse tripped. It had to be Buchan. She had imagined someone older, and gray haired.

"Where is my ward?" he demanded testily, causing her heartbeat to ramp higher. "Come now, my time is important. Please don't waste it."

Sister Agnes approached him quickly, nodding and extended an arm toward Tara. "Mistress Iverach, this way."

Tara moved quickly as well, not wishing to be barked at for tarrying overlong. All along her way, the ladies stood back, watching the moment unfold. As she drew near, three pairs of male eyes latched onto her. It had been years since she had drawn the attention of anyone besides that of her fellow ladies. Her cheeks betrayed her self-consciousness, filling with heat.

Her gaze met the earl's for the briefest moment—and his eyes struck her through with their intensity.

"My lord," she murmured, bowing her head and curtsying as her mother had taught her to do so many years before, arms slightly extended.

"Mistress Iverach," he said in a low voice. "How . . . lovely you are."

"This way," said Sister Agnes.

Tara held back, waiting for the men to follow, but they only stared at her in darkly amused silence.

The earl gestured that she should go before them. "I insist."

She lowered her gaze and followed Sister Agnes. The heavy fall of their boots sounded on the stones close behind her and she felt their stares on her back. Perhaps it was only her lack of familiarity with men, but there was something distinctly unnerving about the earl and his companions. Though handsome and clearly schooled in all manner of noble manners, they cast an intimidating . . . *predatory* energy that put her on her guard. Was it intentional? Her instincts told her yes.

Her guardian was a powerful man—the king's youngest son. She realized that. Still, she had hoped to be meeting a different sort of man, someone warmer and kinder, who she might look upon as a fatherly sort of figure.

Yet . . . wasn't it wrong of her, and more than a little foolish, to render judgment based on just a few moments spent together? She was only nervous, having never met them, and unused to the company of men. And most certainly Arabel would have warned her if the earl was anything less than honorable.

No doubt Buchan and those who accompanied him were simply travel-worn and hungry, and not at their best, just as she would not be under the same circumstance. She must express gratefulness that he had traveled out of his way to visit her, and more importantly, keep her heart and mind open. Her mother, if she were still alive, would insist upon it. Also, if she impressed him perhaps he would allow her to leave the cloister for a life outside the walls, if that was not already his intention.

Sister Agnes led them to a room, in which a large table had been laid out with an extensive breakfast. Only as Tara and the men went inside, the sister drew back, remaining near the door like a sentinel statue, silent and watching. The scent of baked bread, meat, and eggs hung in the air, driving a stab of hunger through her stomach as she had not yet eaten, but she assumed they would break their fast together after introductions. Tara moved toward the hearth until she felt its warmth through her clothing, and turned to face her visitors with what she hoped was a welcoming expression.

"Welcome, my lord," she said. "I am so pleased to finally meet you."

"Hmmm, yes," the earl answered. He approached her, coming to stand so close she smelled the scent of earth and mist carried on his garments. "And I, you."

He smiled, his mouth drawing back on one side, enough to show teeth . . . something that struck her as a display of arrogance rather than a greeting of sincerity and warmth. His eyes, sharp and scrutinizing, moved over her face—and then her person—in a way that made her want to step away. To *turn* away. Instead, she forced herself to hold still, her arms at her sides, and her shoulders straight.

She heard one of the earl's companions chuckle, though she knew not which.

Inside, she bristled, for the laugh offended her. It was neither noble nor gentlemanly to make a young woman feel as she did now, as if she were the object of some private jest.

She looked at her guardian, with all hope and expectation that he would, in the next moment, redeem himself.

But Buchan's smile widened by a degree—as if he too were deeply amused by her—and then dropped from his lips completely. He peered down his nose at her as he removed his leather gloves, one by one.

"As you have surmised, I am your guardian, Buchan. These are my sons . . . Duncan Stewart, my elder—" With the hand that held the gloves, he gestured to one, with a wider face and a lock of hair that fell across his forehead, who nodded solemnly—and then to the other, who boldly held her gaze like a sharp-eyed, overconfident wolf. "And that is Robert."

They were indeed related, then, as she had surmised. Although she had already decided she did not like either of them very much, Tara acknowledged each of Buchan's sons with a nod.

He tucked his gloves into a wide belt at his waist—but his eyes . . . his eyes consumed her.

"And you, Mistress Iverach are . . . a child no more," he murmured. The earl moved closer to her, slowly circling her, coming so near she could feel his breath against her cheek and the heat of his body through the leather he wore. So close the skin at the back of her neck pricked in alarm. "A woman full grown."

He stood *too close*. And the way he looked at her . . .

"A woman full grown indeed," he growled, low in his throat.

He made her *very* uncomfortable. She looked to Sister Agnes for reassurance, but the woman stood motionless and stone faced, watching in silence.

All of a sudden, his arm came up behind her, and he caught her by the shoulder. She gasped, startled.

"Don't be frightened," he murmured intimately.

"I am not frightened," she answered, between clenched teeth.

Should she be?

At the moment she was merely appalled. She just did not like his touch—a forceful half-embrace, which joined her to his shoulder and his hip. It was too abrupt and intimate, and clearly intended as proof of his power over her.

But he was her guardian, and she must submit . . . mustn't she? It was what she had been taught, since birth, as a well-bred young woman. To respect her father, and those men her father respected, and her father had chosen this man to be her and Arabel's guardian.

"What do I see here?" he said, as his other hand came up.

She flinched, knowing he intended to touch her again.

"*Sir*," she protested softly, but firmly.

"Be still," he commanded.

He caught her chin, and forced her to look into his eyes, their faces so close she tasted his breath . . . smoke tangled up with ale, and night. Yet then he released her face and with a turn of his wrist deftly removed her veil.

She stood rigid and unmoving as his gaze moved from her face—to her hair.

His eyebrows rose, as he looked.

"How very . . . uncommon," he breathed, nostrils flaring. His grip tightened on her arm. "The color . . . so unlike your sister's."

It was often remarked upon that she and Arabel looked nothing alike, but that wasn't true. Their features were similar. It was only that her hair was red, like their father's, while her sister's was brown. Red hair was common enough, but she had been told more than once that her particular shade—

The earl's voice grew husky. "Hair like that puts wicked thoughts into a man's mind."

Her stomach clenched. The sisters of the cloister had expressed similarly mortifying opinions.

Still held in his powerful vise, Tara's cheeks flamed as the earl's gaze raked over her with far more interest than proper, given that he was her guardian and, last she knew, a married man. Her head pounded with the wrongness of the moment.

Dangerous.

Yes, he did frighten her.

She wrenched free from his grip, and stepped back several steps, turning toward the fire. She breathed deep, trying to calm herself. Trying to think of how she must speak to him, to instill a proper space and manner between them. Respect. She must command his respect.

She turned toward him, imposing a placid expression on her face.

"My lord, tell me, how does my sister fare?" she asked, her voice only slightly unsteady. "Arabel. What news can you share of her?"

Perhaps she ought not to have met his gaze again— for what she found there sent a strike of dread through her bones. Something beastly and cruel stared back at her, from the nether reaches of his dark eyes.

Behind him, his sons observed in sharp-eyed silence.

The earl's attention shifted over her shoulder, to Sister Agnes. "Could you . . . leave us alone, please? So that we might speak privately?"

Tara rarely prayed outside of morning, midday, and evening prayers, but she prayed now, and fervently. Under no circumstance did she wish to be left alone with this man and his wolfish sons.

Sister Agnes responded unwaveringly. "Forgive me, my lord, but I cannot. It is not convent practice to leave a young lady alone with any man who is not her father or her husband."

Tara held in her sigh of relief.

A sour expression flickered across the earl's face. His nostrils flared, further conveying his displeasure.

"I am her guardian," he answered imperiously.

Her relief evaporated. Would he demand and argue until he had his way?

The nun answered, with complete composure. "Which is *not* . . . her *father* or her *husband.*"

Tara decided, in that moment, that she loved Sister Agnes.

Buchan squinted his eyes menacingly, and scowled. "Must I remind you of the generous support I provide to the sisters of this abbey, in exchange for the care of my ward?"

Tara's pulse rose as he continued to insist.

"No, my lord," Sister Agnes replied, her expression unchanged. "You need not."

The earl smirked in triumph. "Then—"

Sister Agnes stood straight, her slender hands clasped at the waist of her nun's habit. Her eyes gleamed with challenge. "As I said, it is *not* . . . convent practice . . . to leave a young lady *alone* . . . with *any* man who is not her *father* or her *husband*."

Buchan rolled his eyes and let out a condescending *huff*. Duncan chuckled, amused, and strode to the table, where he poured himself a goblet of ale, and lowered himself, sprawling, into a chair. Robert joined him, sliding a goblet for his brother to fill. Behind them, the window shutters rattled, harried by a strong gust of autumn wind.

The earl thrust her crumpled veil into her hands. Crossing his arms over his chest, he paced a few steps. In the next moment, he turned to her, eyes narrowed, and pronounced, "I have come to see you because it is time, my dear child, that you are wed."

The ground shifted beneath her feet—or very well seemed to.

"Wed," she repeated softly.

Did he speak generally or had an agreement already been made? She had hoped to go to court and to live life away from the abbey and its restrictions for a time, not be married to a stranger straightaway—

But in light of the previous moments, she warned herself to tread carefully with the earl. Arabel's words returned to her then, warning her to be patient, when she had complained about being left overly long at the nunnery. Not to displease the earl—

The air left Tara's lungs. Perhaps her sister *had* warned her as best she could, and she, in her innocence, hadn't understood. Perhaps Arabel couldn't convey the truth to her. What if she'd been prevented from doing so? Someone could have read her letters. A servant in service to the earl . . . anyone. And refused to deliver anything that did not meet with his approval.

It was a terrible thought—one she didn't want to believe. But true? She did not know. Perhaps she was conjuring wild untruths, when in reality her sister had never made any real mention of the earl's qualities because he was an absent guardian, just as he had been to Tara. One who traveled extensively, immersed in his own affairs. That explanation made just as much sense.

She would only know the truth once she was reunited with her sister. Really, that was all that mattered. That she and Arabel were together again, if only for a time. So that she could see for herself that her sister was safe and well and happy. The only way to achieve that wish, was to remain in the good graces of their guardian, at least for now.

"Yes, my lord." Dutifully, she bowed her head even as her heart sank in her chest.

One corner of his lips turned upward, offering half a smile. Lifting a hand, he grazed a knuckle down her cheek.

"Good, obedient girl."

Turning toward the fire, he extended his hands and rubbed them together, warming them.

"My sister," she began in a soft, conciliatory voice. "It has been five years since I saw her last. I would very much like to see her before I am married. Is she in Edinburgh, or—"

"A beneficial betrothal has already been arranged for you," he said, speaking toward the mantel, as if he did not hear her. But she knew he had. "You will be conveyed to your new home posthaste, and married to the son of the Chief Alwyn, a powerful northern laird."

The Chief Alwyn.

Though she knew nothing of the Highlands, her heart filled with sudden brightness at hearing that familiar name—one mentioned in her sister's last letter, as the name of her own betrothed.

"To a younger son of the chief?" She nodded happily. "And so my sister will be there as well, with her husband, the Alwyn's elder son?"

"No," he answered abruptly.

He moved toward the table where his sons devoured their meal with ravenous fervor. He perused the repast that had been laid out.

"No?" she softly questioned.

Glancing at her over his shoulder, he shook his head, looking distracted. More interested in the food now than her. He took up Duncan's goblet and drank from it, and reached toward a platter. "It is you who will have the good fortune to marry the eldest son. His name is . . . Howard or"—he waved a hand—"Hugh." He paused and nodded. "Yes, that is it. Hugh."

Hugh. But that was the name of her *sister's* betrothed. Her chest went tight.

Tara drew closer. "Was not Arabel to have married Hugh?"

Buchan turned to her, a capon leg held in his hand.

"She can't very well do that now, can she?" he said quietly.

The earl took a bite, and chewed slowly, his lips shining with juices, as his gaze hardened . . . and narrowed on her. Tara's heart skipped a beat, stumbling over some unknown warning, some instinctive fear.

"I don't understand what you are saying," she whispered.

His sons paused in their eating, glancing at their father, and at each other.

The earl swallowed, and his eyes grew dark as a crow's. "What I'm saying is that your sister is dead. And that you will take her place."

A hole opened beneath her feet, and in that moment, Tara felt as if she was falling into darkness. Arabel. *Dead?* She prayed she had misheard. That this was a terrible dream, and that she would awaken, but she did not. Instead, Buchan's words echoed inside her ears and her heart broke. A powerful tremor of grief rippled through her, so strong she had to struggle . . . gasp for her next breath.

"How?" she rasped, tears flooding her eyes. "When?"

"Perhaps a fortnight ago. A fever . . . I believe." He looked at Duncan. "Or was that the old war horse, Mc-Grayvan's, wife?"

Duncan shrugged.

Buchan looked at her again, his expression blank. "I am an important man, dear. I receive many important letters, about many important things. Certainly you understand I cannot be expected to remember all the lesser details. She is dead. Is that not the only thing that matters? And now, we must carry on."

Carry on? Could he be any more dismissive of her only sibling's death? Any more cruel in his conveyance of the news? Oh, Arabel . . . her dear sister! Her friend. The only family she had left.

Tara stared at him, dizzied by sadness and outrage. "I will not marry my *dead* sister's betrothed."

She would not do anything this awful man said. She would assert her own path, from this moment forward.

The earl rolled his eyes, and examined the gleaming bone in his hand. "Don't be tiresome. Of course you will. It is what young ladies of good breeding do. They marry."

He looked piercingly at her again. "They do as they are told."

She stood taller. "I would have you dissolve the betrothal agreement, as I intend to return to Menteith."

Her family's ancestral home. "I am twenty—and I will live there from now on. The steward will assist me with whatever needs to be done—"

"If only that were possible," he answered, tearing off a chunk of bread and stuffing the bite into his mouth. "But Menteith, like Arabel, is no more."

The words repeated inside her head. "What do you mean, no more?"

Dread consumed her. She was both desperate to hear, and fearful of the words he would speak next.

He nodded, drinking from his cup. "Granted to me—"

"*No!*" she shouted.

"—by *full agreement* of your sister," he bellowed back, his face a mask of fury . . . before again normalizing his voice and his features to their former calm. "Did she not inform you? For that I am sorry. That was wrong of her, truly it was, but it all made sense. The properties were so distant from her new home, and she—nor you—without the maturity, wisdom, or ability to oversee them."

"You stole them from us," she hissed.

Arabel had always been gentle, and trusting. She could only imagine how she had been bullied or tricked into agreeing to Buchan's wishes.

He gaze narrowed on her. "Careful with your accusations, child. I would not wish for our loving guardian-ward bond to be destroyed. Your estate received due compensation, and as sole heiress of the Iverach estate, you will inherit it all—"

"Give me my fortune, then," she demanded, swiping the tears from her cheeks.

She would not fall into helplessness. She would go and live elsewhere. Anywhere, abroad, if necessary—away from this man and his machinations.

"Indeed," he answered, easing back in his chair. "I will gladly convey your inheritance, in its entirety . . . *to your new husband*, Hugh of the Alwyns, in the form of your *tocher*."

She had awakened to a new day only hours before, and in that short time her life as she knew it had been ripped away. She wanted nothing more desperately than for her mother and father to be alive. Her sister. To be at Menteith, surrounded by familiar faces and belongings. For things to be as they had once been. But life would never be the same again.

"What a despicable man you are," she said, backing away, already making plans for escape in her mind.

She had many skills. Fine embroidery. She could read and write, in more than one language. She would find a place in a noble household as a maidservant or tutor if necessary, and live under another name until she educated herself on what to do. How to legally petition the courts to end Buchan's guardianship over her. There had to be a way.

Moving toward the door, she found Sister Agnes waiting there, her eyes filled with sympathy. The nun reached for her, and placed a comforting arm around her shoulders, while opening the door.

And yet, before they left the room, Tara froze at hearing Buchan's voice call after her.

"Mistress Iverach."

She stood rigid, listening.

"Be prepared to travel at morning's first light. And Duncan . . ."

"Yes, my lord," his son answered.

"Place guards outside Mistress Iverach's chamber, and below her window as well. I wish her to rest well tonight, rather than tiring herself attempting to carry out any childish, unwise plans."

Chapter 2

A sennight later.

Sometime between first cock's crow and daybreak, Magnus awakened to the cold darkness of his chamber. Wind hummed and moaned through the shutters.

He was a Kincaid.

He had always been a Kincaid.

The blood of his ancestors thundered in his veins.

A spark flared instantly—hot and raging, deep in his soul—the tinder, his hate. A sennight had passed since he had left the bonfire at Inverhaven, his life forever altered. His path in this life, forever changed. Yet anyone watching, not privy to his thoughts, would have observed no change at all.

For since returning to Castle Burnbryde, he had gone through the motions of his days just as before, holding silent on all he had learned and giving no outward glimpse of the vengeful intentions he carried inside. He had gauged the power of his hate, and strengthened his control over it, and observed, through the watchful eyes of an assassin, the man he intended to destroy . . . the Laird Alwyn.

Not his father.
His father's murderer.

Once the fog of anger from that first night had cleared, the first question he'd had to answer for himself was whether the laird knew the truth of his identity. Whether he had any part in the years-long deception that had become his life.

Magnus—for he was not yet comfortable thinking of himself as Faelan—had briefly considered the possibility he'd been brought at the age of ten to Burnbryde as a war prize, to be gloated over and tormented for the entertainment of the man who'd destroyed his clan. He had quickly discounted that notion. The only torment the Alwyn had inflicted on him as a boy had been a complete and utter indifference that extended to this day.

Laying on his back, he exhaled and stared up at the ceiling. His breath clouded the frigid darkness. This was the time of day he liked the best, when he could think in silence, and ruminate . . . and plot.

Neither was the Alwyn a kind or merciful man. It simply wasn't possible the laird had discovered him—the son of his enemy—alive after the battle that killed his father, his mother, and so many other Kincaids, and out of the benevolence of his heart, brought him to Burnbryde to recover from his injuries in the care of a cast-off mistress, who would henceforth be required to claim him as a son. A *bastard* son, who as soon as he could speak again, was torn from his mother's hearth, at the order of his "father" who never once called him "son"—commanded to act as his cupbearer in the hall at Burnbryde or when hunting or visiting neighboring clans, and made to feel fortunate to sleep on the cold stone floor of the great hall, with the other servants and the dogs.

Even then, the Alwyn had shown no interest in him—other than the one night, during a feast, when he called

Magnus to stand before all the men of the great hall, next to his younger, legitimate brother, Hugh, for the sole purpose of pointing out Hugh's stature, intelligence, and highborn qualities—and how Magnus lacked all those things.

After that, Magnus had gone to the weapons master and begged to be trained with the other peasant boys of the village to defend the clan. The laird, seemingly amused by his feeble bastard's folly, had allowed it.

Magnus shifted, tucking his hands behind his head, stretching the muscles of his arms and shoulders, which were sore and tight from the previous day's sword practice.

Only through Magnus's own fierce determination had he grown stronger, and harder—both mentally and physically—and dangerously skilled with a sword.

No one was more surprised than the Alwyn himself, when Magnus rose through the ranks to become one of the members of his own personal guard. And yet even then, never had there been one hint of pride in the Alwyn's manner toward him. Not one smidgeon of a father's acknowledgement or esteem.

No . . . any amount of respect he had gained in the clan had not been allowed by the laird's generosity or guilty conscience, but earned by his own efforts, alone.

Magnus felt quite certain the only person who knew the truth of how he had come to be at Burnbryde was Robina. Those years ago, she had led him, a weak and deeply damaged boy, to believe her untruths. Yes, he felt anger over it. But he wasn't angry at *her* for it. Not anymore. He'd had had time to think. To be rational.

It was for that reason he had not yet visited her. Once he questioned her about the truth, the mother and son bond between them would be severed forever. And yet he could not put off their meeting forever. He would visit her soon enough, when it became necessary for her safety to be informed of his intentions.

A gust of wind rattled his shutters, sending a deeper wave of coldness through the room. He returned his arms beneath the wool blanket, greedily pulling its warmth higher, against the bottom of his chin.

For now, he knew the only truth that mattered . . . that the Alwyn remained completely unaware that a vengeful Kincaid son sat at his hearth every night, watching, listening, and waiting. It was an advantage he intended to exploit to the fullest, as he plotted to exact his revenge.

His revenge . . . how did he envision it?

Magnus took no pleasure in killing, but yes, he would, without hesitation, kill the Alwyn for what he had done.

Truly, he had no other choice. The Alwyn's royal ally, Alexander Stewart, the Earl of Buchan and the king's youngest son by his first wife, had recently been appointed Justiciar of the North, and now imposed Robert II's laws in the Highlands with the full authority of the Crown. Magnus wasn't a fool. There would be no justice granted against the Alwyn by any sheriff or court under the earl's control. As such, nothing would come of seizing him as a prisoner, declaring his crimes for all to hear, and insisting on a trial.

He was grateful, really, for having the choice taken from him. Death truly was the only rightful justice for a murderer.

In that moment, hate numbed his skin, not the cold that consumed his small chamber. From somewhere in the distant corner came a rustling in the rushes, and the faint *squeak* of a mouse.

Magnus felt no animosity toward the rest of the clan, and would do his best to leave the others living—even Hugh, for he would not kill the son for his father's sins. Nonetheless, he would face Hugh again, of that he had no doubt. Indeed, he looked forward to the day, for he bore a lifetime of grudges against his "half-brother." Most recently, his assault of Elspeth MacClaren while at the Festival of the Cearcal, in an attempt to force a marriage between Hugh and Elspeth, though it had been Niall's honor to punish the man for that transgression. Hugh's face still bore the bruises.

Once the Alwyn was dead, Magnus would flee Burnbryde and rejoin Niall, and from Inverhaven, either negotiate peace with Hugh and the Alwyns—or meet them, with the rest of his Kincaid kinsmen, on the field of battle. There, he would endeavor to challenge Hugh, and Hugh alone, and end the conflict by a personal contest of swords.

His muscles tightened, more than ready for that fight. Faint blue light crept through his window, heralding morning. Would he have his revenge today?

Likely not. Because before any of that could occur, he must have a confession. In order to hold his own conscience clear of any death that he might inflict, he needed to hear the truth from the Alwyn's lips. He would know why . . . and how . . . and *who else* had been involved, besides the MacClaren, who had already been dealt his punishment. Most importantly, who had provided the unidentified warriors who had laid waste to his clan? What northern chief remained unnamed—and what had he gained for his part in the betrayal of the Kincaids?

He must remain close to the laird and those who surrounded him. To keep their trust, and to act on any opportunity to extract the admission. Instinct told him he would not have to wait long. With the conflict between the Alwyn and Niall growing fiercer by each day, the past, which had only been whispered about by the old warriors like a shameful secret, would certainly be resurrected. He would make sure it was so.

He could not miss any opportunity, and the laird would rise soon to break his fast in the great hall. Easing up, Magnus carefully disentangled himself from two pairs of smooth arms, legs and soft, fragrant hair—

The cock crowed, shrill and loud, from the bailey.

"Oh!" Kyla bolted up beside him, her hazel eyes sleepy, but wide. "Was that . . . ?"

Her *léine* slipped off her shoulder, but with a turn of her head, her long honey-colored curls covered her bare skin.

"It was," he answered.

"Laire," she exclaimed. "Awaken! Before that tyrant in an apron comes looking for us."

Laire groaned from beneath the blanket, and snuggled closer to Magnus's side, which made him chuckle. Kyla reached across his torso and gave her shoulder a hard shake.

"Make haste," she urged breathlessly, springing from the bed.

Kyla reached for her kirtle, which had been discarded onto the stool the night before, then circled around to tug at the blanket covering her friend.

"It's too cold!" Laire complained, holding on tight.

"Come along now." Kyla won the battle, yanking the blanket free. "We're already late."

Magnus stood, and walked on bare feet across the frigid stone floor to the basin.

Aye, the room was cold, but it was autumn and to be expected. He gritted his teeth a half second before he splashed a handful of frigid water against his face and neck.

"*Stop*," exclaimed Laire, scowling at Kyla, who pulled

her up by the arm. "I'm awake. Mind yer own self, and leave me be."

Kyla did so, taking up Magnus's comb from where it lay with his other belongings, and pulling it through her hair before quickly braiding it, while Laire grumpily searched the floor for a wayward shoe. When they were dressed, they stood side by side, looking at him, suddenly both silent and still. Both blushing wildly.

He took up a clean swath of linen from the table and dried his face.

Kyla's gaze descended over his bare chest, and lower, to where his *braies* hung from his hips.

She sighed. "Again . . . *thank you.*"

Laire's dark hair gleamed in the dim morning light— but her dark eyes shone even brighter. "Yes, thank you for being so . . . unselfish."

"'Twas nothing," he shrugged, one corner of his lips turning upward.

How could he not smile? They were both lovely young women.

"I hope we can . . ." Kyla began, clasping her hands. "What I mean to say is . . ."

Her blush deepened.

"We hope we can do this again," Laire blurted, smiling.

They looked at him hopefully.

He cleared his throat. How to choose the right words? He cared for them both, of course, but he didn't want them here *every* night.

"If there is a *need*, such as occurred last night," he answered, with all sincerity, "my bed is always open."

They were on him then, up on their toes to embrace him, their hands touching his hair, his arms. Pressing warm kisses to his face.

"Magnus, you're *wonderful!*"

"A man like *no other*."

He grinned because he liked their attentions. It would be a lie to claim otherwise.

A piercing screech came from elsewhere in the stronghold.

"Where are me kitchen maids? Lazy wenches!"

Then came the clatter of something that sounded like a wooden bowl being flung to the floor.

Kyla's eyes widened in panic. "We must go!"

He laughed, eyebrows going up. "You must."

They rushed through the darkened outer chamber, and after cautiously peering into the corridor they both disappeared through the door. With them gone, Magnus took up his trews from where they lay across a wooden trunk, along with his tunic. From the outer chamber, there came a rustling sound.

"Oh, Magnus, you're *sooooo* wonderful!" said a sleepy male voice, yet high and affected, in the imitation of a woman's. Quentin, from his pallet near the hearth.

Magnus's smile widened.

"A man like *no other*," exclaimed another groggy falsetto. Adam, of course.

A host of deep voices chuckled then. He moved to stand in the portal, looking outward as numerous pairs of eyes peered up at him from their blankets. His companion warriors. His brothers in life, if not by blood. His friends. All outcasts, like him, at least when they had been young. Bastards, orphans, or simply unwanted, their band of thirteen had befriended one another as youths and together they had grown older and stronger, and become men.

The warriors of the Pit—named for the dark, narrow chamber they inhabited each night, along the defensive wall of the castle—had earned a formidable reputation among the clan's fighters, and a place of honor in the laird's hall. A number of them, like Magnus, held positions among the laird's personal guard. Magnus had emerged as their leader, after proving himself, time and time again, the strongest, fiercest and most cunning of them all, no doubt because he had so much to prove to a man who found him worthless.

And yet he had confided the truth to none of them, that he was a Kincaid.

For as long as any of them would remember, the Kincaids had been their enemies, just as they had been his. They had done as their chief had told them, as warriors were trained to do, taking his grievances as their grievances . . . his enemies as theirs. Would they hate him if they knew? Magnus wasn't ready to find out. Though he trusted each man equally with his life, revenge was a plot best carried out with the utmost secrecy. He could take no chances that one or all would reveal him, intentionally or unintentionally, before his plan was in place.

When the time was right, he would give them a choice. Join him, or take arms against him. No matter what they decided, he would respect them for it. For now, things were as they had always been between them. This was one of the many lighthearted moments of camaraderie he'd cherish forever.

After pulling his tunic on, he arranged his plaid over his shoulder, grinning. "You are all just jealous. Perhaps you should refine your methods *and* your manners and you would find yourself as fortunate as me."

Someone's trousers hurtled toward his face. He ducked, laughing, and strode into the corridor.

The talk was all jest, and every man knew it. Though he was a healthy, hot-blooded man who enjoyed the affections of a beautiful woman as much as any, the only wickedness that had taken place in his bed the night before, as he lay between the lovely Kyla and the ravishing Laire, had been fleeting—and *only* in his mind—in the brief moments before he fell fast asleep. He'd not touched either one of them, other than allowing them to burrow like squirrels against his sides in the cold night, as his bachelor's bed was very narrow.

Just as the laird had a personal retinue of warriors, so did Hugh. Only his men lacked the discipline of their counterparts, and Hugh, of late, turned a blind eye to their misbehavior and their crimes. It had not been the first time, late at night in Burnbryde's great hall, that Magnus had intervened when one of Hugh's men, in a drunken lust, had sought to abuse a young woman. This time there'd been two.

Afterward, he'd given the two maids—young women from the village that he had known since he was a boy—a safe haven in which to pass the night, where they could awaken in the morning with their virtue preserved for the husbands they would one day wed. He could not imagine a lower creature than a man who would force himself on an unwilling woman.

He moved along the corridor, in utter blackness, as neither candle nor pitch were wasted in this part of the castle for fighting men who neither required nor requested such luxuries. He knew the way along the narrow tunnel, and up the stone steps.

He emerged into wane light, cast down through narrow windows high above, and moved toward Burnbryde's gathering hall, and the sound of voices. How strange it felt now, to exist here, within these familiar walls, knowing what he knew.

Castle Burnbryde had been a place of abject unhappiness for him—but his home all the same. While he had found no place of honor at the clan chief's side, as a son, he felt kinship with the Alwyn warriors and clanspeople.

For that, he could not help but feel a fissure of remorse for the shock he would inflict upon them. But there were other leaders among the clan. Good and noble men, who would make decisions based on the good of their people, rather than plotting against allies out of greed and an all-consuming hunger for land and power. When the Alwyn—and Hugh—were gone, the clan would be better for it.

Entering, he found only a cold morning repast laid out and an army of servants vigorously cleaning every nook and cranny, under the direction of the castle's shrewd-eyed housekeeper. Lady Alwyn, herself, was rarely seen. In recent years, she'd kept more and more to her chambers in the west tower, eschewing the coarse society of the keep below, where her husband and his warriors did as they pleased, rather than respecting the refined courtly manners and courtesies she had so painstakingly installed when she'd come here as a new bride, or so he'd been told by Kyla. Without the lady's influence, the stronghold could at times decline into shadows, filth, and shambles, but the pile of stones cleaned up nicely with effort.

Magnus joined a number of the Alwyn's warriors seated at one of the side tables, and was greeted by a round of nods and grunts. Lorna, the "tyrant in the apron," took up two empty trenchers from the table, scowling as she hurried about.

"What? None of your magnificent sweet buns this morn'?" he teased as she passed by. "How I can survive the day, without them to start me at my best?"

"*Och*, ye!" she exclaimed, her mouth breaking into a wide smile. Patting his shoulder affectionately, she leaned closer. "Bide ye reit thaur. A gart a batch, special fur ye, usin' 'at fine Persian cinnamon ye brooght me frae th' Torridon market."

She trundled off.

Diarmid, a happy giant of a man, who in a long-ago skirmish had lost all the fingers on his left hand, leaned close. "Yoo'll be sharin' those sweit buns wi' yer guid friend Diarmid, won't ye?" He pointed his lone thumb at his chest.

"Indeed. I am looking out for both our stomachs, always." Magnus grinned. "What is happening here theday?" He indicated all of the servants, bustling about.

Diarmid shrugged, eyes sparkling. "Ah, don't ask questions—unless they ur abit food."

Kyla passed by with a shallow, circular basket, strewing handfuls of herbs on the stone floor. Magnus asked over his shoulder. "Why all this? Are there to be visitors?"

Over his shoulder, because he did not wish her to be reprimanded for flirting and dawdling. It was an unspoken rule that only Lorna could flirt and dawdle.

"Oh, aye," she answered in a discreet tone. She leaned in his direction, sprinkling a few herbs as she spoke. The scent rose up between them to fragrance the air. "I have heard we are expecting the—"

"*Ye* are expecting no one, *serf*," a man's voice interrupted, thick and taunting.

The muscles along Magnus's shoulders tensed. Kyla jerked upright, rigid, the color draining from her face. It was Ferchar, Hugh's captain, and the same transgressor who had laid hands on Kyla the night before.

Behind him, Hugh and four of his men meandered past, chuckling and smirking, as they made their way toward the chief's table, closest to the hearth.

Normally they were spared such unpleasantness this early in the morning. Hugh and his band of hangers-on rarely made an appearance in the hall before noonday. Kyla sought to step away, but Ferchar seized her by the shoulders and boldly pressed his body against her back, his hand splayed possessively across her stomach, his features tainted by the split bottom lip and purpled cheek he wore, courtesy of Magnus's fist.

The maid stood rigid, the basket clenched in her hands, her eyes clasped shut.

"Let her go," Magnus commanded.

Ferchar cast him a menacing glare through bloodshot eyes. In the dim morning light, broken only by the fire at the end of the hall, his skin gleamed sallow. A deep frown pulled at his lips. Clearly, he still suffered from his excesses of the night before . . . but he radiated the same dangerous unpredictability as always.

Beside Magnus, Diarmid shifted, his boots scraping the floor, clearly agitated as no doubt others were all about the room. Everyone loved Kyla. It took every bit of Magnus's willpower to remain in his seat, but he had to show caution. They all did—for her sake.

Magnus did not fear a fight with Ferchar. Ferchar, like Hugh, ate too richly, drank too much, and as a habit, slept overly long.

But he had already humiliated Ferchar the night before, in a shadowed corridor, when the man was very drunk. To challenge Hugh's man here in the Alwyn's great hall, in the light of day before a host of witnesses, would not only be a challenge against Hugh, but the Alwyn himself, which could lead to dangerous repercussions not only for himself—but for Kyla, who would certainly be punished for her part in any confrontation, no matter how blameless she might be.

He stared into her eyes, willing her to be strong, all the while feeling *boundless* hate for Hugh, for sitting by and doing nothing.

"Y' dare blether aboot the affairs of your betters?" Ferchar growled near Kyla's ear.

"I meant no offense," she gasped, clearly desperate to be free of her tormenter, yet the warrior's grip on her only tightened, digging into her flesh.

Ferchar's gaze raked downward over Kyla's shoulder, to her breasts. His lips curled in an outright leer.

"Everything about you . . . filthy servant, *offends* me. Especially your smell." He sniffed exaggeratedly. "Did you know that you *stink?*" Ferchar's smile broadened with obvious pride at striking such a nasty verbal blow.

Kyla made a miserable, choking sound. Magnus's eyes narrowed on her tormenter.

"Ferchar—" he warned, through clenched teeth.

From his table, Hugh shouted. "But that's tae be expected, when ye lie doon w' dogs."

His companions all laughed loudly, nodding their heads in agreement. Boot lickers, one and all.

A shudder rippled through Kyla, and her shoulders twisted as she struggled to be free.

Instead of releasing her, Ferchar laughed—"*Slut.*"

He licked her cheek.

"*Enough.*" Magnus lunged from the bench—

Shouldering between them, he swept Kyla behind his back, and stared at Ferchar.

"The lass has offered her apology, as observed by all these witnesses," Magnus growled. "Are ye not *man enough* to accept?"

The warrior straightened and spread his shoulders in an attempt to look larger, and more threatening. "I'm man enough a'right. Tae much man, apparently, for her."

Just then, Lorna entered, holding a basket. "There ye be, Ferchar. See here, I've made yer *favorite* sweet buns."

Though she pretended to be oblivious to the confrontation she interrupted, Magnus knew she did her part to diffuse the tension. As stern as she was with the girls who served under her purvey, she held them all in great affection and would do anything to protect them.

The room fell silent, as everyone waited for Ferchar's response.

He sneered at Magnus. "Have 'er, then. It's not as if she's some prize. Nay, she's jist an overused castoff."

He huffed, backing away . . . grinning triumphantly, as if he had won some fight.

Yet the pale, grim faces all around told he'd only proven himself, again, to be one of the most reviled persons at Burnbryde.

Turning on his heel, he joined the rest of those reviled persons at the far table. Hugh laughed and nodded in encouragement, while the other four warriors raised their cups in salute, and pounded him on the back like a returning hero.

Magnus glanced over his shoulder at Kyla, who dimly smiled her thanks before hurrying toward the kitchen.

Diarmid muttered under his breath. "Thaur go our sweet buns."

He'd been so focused on Ferchar, it was only then that he realized Quentin, Adam, and Chissolm stood there, as well with several other of his Pit warriors, their jaws rigid and eyes sharply gleaming toward the men at the far table.

Chissolm edged close, muttering. "We'd have willingly gone to the dungeon with y', Magnus, if y'd wanted to knock his teeth out."

"Didn't know 'e had any teeth left," Quentin hissed.

Adam muttered, "What a sot."

Magnus nodded, his hands on his hips. "Being thrown into the dungeon for the next sennight would do none of us any good. Especially Kyla and the others."

Suddenly, everyone seated at the benches—stood. The

Alwyn had entered, and made his way toward them, his close-shorn gray hair shining in the firelight. He wore a fine woolen tunic of blue, edged with thick gold embroidery at the sleeves and hem, and several heavy chains at his neck. Even as an older man, he was tall and strong, and had eyes that pierced one through.

Magnus's body tensed and his soul seethed in response, as occurred each time he came in contact with the chief. All his senses growled that *this* was the man who had conspired to have his father murdered. *This* was the man who had destroyed the life he would have lived. And yet he welcomed these moments because they allowed him to assert control over his anger and his emotions, with the promise that one day, and one day soon, he would unleash himself and *act*.

All around him, men offered their morning greetings to their laird. After stopping to speak to one or two warriors along the way, the Alwyn strode directly toward Magnus and his companions.

Chapter 3

The chief must have observed his confrontation with Ferchar. Magnus did not know if, as a result, he would receive a mere word of caution—or a blistering rebuke. It all depended on the Alwyn's mood, which had been poor of late, as the previous fortnight had been a disappointing one for the chieftain, all in all.

Near a fortnight ago, Hugh's betrothed had died while at Burnbryde, of circumstances he'd never heard explained. Because the girl—Arabel Iverach—was also Buchan's ward, the Alwyn feared her death would throw him into disfavor with his ally. Immediately after, the chief had failed to force a marriage between his newly unencumbered son and Elspeth MacClaren, thereby denying him a claim to the extensive lands surrounding Inverhaven, and the magnificent castle there.

"Magnus," he said in a cool, brisk tone.

Magnus bowed his head. "Yes, laird."

The Alwyn gripped his shoulder. Magnus flinched inwardly at the touch.

"Today," said the laird, "I would have you take your

Pit warriors and ride down through the valley. Be as visible as you can be among the villages there, stopping to talk to and reassure the people." His lip curled. "They are increasingly anxious over the *pretender's* claim to be the Kincaid. They reside on disputed land and fear he will come with that mercenary army of his, to murder them in the night." A cold smile turned his lips, and he tapped a finger against the front of Magnus's chest. "An army that I know . . . *I know* he cannot maintain more than a fortnight longer, if even that. When he can support them no longer, they will abandon him, leaving him with the shoddy remnants of the Kincaid clan, and *we will be ready.*"

Magnus did not know how long Niall would be able to sustain his mercenaries. It did not matter to him. His path remained set, regardless.

"Aye, laird," he answered. "As you wish."

The laird nodded, his eyes glowing even brighter now. "And . . . upon your return, no later than noonday, do y' *ken*, hold watch over Glen Comyn. A courier arrived early this very morning with word that we should expect a most important visitor—the Earl of Buchan himself."

Magnus's heart stopped. He had known the Alwyn had threatened Niall with intervention by the Crown, and had dispatched numerous letters to Buchan, but had not expected the earl to respond so swiftly.

The laird nodded, looking from one warrior to the next, while Magus silently considered the implications of his announcement.

"When he arrives, you, Magnus, will extend to him a warm greeting on my behalf, and escort him here. Be sure to send one of the men ahead with word so that Hugh and I, and Lady Alwyn, will be prepared to welcome him here, in a manner that befits his royal stature."

"Indeed, sir," said Magnus. "So we shall do."

Already the Alwyn looked away, and proceeded to the table where Hugh watched them, his gaze narrowed in obvious displeasure that Magnus had been given a task of such importance. Once, Magnus too would have looked upon the chief's order as a great honor, one which might earn him greater respect. Now he could only think of how he would send word to Niall that Buchan—and no doubt a large force of men—were expected to arrive.

"Good morning, son of mine," the Alwyn called cheerfully, raising his hands in greeting. "Tell me, what marvelous things will you do this fine day?"

Hugh shrugged, unsmiling. "I am here, am I not?"

Magnus turned to Quentin, who acted as his second-in-command. "Let us be on our way then."

Under a darkening sky that threatened rain, they made their way from farm to farm, village to village. Though none would notice, Magnus hung back, allowing Quentin and the others to offer words of reassurance about the protection offered by their laird. Near noonday, they arrived at an overlook that gave them a wide view of Glen Comyn and its broad, sweeping plain, and they waited. And waited another three hours more, as the wind rose higher and a cold rain fell.

"What do you suppose we should do?" Quentin asked, water streaming over the hard planes of his cheeks.

Magnus scanned the valley. "Send Adam with word to the Alwyn that Buchan has not yet arrived."

"What of us?"

Magnus lifted one brow. "You know the answer to that. Unless we receive instructions to return, we wait."

"We were to have arrived at Castle Burnbryde by nightfall," said Sister Grizel, from the pitch-black darkness beside Tara, her tone more fretful than before.

They sat shoulder-to-shoulder, tightly bundled in blankets and furs, but nonetheless damp, half frozen and miserable, just as they had for the past six days as they'd traveled in the small, barrel-shaped carriage over increasingly difficult terrain. The horses' hooves thudded over the earth. With each turn of the wheels, the carriage creaked and groaned.

The carriage gave a hard bounce. They both braced for the violent movement, seizing hold of anything—the wooden window frame, the cushions beneath them—to keep from being tossed off the bench.

"No doubt we will arrive at Castle Burnbryde at any moment," Tara assured her, peering out through a crack in the window which they'd kept closed against the frigid wind and bedeviling rain. "Otherwise, I'm certain the captain would insist that we stop for the night."

Not that she had any wish to arrive at their destination—the place where her sister's life had come to a tragic and early end. Truth be told, she had remained vigilant throughout the journey, looking for any opportunity to steal away, but Buchan's men had clearly been informed of their duties and watched her relentlessly.

Aye, any journey undertaken alone would certainly be fraught with danger, but she despised her guardian just that much, and would do anything to thwart his control over her.

"I pray that you are right," declared the older woman, with a weary sigh. "My old bones have had enough."

Their journey from the priory had been beset by delays. Given the remoteness of their destination, they'd expected their progress to be slow, and the terrain challenging. But their carriage had suffered not one, but three shattered wheels, requiring replacements from the wagon traveling behind them, that also carried all of Tara's belongings, save for her mother's pearl and ruby necklace, which she wore around her neck and tucked under her kirtle for safekeeping. With her fortune under Buchan's control, the necklace was the only true object of value she possessed—and though she treasured it because it had belonged to her mother, it would finance her escape from Burnbryde. There, she would not be watched so closely and at the first opportunity she intended to flee, by land or by sea, before any wedding could take place.

The voice of the driver carried back on the wind, urging the horses on.

"I can smell the ocean," said Tara, inhaling deeply. "So we *must* be close."

She had learned from the kindly old driver that Burnbryde perched alongside the sea.

Her companion sniffed the air.

"Oh, *yes*." She straightened in her seat, her pale face peering out from her even paler wimple. "Yes, dear girl, as can I. If we keep watch, I know at any moment we'll be rewarded with a glimmer of torches on the battlement." She waved her mittened hand grandly. "Do open the window, just for this last little while. As a young bride, you'll forever remember these moments, when you arrive at your new home."

A home she had no intention of settling into.

But the elderly woman beside her did not deserve such discomfort, and after days and nights of endless damp and cold, a warm bed from which to plot her next move toward freedom *would* be nice.

She wondered if she would sleep in Arabel's bed. How she missed her sister. She had spent the hours inside the carriage recalling every possible memory. Every happy time. At times the grief seemed too much to bear, and threatened to smother her, as it did now that she drew closer to the place where her sister had died.

She pushed open the wooden shutter. Cold wind struck her face, heavy with the scent of brine. The sister tucked their heavy furs more securely around them both, and fussed over Tara, insisting on securing her woolen veil across the bottom half of her face, before doing the same with her own.

"I've never seen such darkness," Tara murmured, her breath warm against her lips. "If we strayed from the road, would the driver even know?"

"Don't even think it. Of course he would," assured the sister with a nervous laugh. "That's why we have the outriders, with their torches. To lead us safely along our path. You see them up ahead . . . don't you?"

Tara squinted . . . and stretched to look outward. "No. I don't."

Just then, there came the sound of horse's hooves upon the earth, the rear outrider riding from behind, a lantern swinging from a staff. The wavering orange light revealed tree trunks and branches—a forest all around. His animal carried him at a swift canter, forward and through the trees, out of sight, where she assumed he joined the other two who rode ahead.

"There, do you see?" Sister Grizel assured her. "We've nothing at all to worry about."

Tara eased back against the cushion, and closed her eyes, telling herself her companion was right. They would arrive at Burnbryde soon enough, and she would have her answers about Arabel's death—before leaving.

From the darkness, a man's voice shouted. No . . . more like *screamed*.

Tara sat up straight.

"What was that?" she hissed.

Sister Grizel clenched her arm. "I heard it too."

The carriage slowed . . . and rolled to a stop.

The horses snorted and stamped.

"Driver?" she called.

"I see something," he answered faintly. "Up ahead."

Horse hooves sounded, rapid at first, then slowing. And again . . . the dim light of a lantern appeared out of the nothingness.

A man's face appeared at the window, blood streaking across his nose and cheek. She recognized him as one of the outriders. Tara and Sister Grizel both cried out, alarmed.

"Brigands!" he bellowed. "Flee to the forest. Save y'selves!"

He lifted his sword high, before swinging away.

Terror struck straight through Tara's heart. *Brigands*?

In the next moment, the forest around them erupted with shouts.

"Should we do as he says?" she cried, her thoughts immediately moving toward their defense. Curse the earl, who had personally divested her of the dagger she had intended to carry on the journey, as if she would actually commit murder in her attempts to flee.

"No! We will barricade ourselves here. Secure the door!" Sister Grizel commanded, pointing.

Tara wavered for a moment, undecided, then seized the bar—

Only for the door to fly open, yanking her into the night. She slammed to the ground, teeth snapping. Moisture soaked through her cloak and garments, dampening her hands and knees.

The forest echoed with the sound of male voices. Curses. Swords striking. She stared into the face of the carriage driver, who lay on his back, staring up, wide eyed—

In shock . . . or dead?

"Sir?" she cried, planting her hands against his chest and shaking him.

A gravelly voice chuckled above her. Her head snapped up.

A giant of a man towered above her, and another behind him holding a blazing torch clenched in his hand. Dark hoods concealed their faces and heads. Ominous black holes stared down at her.

"Y've dared ta trespass on *Kincaid* land," the largest one growled. "By territorial right, we declare yer person under our command—and all yer possessions, forfeit."

Kincaid land? An unfamiliar name. Certainly not Alwyn. They *had* strayed off the highland road then.

She scrambled to her feet, heart pounding, and stood with her shoulders straight and head high, trying desperately not to look as frightened as she felt.

"You must release us," she demanded. "We travel under the protection of Alexander Stewart, the Earl of Buchan. The king's own son. I am betrothed to the eldest son of the Laird Alwyn. I'm certain you must know of him."

She suffered no qualms over invoking either man's name, if it would mean their survival.

The man leaned closer, peering at her. She glimpsed the whites of his eyes.

"All th' more reason I'll be havin' tha' loovely necklace yer wearin'."

Tara's gaze dropped to see the glint of rubies and pearls at her bosom. Her mother's necklace had slipped free during her fall. She covered the chain with her hands, and backed away, her pulse frantic, realizing these men respected no higher authority and would do whatever they wished.

"There are much finer things in that wagon, over there," she shouted, pointing.

"I'll be havin' the necklace," he intoned, stepping toward her. "*Now*, if y' please."

A banshee shrieked behind her. Whirling, she saw a shadow that could only be Sister Grizel hurtle from the carriage, her pale veil streaming back, and slam into their attacker.

But it was as if the old woman struck a stone wall. She bounced off his chest and staggered in a sideways direction, only to pivot toward Tara, arms flung wide.

"Run, lass," she shrieked. "*Run.*"

Tara couldn't possibly abandon her companion—a defenseless old woman, no matter how dire the consequence.

But in the next moment, Sister Grizel darted into the night, abandoning *her.* The man holding the torch ran after her.

Left in darkness, she seized up her skirts she started in the opposite direction, running as fast as she could.

Heavy boots thudded on the earth behind her, as she's known they would.

"Y' can't run. Y' can't hide." He laughed wickedly. "I'll find ye."

The words sent a chill down her spine. She quickly changed direction, hoping he wouldn't realize and follow. She scoured the ground for a branch. A weighty stone. Anything she might use as a weapon to defend, but darkness obscured everything—including a tree root— *thunk*—which struck her shin. *Pain*! She gritted down a cry of agony and raced on. Entering a small clearing, she ran faster—

Only to have the toe of her boot sink deep into the earth. She stumbled. *Fell*. Into a wide puddle. Water . . . and mud, splashed up to strike her full in the face, cold and shocking.

Gasping with dread, she pushed up to stand and heard footfalls *squishing* heavily behind her. She whirled, backing away, skirts heavy now, and tangling at her ankles as he advanced.

"Stop runnin', lass," he growled, breathing heavily. "It willna do y' any good."

He drew his sword—

Panic rippled through her. Her lips went numb, and the hairs along the back of her neck stood on end.

Did he . . . did he intend to *kill* her?

Again, she turned and ran—

But something tugged *hard* at her neck—then *released*, leaving her skin stinging.

Touching her chest, she found the necklace missing. She spun round to find the man holding her mother's necklace in his hand.

"No," she bellowed, outraged. Forgetting her fear and his size, she lunged, reaching with both hands, determined to take back her one treasure, her only means of freedom.

Thud.

Suddenly, her attacker slumped to the side—along with the other man who had struck him.

"*Aagghh.*"

From the darkness, she heard the sounds of splashing, thrashing, and groaning.

She turned, squinting into the darkness, and could just make out the sight of a man, on top of the first attacker—the glint of a blade—a short sword, and a shimmer of pale hair.

But he was thrown off.

Both men cursed . . . rolled . . . leapt to their feet—

Her attacker lunged sideways, as if to flee. The other man—the blond one—lunged sideways as well, meeting him face-to-face, and with a commanding upward strike of his sword—

The air *sang* with the clash of metal.

Again, and again.

"So you wear a mask," taunted the blond man, in a smooth, deep voice. "*Very* courageous of you."

They splashed near, their arms swinging their swords

with terrifying power. Tara crouched, fearing her head would be cut off.

"Would I recognize you?" he added, still teasing. "I suspect so. So let's see who you are."

More clashing, until there came a loud, long *scraping*—their blades sliding heavily against the other—and a *whooshing* through the air . . .

Followed by two distinct thuds, some distance away.

The sound of their swords falling.

More cursing, grappling, growling and swinging fists.

Her rescuer, if that's what he was, was younger, leaner, more agile, and now—without a weapon.

She ran to the place she thought they'd landed and searched the ground, bending to touch the grass and tapping about with her toe. Her shoe struck the hard metal of a hilt. *There!* And yes, not far away, the other. She removed her thick mittens and quickly judged one more finely crafted and evenly weighted than the other. She returned to where the men fought, carrying the one aloft and dragging the other by its hilt, behind her, and dropping it into the muck.

"You there," she cried, attempting to edge nearer to his side, desperate to help him—because she did not wish to be left alone with the other man again. "You there. *I have your sword!*"

But with a roar, the hooded man seized hold of the blond man's tunic. The blond man bent at the waist, and in one quick movement, freed himself from the garment, causing the hooded man to stumble back. In the next second, the now-shirtless man lunged at the other's torso, tackling him to the ground.

Scrambling atop him, his arm—*his fist*—rose and fell with terrifying swiftness, a blur in the night.

Thud.

Thud.

Thud.

He stopped. Breathing hard, he reached for something—his tunic, she surmised, and stood. His opponent did not move.

Had he just killed the man? With his *hands?*

Tara stood frozen, staring at his back, he only a shadow in the night. An immense, imposing shadow.

He turned to her.

Dangerous, her instincts warned.

She stepped back, lifting the sword.

Yes, he had saved her, but for what purpose? Ah, she was a fool. Why had she not run while they fought?

He came nearer, his boots crunching over the earth, slowing to a stop just beyond the point of the blade. The night concealed his features. There was only the faint, silvery gleam of his hair.

"Let me understand this," he said quietly. "I have valiantly saved your life, and now you think to kill me, with my own sword?"

She heard amusement in his tone, genial and teasing—so unlike the cruel taunts the first man had employed. Nonetheless, she continued to point the blade at his chest. His *bare* chest, though she could see nothing of it, save it being a lighter shade of shadow in the night.

"How do you know it is your sword—and not his?" she asked inanely, believing as long as they were conversing, then things would remain civilized between them.

"Because the blade speaks to me, even from your hands," he answered.

What a ridiculous thing to say.

"That's not true," she retorted.

"Of course it's not true. I'm only guessing it's mine," he replied, chuckling low in his throat. "It's very dark, if you hadn't noticed. Now give me the sword so that I can decide for myself," he said in a brisker tone. "And then we'll go back and see who's still alive back there at the carriage."

He stepped toward her. Again she stepped back.

He paused . . . and shifted his stance. He stood easy and relaxed, but remembering the way he had moved in the darkness, she knew she must not let her guard down.

"We're still not friends, I see," he observed.

"Of course not," she replied. "I don't even know who you are. You could be just as dangerous as that Kincaid over there."

She pointed the tip toward the man on the ground. He still had her necklace, and she must retrieve it, but she didn't want *this* man to know about the existence of her valuable jewels, because he might thieve them as well.

"Kincaid, you say?" he answered, his voice deepening.

Och, the sword grew heavy, and her arms shook from the strain of holding it extended.

"Are you familiar with the Kincaids, then? Did you recognize him?"

"Unfortunately this dark is too dark for even my astoundingly keen eyes," he answered. "I shall have to return with a torch, if one can be found, and look at his face. Now back to this I-don't-know-you-and-therefore-can't-trust-you-nonsense."

"It isn't nonsense," she replied. "I'm a woman traveling through unfamiliar lands. For all I know, you could be a brigand, just like him."

"Well, I'm not." He chuckled, emitting a raspy sound from deep in his throat. "At least not tonight."

"I'm not reassured."

"In all fairness, I don't know who *you* are either," he countered. "Perhaps it is I who should not trust you. Especially since you so unkindly refuse to return my sword.

A female brigand, that's what you are. Thieving swords from innocent young men in the night."

She smiled. A foolish reaction, which she quickly corrected.

"Perhaps the sword on the ground . . . *there* . . . is yours," she said, pointing in the opposite direction of the sword behind her, thinking that once he turned to search the darkness, she would flee.

"I'm not interested in that sword," he answered softly. Almost . . . seductively. "The one you dropped on the ground behind you."

A shiver went through her—one, she attributed to the cold and her damp clothes, though she knew full well it hadn't been that sort of shiver.

"Why not?" she said, putting another step's distance between them, and shifting her position sideways, just a bit.

He rotated on the heel of his boot, keeping his gaze fixed on her so pointedly she wondered if he *could* see in the dark.

"Because you aren't holding it."

Heat rose into her cheeks.

This dangerous man was trifling with her, and as much as she knew she shouldn't, she *liked* it, just a little.

She ought to be scared of him, but she wasn't. Not really.

Instead, he intrigued her, an unwise reaction, being that she couldn't even see his face, and faces revealed so much about a person's intentions. It was time to end their verbal flirtation, or whatever this was going on between them and distinguish whether he was friend or foe.

She straightened, still wielding the sword, and peered as best she could at him, out from the depths of her cowl. "I am Tara Iverach, ward of the Earl of Buchan. I have come at the invitation of the Laird Alwyn, as I am betrothed to his eldest son."

He remained quiet for a long moment.

"Is that so?" he answered quietly.

"Yes."

He let out a sound—a laugh, she thought. "Indeed."

"Well, then . . ." His voice went husky. "How fortuitous that we should meet."

Lifting his hand, he touched the tip of the sword, and commandingly pushed it down, moving closer. She—finding herself unwilling to wrench the hilt higher and stab the blade through his chest—could only allow him to do so.

"Being that I *am* the Alwyn's . . . eldest . . . son."

Tara's breath caught in her throat.

She inhaled softly. "*You?*"

This was the man from whom she intended to escape? With whom she intended to break her troth?

What would it mean to have a man like him as a husband?

Despite all her caution, something like pleasure speared up from her stomach, warming her neck and her cheeks, and her breasts. Gently, he took possession of the sword—his hand closing over hers for a moment as he claimed the hilt, and closed the space between them, peering down at her. Her heart raced.

She did not step away this time—she felt anchored there, caught up in his power and presence.

"Indeed," he answered in a quiet voice of command. "Which I believe . . . entitles me to a kiss for saving you."

A kiss.

She had never been kissed before but . . . perhaps she did want to be kissed by him.

She didn't even know what he looked like, but somehow his face didn't matter. His voice. His manner. His skill as a warrior. The way she felt *now*, deep in her soul. It was all she needed to open her mind to the possibility of him.

"May I, then?" he murmured.

She did not answer.

She listened, instead, to a soft whisper that seemed to come straight from her soul—

Reminding her that he had been Arabel's betrothed first. Though dead, Arabel was not gone from her memory and most certainly not her heart. She still deserved a sister's loyalty and respect. Even a sister's guilt, for being alive . . . for being here in her stead.

That whisper faded when his arm came around her suddenly, pulling her close against his body.

He was hard—*everywhere*—constructed of muscle and strength. She took a step, but not away—just to steady herself, her hands coming up flat against his chest— his *bare* chest, cool, firm skin, underscored with heat. *Her* betrothed . . . if she so wished.

The sensation *of him* shocked her senses. Dizzied her.

He stepped too, aligning his body to hers—still clenching the sword low and ready—a warrior's stance.

It was like a dance. A wonderful, mesmerizing dance. An intimacy not forbidden, because by the law of the land, they were already bound to one another, just as surely as if they were married.

Unless she fled, as she had planned to do all along.

"Come here," he said huskily, lowering his head, his face into her cowl—

His voice . . . the words he spoke, sent a flush over her skin, a sensation of heat.

To accept or deny him? Her pulse surged high with excitement and uncertainty, for she knew not what to do. Instead, because it was easier than making that choice . . . she did nothing. She closed her eyes . . . and waited.

She felt pressure against her lips—but the sensation of cloth, *not* his lips.

Her eyes flew open. Her veil! Even she, lost to the thrill of the moment, had forgotten its presence.

"Thwarted." He chuckled deeply—a distinctly masculine sound. She felt the rumble of his chest, under her palm. "And cruelly so."

He gently tugged the swath of linen lower and she felt cold air on her lips and her chin.

"But I wilnae be denied again." He dipped, lowering his face—

As right as the moment felt, something still felt *wrong*. She went stiff in his arms and turned her face away.

"What is it?" he asked in an intimate tone.

"Arabel," she whispered. "She was my sister."

"I never kissed her," he murmured. "But I will kiss you."

The sudden brush of his lips against hers sent a shock rippling through her. She exhaled, unsteadied by the rapid beating of her heart. And yet the kiss did not end. Before she could take another breath, his mouth closed on hers with deliberate passion.

He gathered her nearer, so that their hips . . . legs . . . stomachs . . . *hearts* . . . aligned, their bodies standing, but entwined. His kiss deepened, his mouth and tongue coaxing her response. Gasping, she inhaled his scent: rain . . . peat smoke . . . and male skin. Even as her instincts insisted she be wary, his power consumed her, and laid siege to her thickly bastioned soul.

She sighed, surprising even herself when she yielded, her arms slipping around his waist, her hands flat against his back. She clung to him, savoring the flex of his muscles beneath her hands, so foreign from anything she'd ever touched.

Distantly, she heard the wind rush through the trees, felt the wet and cold against her skin and her feet, but in his arms, in that moment, she felt warm and safe and shielded from the shock and sadness of the previous days. His hand cradled the back of her head. Tilting his face, he kissed her again.

Was it wrong?

Was it *wrong* to hope that something meaningful existed between them, from this first moment?

A low growl emitted from his throat. He pressed his lips hard against hers, before releasing her.

"Best we go and find the others," he asserted, stepping back. "Before they come looking for us."

She blinked, dazed, and watched as he moved in the darkness, lifting his arms over his head as he pulled on his tunic. He came near again, placing his hand at her back, as if it were the most natural thing to do, and led her away.

Only now he wasn't overwhelming her with his kisses, and with each step, her mind grew clearer. Regardless of whether this man was her betrothed . . . *regardless* of how nicely he had kissed—he was still a stranger. Just because they had shared a moment of passion did not mean he warranted her trust.

Her necklace.

"Wait." She dug in her heels. "What about the Kincaid?"

"The Kincaid? Oh . . ." He glanced over his shoulder. "He is gone."

The words shattered her calm.

"Gone?" she cried. Her heart fell. She broke free from him to turn and search the darkness. She found the space of ground empty, her attacker gone.

And with him, her only guaranty of freedom.

"Aye," he answered, catching her hand, and gently pulling her along beside him. "Somewhere between I-don't-trust-you and my-name-is-Tara-Iverach."

"I thought you'd killed him," she whispered.

Numb with shock and loss, she walked alongside him through the frigid ankle-deep muck, in torment over the lost necklace, not even caring that she'd left her mittens behind. One foot sank unexpectedly deep, and she stumbled—

Only to find herself lifted up into strong arms, and held against the bulwark of his chest. Held thusly, with her arms around his shoulders, she realized he was even larger and stronger than she'd believed.

"Killed him?" he repeated, his mouth near her ear. "We're not savages here. We don't kill each other. Well . . . sometimes we do, but mostly we just enjoy a good fight."

"He took my mother's necklace," she said quietly, looking into the night. "The only thing I had left of hers."

"I'm . . . sorry," he answered, in his deep brogue, sounding genuinely regretful. "You should have told me, I did not know. Tell me what it looks like so that if I see it again, I will know to take it back for you."

"Rubies and pearls."

"Rubies and pearls. I will not forget."

She found his voice soothing. And yet she could not be soothed. Instead she was grateful for the dark, so he would not see the angry tears gathered in her eyes. Yes, anger, for she was angry at herself for surrendering so easily to a stranger, for allowing herself to be distracted from what mattered most. For liking the way it felt to be held like this in his arms.

"Where is Buchan?" he asked. "It was he whom the courier informed us to expect."

She flinched, at hearing the name.

"Called away at the last moment by some duty or another," she answered. "I bear a letter from him for your father in which he sends word that he will come in a fortnight for the wedding."

A wedding she'd intended would never take place. *But now?* Would she consider this man as her husband?

She did not know. She needed to think . . . and she found it difficult to think with his arms around her, and while his kiss still lingered on her lips.

They arrived at the carriage, where to her surprise, in the darkness, she discerned the driver on his perch, rubbing his head. Her betrothed slowly returned her to her feet, his hands lingering on her waist for a long, deliberate moment before he stepped away.

To her great relief, she also spied Sister Grizel— recognizable in the dark by the white wimple encircling her face.

The old woman rushed toward her, hands raised to her face. "Thanks be to God! You are spared. Filthy brigands."

There were other men there. Warriors, by their stature. They returned Tara's chests to the wagon, and calmed the horses.

"Where are Buchan's men?" her betrothed asked, in a clear tone of authority—and the men all paused in their efforts to respond to him.

"The outriders?" One of his companions snorted. "Gone."

"Fled," said another.

A third growled. "Cowards. We saved what we could from the wagon. We don't *ken* if anythin' is missing. The lady will have to look ance we return tae Burnbryde."

She did not care about gowns or shoes or linens.

Nothing but her mother's necklace mattered, and it was gone.

"You're safe now, with us," said her betrothed.

He seemed sincere, and her old self might have believed him. But she wasn't safe. Even here, she felt Buchan's shadow looming everywhere. She feared she'd never feel safe again.

"We'll go straightaway to Burnbryde," he added, pointing west. "It's not far."

She could not help but notice, and admire, the way he moved and spoke with such decisiveness and confidence, quietly instructing one man to ride fast ahead to inform the laird of their impending arrival, and the others to ride behind the wagon and on either side of the carriage, for defense, if necessary. She also grew more curious with each passing moment, to know what he looked like.

"Then we are not on Kincaid land, as the brigand claimed?" she asked.

He paused, silent for a moment. "Nay, my lady. This is Alwyn land. We were waiting for Buchan to arrive at the glen just north of here when we heard shouts and screams from the direction of the forest road."

She caught a pale glimmer of his hair in the shadows, as he opened the door to the carriage. He carefully assisted the elderly sister inside—before turning to her.

"Up now, you." Though he spoke the words in a tone of teasing affection, his manner toward her seemed quieter now. More reserved, and distant. His hands at her waist, he lifted her inside.

Pausing in the open door, he peered at her in the darkness as if he had something to say.

"Yes?" she inquired.

After a moment he answered, "I'm glad we were here. That is all."

Backing away, he secured the door, and was gone.

Tara leaned nearer to the window, thinking to watch him go, but it was too dark to see anything. There was only the sound of his boots crunching over the earth.

Suddenly . . . she could not wait to see him again, to match his voice with his face.

Would she find him pleasing? Would he be pleased to see her?

Would he kiss her again, tonight, before she slept? And would she allow it?

She did not know. How would she feel, arriving in the place where her sister had died? Sad . . . of course. And eager to have answers about Arabel's death.

I never kissed her.

Why hadn't he? The words had not been spoken unkindly. Perhaps he and Arabel had been good friends, without the romance that sometimes blossomed during a courtship. Perhaps he grieved Arabel too, and they could exchange memories of her. Perhaps she had been too hasty in deciding she could never marry him, and should at least give him the chance to convince her otherwise. She must be smart, and judge her choices carefully, and not cut off her nose to spite her face just to defy Buchan.

Perhaps despite the earl and his schemes, she could indeed find happiness here.

"You're freezing!" Sister Grizel declared, tucking blankets about her. "And where are your mittens?"

She did not answer. Her attention lay elsewhere. With him . . . outside the carriage, and just down the road, where her journey would end, at least for tonight. The place where Arabel had taken her last breath. She heard the sounds of the men climbing into their saddles. They set off then, at a rapid pace. Bursting out of the forest, they traveled down a wide, sweeping hillside before climbing again, up a stony incline that seemed to go on forever, as silvery as fish scales in the clouded moonlight, until in the distance, a shadow rose up, enshrouded by mist, along with the distant crash of ocean waves. Flames wavered against the stone. A chill rippled through her.

At long last, she'd arrived at Burnbryde.

Chapter 4

As they neared the castle, she could discern very little of the actual structure, other than to believe it resembled a sleeping black dragon perched on a cliff. The carriage crossed over a wide, stone bridge, which she could only suppose gave them safe passage over a ravine or a moat. Fires burned in large metalwork cages on either side of the high, broad gates, which they passed through.

Faces appeared all around, pressing close, peering inward with curious eyes. Villagers she could only suppose, from their rougher garments and speech. Their voices clamored loudly in welcome. Her heartbeat increased with anticipation of the moments to come. Would she be made to feel welcome, and as if Burnbryde were her home?

Scores of men spilled from the immense front doors of the stronghold, into the courtyard, holding torches aloft, lining the carriage's way—an impressive and primeval sight all at once. They bellowed greetings.

"Just look at them all," Sister Grizel murmured beside her. "This, all to welcome you."

"No—to welcome Buchan. It was he they expected."

Although suddenly . . . instinct told her he might never come. That she had been sent alone intentionally, as an appeasement. As a sacrifice.

Remembering her betrothed's kiss and his forthright manner, she brushed the feeling of apprehension away. If the earl never came, she would be glad for it. She would be happy to never see him again.

The driver drew the carriage to a stop.

She shivered from the cold that crept up her legs through her sodden shoes, hose, and kirtle. At last. There would be a fire inside. She could not wait to be warm. She wanted to see her betrothed again, without the darkness that had concealed their faces from one another, and know if her fears could be set aside.

Through the window she observed a tall, silver-haired man descend the steps, gold chains gleaming around his neck, atop a heavy tunic. He wore a rich fur cloak draped across his shoulders. No doubt this was the Highland ally of whom Buchan had spoken, and her intended father-in-law, the Laird Alwyn.

The door of the carriage opened. Tara's heart raced, thinking that Hugh would step forward to present her. But it was another man who stepped forward to offer his hand. An old warrior, who grunted in welcome as she stepped down.

Now that they'd arrived, where had her betrothed gone? The crowd pressed close all around, and though she looked everywhere, she did not see his face.

"Mistress Iverach? *Fàilte!*" the laird bellowed, descending the steps toward her, his steps quick, his demeanor urgent. His gaze moved over her sullied garments, and his brows gathered. He scowled. "Thank God you are safe. Tell me, someone, what has happened?"

"Brigands, my lord."

Her breath caught in her throat. It was *his* voice, deep and rich, just behind her.

Her body responded, going warm and aware. Though he did not touch her, just knowing he stood behind her, reassured her.

"Brigands, on Alwyn lands?" the laird thundered, his brows gathering sharply together.

"Indeed."

"An outrage," the chief seethed, his nostrils flaring. "Did you capture them?"

"Nay, sir."

She wondered why he did not mention that their attackers were Kincaids. But she would watch and listen for now. Certainly he and his father would confer once they went inside, and all such details would be shared.

The laird looked behind her to the carriage, as if expecting something more. "Where is Buchan?"

"I have brought a letter for you." She smiled, hoping he would be satisfied. "He will come for the wedding in a fortnight's time."

The Alwyn's face darkened with obvious disappointment. Perhaps even anger.

"A fortnight," he said, with a jerk of his chin. "I see. I look forward to reading the letter. I trust he will do as he promises and we will welcome him them."

"What is this?" called a man's voice from behind him.

A black-haired young man stood at the top of the steps, his face swollen and flushed. Finely dressed and wearing more gold chains than even the laird, he peered at her through glassy, darkly shadowed eyes, and wavered unsteadily on his feet, either ill . . . or very drunk.

"There you are," said the laird, lifting a hand, indicating the young man should come closer. "Mistress Iverach, I would have you meet your betrothed."

His words thundered in her ears. A sickly feeling crept into her stomach.

"My . . . betrothed?"

"Yes, child. Come, come," he urged. Turning away from her, he gestured to the man on the steps . . . *not* the man behind her. "Hugh, don't just stand there gaping at her."

A hand touched her back, the touch sending a jolt through her.

"My apologies," murmured his voice near her ear. "I am the *wrong* . . . eldest son."

Then the hand was gone. She felt him brush against her, moving away.

She stood rigid, in shock, but did not turn around to look after him. She would not give the offender the satisfaction of her dismay. She did not understand exactly what his words meant, but she did know a cruel trick had been played on her. That she had been betrayed by someone she had hoped to trust.

Instead she gathered herself to greet another man. The betrothed that Buchan had chosen for her.

Her intended shambled drunkenly down the last few steps, followed by a contingent of men, all glassy eyed, all as intoxicated as he.

"Is that *her*?" he squinted, scowling. His lip curled, and he let out a ragged sigh. "*Look* at her. She's *filthy*. And plain . . . and dressed like a nun. She's a plain, filthy nun." He teetered there, his knee bent, his booted foot hovering above the last step. The men crowding the steps behind him snorted with laughter.

"I liked the last one better," he declared, stepping down.

The last one. Arabel.

He landed hard and swayed . . . losing his balance. He attempted, with outstretched arms, to right himself—

then pitched forward, limbs flailing. Though several warriors lunged, reaching, grim faced, to catch or steady him, he tumbled headfirst, landing on his hands and knees at Tara's feet. Another moment more, and she would have recovered her self-control and reached to help him, but—

His shoulders bunched and with a groan he retched on her shoes and the hem of her gown.

She peered down, aghast.

"Good god," the Alwyn muttered, plainly annoyed.

Reaching, he took her firmly by the hand and guided her around his fallen son, who remained on all fours, heaving. Tara's cheeks burned with mortification. Tears stung her eyes. What an ignoble welcome. One she would never forget.

She thought of the necklace then, and how badly she wished she still had possession of it.

Together they ascended the stairs. Looking back, Tara saw that Sister Grizel followed, wide-eyed, her lips thin with disapproval. Her gaze searched the crowd, wondering if *he* watched, laughing.

"You must forgive my son," the laird said. "He was very eager to meet you, and when you did not arrive, he feared greatly for your safety. He must have had too much wine, while waiting for word. Come inside. Come inside, dear girl. You've had a very trying journey, and we must get you warm and fed."

However, at the top of the steps, someone else waited—a woman wearing an exquisite blue gown and a resplendent black robe, embroidered with colorful thread. She could not see the color of her hair, for she wore a head covering, but jewels sparkled everywhere, at her throat, ears, wrists, and fingers.

"Welcome to Burnbryde," she said, smiling warmly. "I am Lady Alwyn."

Tara curtsied. "I am pleased to meet you."

The lady tipped her head in response. "I've had your chambers prepared, and a meal and a bath are waiting."

The laird cut in, his smile turning into a scowl. "A feast has already been prepared, in anticipation of Buchan . . . and our new daughter's arrival. I know it is late, but I do not ken why the both of you cannot come and enjoy a celebration at least for a little while, so that Mistress Iverach may converse with Hugh, once he is recovered."

Two men hauled Hugh past them, up the stairs, carrying him by his arms and shoulders. His booted legs dragged behind.

The laird looked at Tara and smiled tightly. "Which would only be a few moments, for he is hearty and strong."

"I think Mistress Iverach has had quite enough of Hugh and everything else for tonight," replied his wife, her manner a shade more abrupt now. "She is wet and cold, not to mention, covered in mud. A delicate creature in need of rest, lest she fall *ill*."

Like her sister had?

The chief glared.

Lady Alwyn extended a hand. "Come with me, child."

Though neither of them touched her, Tara felt as if she were being pulled back and forth between them.

"Of course," the Alwyn answered between gritted teeth, stepping back to allow her to pass. "I have been thoughtless . . . *again*. As I *so* . . . *often* am. According to you."

The lady ignored him. Tara could only conclude that the laird and his lady were not on the best of terms, at least not presently.

"Well, go then," he snarled. The laird gestured with an exaggerated forward sweep of his hand, that Tara should follow the lady of the keep.

Lady Alwyn turned and disappeared into the darkness

of the castle. As she did so, two female servants, so similar in appearance they had to be sisters, dutifully stepped back waiting for Tara to follow, before they fell in behind.

Tara was led through a high-ceilinged entrance hall, barely glimpsing anything for the dark shadows. To the right she saw what appeared to be the great hall—a narrow, vaulted room illuminated with light from a fire just out of view. Servant girls and women in aprons peered out, watching. But the lady went another direction, into deeper darkness until they arrived at a large wooden door, crisscrossed by wide metal bands. Here, two guards stood at either side.

Lady Alwyn produced a ring of keys, and the stones around the door echoed with the grate of metal as she unlocked the door. "My apologies for the locks, and the guards. We aren't always so severe but with the Kincaids threatening our borders, we cannot be too careful with our safety." Once they were all inside, she shut the door and lifted the key to lock it again.

"A moment," Tara called out, realizing Sister Grizel was no longer with them. "My companion seems to have been left behind."

"I'm certain she is tending to your belongings," the lady answered. "She will rejoin you shortly."

Though the lady seemed welcoming enough, Tara could not help but feel ill at ease, leaving Grizel behind. They proceeded up a winding stone staircase, upward into pitch darkness, into a tower. All the while she felt as if she were being swallowed by an immense, dark beast formed of stone and shadows. Dampness hung in the air, along with the scent of the sea. With each step, her mood became more and more burdened by the fear that she would never again leave this dark and gloomy place.

At the top, they came to another door, which Lady Alwyn opened with another key. When they and the servants had entered, she *again* secured the door behind them.

The sound of the lock turning reverberated loudly throughout the room, but even more loudly inside Tara's head.

Suddenly, Tara could not help but wonder if it were truly the Kincaids, or something else the lady sought to protect them from.

They entered a narrow solar, cluttered with too many tables and chairs, and strewn with all manner of luxurious cushions, embroidered footstools and silken cloth. A large tapestry above the hearth depicted Adam and Eve, their arms entwined and jointly holding a bright scarlet apple. Ivy vines concealed their nakedness, and a serpent encircled Eve's ankle. It was a woman's domain, with no trace of a man anywhere to be seen.

They passed along a short corridor, coming to the room at the end. There, Tara found a small but well-appointed bedchamber, with a small hearth and fire, two chairs, a table, and a narrow bed draped in curtains. Two female servants scurried past, with empty buckets, leaving behind a steaming wooden hip tub beside the fire. On the table, she spied a goblet, and a small trencher of chicken, cheese, and bread.

"This was also your sister's room," the lady said, running her hands along the back of a chair. "I hope that does not cause you too much sadness."

Tara felt a sudden tightness in her chest. Grief weighed on her heart.

"It does, a little," Tara confessed. "But I would have it no other way."

Lady Alwyn tilted her head in sympathy. "'Twas not so very long ago that she passed on. You still grieve her loss." She smiled sadly and nodded. "As do I."

Tara hoped, more than anything, she would be left

alone so that she could recover from the journey in solitude—and perhaps even indulge in a good cry.

But with a wave of the lady's hand, the two attendants came near, the older one reaching to assist Tara with her cloak. To be assisted with one's bath was an accepted custom, but it had been so long since Tara had been the center of such effort, and then only by the nuns she knew well.

Tara's cheeks flushed as her head covering and cloak were taken away, and then her kirtle and underdress. Her linen *liene* was untied and unlaced and pulled over her head, all while her future mother-in-law watched silently.

She stood naked and shivering, her hair falling down her back, her hands covering her breasts, as the servants knelt on either side of her to roll down her wet stockings. Taking them, along with her muddied shoes, they stepped away and left the room.

"Hurry, step in," Lady Alwyn urged, moving with her toward the tub. "Even with the fire, it is too cold to tarry, and we cannot risk your health."

Tara stepped into the tub and quickly sat, eagerly immersing herself in steaming water to her shoulders, more for modesty than comfort. And yet still she trembled, as if the coldness of the previous days had settled too deeply into her bones.

The lady took up a basket from the table, and using a wide wooden scoop, sprinkled dried rose petals and herbs into the water. Tara sat rigid in the tub, uncomfortable with this stranger's presence, when she really just wanted to be alone.

Lady Alwyn murmured, "I always wanted more children. Daughters. But there was only ever Hugh." She drew back, setting the basket aside, before sitting in the nearest chair. "I was devastated when your dear sister died. In the very short time that we spent together, I grew very fond of her, and like to believe she felt fondly toward me as well."

Tara's heart softened a degree. The lady of the castle seemed sincere and welcoming—unlike the son who had met her on the stairs and his cold-eyed father. But no matter how she came to like Lady Alwyn, there would be no marrying Hugh. She did not need to meet him again, to recognize that he was a nightmare come to life, courtesy of her guardian.

What of the other man? The man who'd dared to kiss her, when he had no right? Oh, she should not think of him! He did not deserve one moment of her time. She must only think of a way to flee this place. But without anything of true value which to barter for passage away, she did not know how she would escape. She only knew she *must*. She could not remain at this place for the rest of her days. *This* could not be her end.

And yet reality closed in on her, as dark as the shadows in the room, threatening to smother her determination. Had Arabel felt this afraid, before she died? This hopeless?

"How did she die?" Tara asked.

The lady's brows gathered. "Did Buchan tell you nothing? I wrote the letter to him myself."

Tara swallowed hard. "He could not recall the circumstances of her death."

Lady Alwyn's placid expression fell into a scowl. "That *man*." She shook her head, and the luxurious fabric of her veil shimmered in the candlelight. "He has been generous to our family and this clan, but he is nothing if not consumed by his own self-importance and ambitions."

Tara exhaled, relieved from the depths of her soul to hear someone else voice words that mirrored her thoughts. "I cannot claim to disagree."

The lady sighed. "The difficult truth is, Mistress Iverach, that we barely had time to know your sister before she fell ill of a fever. Within days, she fell into a deep sleep, and one early morning soon after, she died."

Tara listened, her eyes filling with tears. So simple a story, one that seemed an unworthy end to one so well loved. She imagined Arabel, small, still, and dying in the bed across the room. She covered her face with her wet hands, the sorrow she carried in her heart, too strong to contain.

She heard the creak of the chair, and felt the softness of linen being pressed into her palm. "There, child. I am certain she did not suffer, and I was there with her at the end, along with our priest. She was not alone. I hope that is of some comfort to you."

"Thank you." Tara nodded, pressing her face into the cloth. "Aye, it is."

However, as much as she wished to deny it, the tears she shed were not just for Arabel but also for herself.

Magnus drew back his legs, as the two men crashed just in front of him. After they rolled past, still grappling, still shouting challenges at each other, he again lowered his boots to the floor. Adam participated in a different sort of wrestling, just across the table, enthusiastically kissing Phyllis MacKinnon, a pretty widow who almost every night cajoled an invitation to dine at the castle from a different warrior. She was always looking to kiss someone.

A group of men gambled in the corner, laughing over bawdy stories. Others, in mixed company, danced drunkenly to the shrill music of two equally drunk musicians.

Every night repeated in much this same manner, at least since the lady of the castle had taken to keeping to the tower, several years before. For a time, he, too, had reveled in the freedom her absence inspired, but as he'd grown older, he found himself bored of misbehavior and debauchery, and wishing for something different.

The Widow MacKinnon giggled, throwing her head back and wrapping her arms around Adam's shoulders. Together, they rolled off the bench onto the floor. For whatever reason, this made him think of someone else . . . Tara Iverach. Hugh's betrothed.

God, he felt lower than dirt for what he had done.

He shouldn't have kissed her. It had been wrong of him to do so. The girl was innocent in this conflict—in everything—and he had never been in the practice of harming innocents.

But when the opportunity to take something that belonged to Hugh had presented itself, he'd acted impulsively, out of long-festering anger. Anger over what had happened with Kyla earlier in the day. Anger for a lifetime of being forced to suffer Hugh's *insufferable* presence, and those of his fawning, unprincipled cohorts.

Admittedly, he had enjoyed teasing . . . flirting with her . . . and her spirited response. He had also very much liked kissing her . . . a peculiar thing as he did not know what she looked like, and wasn't that usually part of it?

How she must have felt when she realized the truth— no doubt betrayed. He was damned sorry for what he'd done, and hoped he'd have the opportunity to apologize.

But if Mistress Iverach chose to tell the chief or Lady Alwyn, or even Hugh that he'd kissed her, and allowed her to believe he was someone else . . . well, he supposed he'd deserve that, and suffer the consequences as they arose.

Just then he saw Hugh hold his goblet aloft and turn it upside down, indicating its emptiness. Laire dutifully approached, pitcher in hand.

She poured the cup full—only to have one of his men—not Ferchar but Ralph this time, clamp an open hand on her bottom, and seize her close. She struggled against his hold and wrenched away, and in doing so, sloshed ale across her bosom—and onto Ralph's face. Scowling, he wiped his sleeve across his forehead, as his cheeks filled with angry color.

Hugh and the others laughed, which only increased his anger to rage.

"Come here, wench, and beg for my forgiveness," he shouted, and moved to stand—

As did Magnus—which earned the attention of half of the hall.

Aye, he was known as a swift and brutal fighter, but a disciplined one who would not be recklessly drawn into an engagement. He knew full well that men and women alike eagerly watched for any opportunity to see him crush an opponent, and even risked small fortunes on his name. But he would not throw fists here. Not with the Alwyn present. He would intercede and distract in some way. Living at Burnbryde, he had long ago learned that the skills of a diplomat were equally as important as those of the fist, dagger, and sword.

But the Alwyn barked out an order. Ralph slowly returned to the bench, still glaring at Laire.

Laire backed away from the table. Lorna waited nearby, urging the girl toward the kitchens. Indeed, she discreetly signaled to all the younger kitchen maids, herding them as she often did late at night, to be secured away and out of sight in the kitchens, leaving only a few sturdy, steely-eyed old warhorses who would not hesitate to smash a pitcher of ale over the head of any warrior who misbehaved.

Only some nights, Lorna's interventions weren't enough. Some nights, Ferchar or Ralph pursued their prey.

Magnus returned to his seat—only to realize Diarmid approached.

"The chief commands ye to his table."

Looking across the shadowy room, Magnus saw the Alwyn glowering at him.

Mayhap the Mistress Iverach had indeed complained of the wrong he'd done. He stood and crossed the floor, accompanied by Diarmid, aware that the entire room had quieted, and all eyes watched him go, as they always did when the father called to his bastard son.

When he arrived, the Alwyn gestured. "Join us."

Diarmid returned to his place near the end of the long table, while Magnus seated himself closer to the chief, beside a brown-haired beauty—Ysenda Firth, a merchant's wife who lived in the village, and whose husband sailed for much of the year. She was known by all to be the Alwyn's current mistress.

Just then, Hugh also appeared, and took a seat beside his father. Still drunk and no doubt more than a bit humiliated by the scene that had unfolded on the front steps of the castle, he glowered at Magnus, displeased to find him in his father's company.

The Alwyn rested his elbows on the table, and leaned forward. "The old nun who traveled with Mistress Iverach has informed us the men who attacked them tonight clearly identified themselves as Kincaids." Looking squarely at Magnus, he asked, "Did you know of this?"

Magnus nodded. "Aye, I was told the same, but I question whether that is the truth."

"Why?" retorted Hugh, his eyes glassy, his voice thick. "Would they not take any opportunity to attack us, and take what is ours? Just as we ought to do to them?"

Magnus shrugged. "Why would they attack in such a small number, when the Kincaid has an army of hundreds at his disposal? Why would they wear masks, only to declare who they were? It doesn't make sense."

The Alwyn stared at him, eyes narrowing. "I suspect it makes some sort of sense, although I know not what."

Magnus shrugged. "It could be that they are a way-ward band of the Kincaid's mercenaries, acting without his authority. Hoping to thieve something valuable—"

"Ah, indeed." The chief rubbed his chin. "Perhaps that is true."

Hugh grunted derisively. "It's the obvious answer, that's what it is."

"Perhaps not," said Magnus. "Again, I do not under-stand the need to announce themselves as Kincaids, which would only invite our response and draw attention to their misdeeds, of which the Kincaid would likely dis-approve, if he did not give the order."

Across the table, Hugh scowled accusingly, as if Magnus had intentionally led him astray.

"If you wish," Magnus said. "I could . . . go to Inver-haven tomorrow and demand to speak to the Kincaid, making use as I have done in the past, of my friendship with Elspeth MacClaren."

"Elspeth *Kincaid*, you mean," the laird replied, his gaze sharpening. "Poor girl, to be deceived so cruelly." And yet his voice revealed no sympathy at all, only derision. "She and her father ought to have accepted my offer, and married Hugh when I presented her with that opportu-nity. Now the MacClaren wallows in his defeat, and we must seize those lands and that castle by force."

Beside him, Ysenda sighed with boredom, and a sec-ond later . . . Magnus felt her hand atop his thigh, moving with determination toward the juncture of his thighs. More than once, Ysenda had made clear she desired him as a lover, and though she was very pretty, he had no de-sire to share a woman with anyone. Most especially a man that until recently he'd believed to be his father.

Under the table, he flattened his hand atop hers, firmly halting its advance.

His gaze did not waver from the Alwyn's. "I shall inform him of the attack on Mistress Iverach and demand that he keep better watch over his men . . . just to gauge his response, to see if he denies involvement. The visit will be twofold of course—I can observe, firsthand, his army to see if they have declined in number. To see if there are any signs of them departing for the winter."

Sighing again, Ysenda deftly freed her hand from his and planted it square atop his cock. Before he could react, she squeezed, inspiring a reaction that was only natural.

Magnus gritted his teeth and shifted, dislodging her hand. He had not been with a woman in some time, but he had no interest in this one, no matter how enthusiastic and determined she might be.

"Yes. Yes, do so," the Alwyn answered, unaware. "Buchan's delay in arriving has left me in a precarious position. I fully anticipated he would arrive this day, with an army that we might employ, to force the Kincaid off those lands. Land intended for me. For the Alwyns. But in the meantime . . . your suggestion is sound, and will allow us to inform the earl of the specific details of their defense the moment he arrives."

Magnus's heart pounded in his chest, and he dared ask, "All this with the Kincaids began so long ago, that I find myself in the dark about what exactly started it all. Would you tell me of the battle . . . of the conflict which led to it? Were others, besides the MacClaren, involved?"

A change came over the Alwyn's face—his features grew hard, and his eyes black.

"I do not *employ you* to ask me curious questions—" he snapped. "But rather, to do as I say. Do y' *ken?*"

They stared at one another across the table.

"Aye, laird." He stood. "I beg your leave, as I intend to get an early start to Inverhaven."

Ysenda smiled up at him, coyly clasping her wicked, wandering hands together near her bosom. "Sleep well."

"Yes," the laird snarled. "Go."

Magnus strode from the great hall, tension pooled between his shoulders, for he feared he had angered the Alwyn in his impatience for the truth. Several of his fellow warriors from the Pit fell in alongside him, accompanying him down the central corridor, and down the long, dark passageway to their chambers.

Chissolm lit a fire. The others collapsed onto their pallets. Magnus retreated to his private chamber along the back wall, a privilege of being their leader. He undressed, and lay down, gathering the furs around him. Curse that wanton Ysenda Firth, his cock was still aroused and hard. Awake now and unsatisfied.

But he didn't want Ysenda. He did not know who he wanted. He had not been with a woman in months . . . the wildness of his younger days seemed to have fallen away to be replaced by something else. An annoyingly shrewd sort of desire. Of late he could find no particular woman's lips that tempted him, no feminine curves that inspired his lust—but he wanted one just the same.

One . . .

It made no sense to him, for as a warrior he was sworn to a solitary life, unencumbered by anyone's needs or feelings but his own. But he wasn't a simple warrior anymore. He was a son of the Kincaid, with the promise of a future. What sort of future, he did not know because he must not look, with any sort of expectation, beyond his present challenge.

For perhaps he would die on the same day as the Alwyn.

He realized then, he did not want to die. Not because he feared death but because he hoped to enjoy some time on this earth, living life as the man that God and his parents had intended him to be. He wanted to live, at least for a while, as a Kincaid. To be his true self, whoever that might be. The one that had been buried beneath lies and secrecy for all these years.

For whatever reason, as he stared up into the low rafters, he thought again of Mistress Iverach, who had wielded his own sword against him with such valor.

Hugh's betrothed. None of his concern.

He didn't even know what she looked like. Hell, he hadn't so much as glimpsed her face, because she'd been all but entombed against the cold, in her heavy veil. The only image he could call to mind when thinking of her, was that of her sister, but certainly they were not *exactly* the same. He had only ever seen the sister, Arabel, once or twice, and then, from a distance. She'd been a pale, dark-haired creature, pretty enough, but meek . . . and "meek" in no way described the young woman he'd encountered in the darkness of the forest, her lips speaking challenges and rebukes.

The same lips he had dared to kiss—and the memory of which lingered, an alluring, unsolved mystery in his mind.

At last, Lady Alwyn and her attendants left Tara dressed for bed, sitting beside the fire so her hair could dry. Her trunks had been delivered a short time ago, but without Sister Grizel, whom she had meekly been told by the younger maid, had been given another place to sleep elsewhere in the castle. Tara could only interpret that to mean Lady Alwyn had not allowed her to enter the tower. The *locked* and silent tower, to which she had no key, and which despite the kindness shown to her by the lady of the castle, made her a prisoner. Even her chamber door had been locked, as the Lady Alwyn bid her good night. This troubled her sorely, for it seemed that in recent days she'd grown so much wiser and become more cautious, and yet at every turn, higher, thicker walls came up all around her.

One of her trunks was missing, taken by the brigands. The trunk had contained her garments—which was why she wore Arabel's night rail—but more concerning, the missive from Buchan to the Alwyn. She knew he would be displeased to know his letter had fallen into the wrong hands.

Let him be displeased. She curled her legs beneath her, and stared into the fire. She hoped to displease him even more by not being here when he arrived. Let Hugh retch on *his* shoes, and see how he liked it. She only had to get out of this tower, and see what was about . . . and devise a plan to get away.

Her mind still danced around something else. *Someone* she wanted to ignore, but couldn't. The man in the forest. The warrior who had fought so ferociously to save her, only to deceive her.

The wrong eldest son.

What had his words meant? She could only guess, perhaps wrongly, that he was the laird's son by another woman, not his wife, and so out of respect—and caution—she had not mentioned him to Lady Alwyn. Besides, it would have appeared unchaste to show even a glimmer of interest in any man who was not her betrothed, when in truth he did not interest her at all. Indeed, she hoped never to see him again.

Well . . . perhaps just *once* more.

Only so that she could satisfy her curiosity about his appearance, and confirm him just as lacking in appearance, as he was in honor.

She touched her fingertips to her lips, remembering the feel of his mouth on hers, and his skin—warm and firm—beneath her hand. His powerful arms around her.

Her heartbeat tripped and she let out a sigh. If only his kiss had not been so memorable. But what did she know about kisses? Nothing at all and no doubt, one day, she would learn his kisses had not been special at all. At least she hoped she would.

When her hair was reasonably dry, she wove it into one long braid. She was tired. Bone tired. She had not rested well one single night of the journey that brought her here, and now, she just wanted to sleep and forget for a time, all that had occurred and the challenges she faced on the morrow.

She lay in the shadows of what had been Arabel's bed, her ears filled with the silence of the tower. She tried to summon her sister's face in her mind, but could only conjure the image of a young girl, as Arabel had been when they were children, when they'd both been so happy and protected at Menteith with their parents. It had been a paradise she'd believed would go on forever.

As she drifted into sleep, his voice—the Warrior Betrayer—sounded inside her head, gently teasing. She tried to be angry with him but his kiss again touched her lips, silencing any accusation. Only she imagined someone else there, watching them from the shadows, and who emanated waves of malice. A man without a face.

She jerked awake from what had become a nightmare—

Only to find it wasn't a dream.

Chapter 5

Tara gasped, and sat up on the bed, seizing her blanket like a shield.

"Hello," a voice muttered thickly, from the shadow in the chair.

It was Hugh.

"You should not be here," she exclaimed, her head pounding out a warning. Her mind ticked off each of the locks that had been secured behind her as she'd entered the tower. How had he gotten in? Should she scream for help?

"Oh, be *quiet*," he snarled, and she wondered then if he would try to hurt her.

"Please leave," she demanded.

"I'm your *betrothed*," he replied, in a cold voice, sounding as if she were the most tiresome woman he'd ever encountered. "And this is *my* castle. I will do whatever I wish. The sooner you understand that, the easier your life will be."

"What do you want?" She prayed that he would inform her that he found her so displeasing that he intended to

end their betrothal and send her back to the abbey.
Please, yes, please. Let him tell her that.

"I'm glad you ask . . . what I want. Your sister certainly
never did." His voice still carried the hazy slur of drunk-
enness. "She barely spoke two words whilst she was
here. Yes, and no." He let out a derisive sound. "Almost
always *no*. Poor thing, not a bright girl."

Anger sparked in her chest. Tara took grievous offense
at Hugh's words.

"Arabel . . . not very bright?" she responded. Arabel
had not been a poor, dim girl! Growing up, they'd both
studied under tutors, and excelled at their lessons. Everyone had always remarked on Arabel's intelligence and her
dry, quiet wit. "How dare you say such things about her."

In an instant, he was there, his hands forcefully brack-
eting either side of her head. "And how dare you challenge
me for it," he hissed into her face, bathing her skin in spit-
tle and squalid breath.

Just as quickly, he released her, stepping away. Her
face burned hot where he had touched her.

"What do I want?" he growled. "I will tell you, dear
girl, and let me also explain that these are not mere requests, but requirements."

Tara listened, her head so filled with pounding anger
that she could barely hear his words.

"You belong to me," he coldly announced. "Do you
understand that? It was something your predecessor, in
her limited capacity, could not comprehend. As such, you
will take special care with your appearance. You're not
pretty, but you will do your utmost to appear refined, as
my position in this clan commands. You will hold silent
in my presence, unless I grant you leave to speak."

She could interrupt . . . argue, but she knew full well
this was not a man who would listen to anything she
might have to say.

He continued with his litany of demands. "You will not speak to other men, unless it is to extend the warmest of greetings to my father. Are you listening, girl? You will defer *to me*. You will make every effort to *please me*. To *serve* me. To show all those who watch, that your devotion is sworn to *me*. And when I command you to come to my bed, you will not deny me."

The ugly words reverberated in the silence, twisting and tangling inside her head.

"I say, *do you understand?*" he barked.

"I do," she exclaimed, with the fire of rebellion already raging in her heart.

She understood indeed. Her mind *thundered* with understanding.

She understood that she despised him even more than she despised Buchan.

"Just as you must understand that I decline to marry you. It is clear to me that you and I are a terrible match. We would never be happy together. I am far too headstrong. I would ask that you speak with your father tomorrow, and arrange to send me back to the priory."

"That will never happen," he answered darkly, stepping toward her. "Neither my father, nor I, would ever allow it."

Her muscles tensed, as she prepared to fight and flee. Tara flinched, as he lifted a hand and touched her face. Her blood simmered, for she could only imagine what misery her sister had been submitted to. It was all she could do not to shove him away.

He stepped back, looking at her in the darkness, as she trembled with outrage.

"Don't make me weary of you, before our marriage even begins."

Turning, he passed through the open door and pulled it closed. From the darkness she heard the turn of the lock. She waited there, frozen, until she heard his footsteps no more.

Don't make him weary of her? As he had grown weary of Arabel? A dark suspicion struck her through. One that questioned whether her sister had truly died of a fever. Or had something else occurred? And did Hugh's mother know that he had a key, and that he would come to her like this, unannounced and in the night?

She looked at the door. If she could just . . . unlock and open it, she would feel better, and not so confined.

Springing from the bed, she went to one of her trunks and searched until she found the set of feasting knives, a remnant of Menteith that she'd never put to use. Returning with one, she tried to insert the blade into the lock, but it was too wide to fit. She went again to her trunks and searched for anything she might use. A hair pin. Yes. But despite all her efforts, the tool did not gain her freedom, it only scrabbled uselessly inside the narrow hole.

Turning, she threw it across the room, panic rising to beat painfully in her chest.

"I cannot stay here," she whispered to herself.

There were no windows. Only narrow openings, covered by shutters, that in times of war might be used by archers through which to shoot arrows at their enemies. She felt smothered. Half mad with needing to be free. She willed herself to be calm. To think.

Often there were hidden passageways. She and Arabel had enjoyed many an adventure at Menteith, finding and exploring them all, and there had been more than one hidden door at the abbey. She prayed there might be one here.

Behind the third tapestry, she found what she was looking for. A small door, with a sliding bar lock. She almost cried with relief when it opened at the first pull.

With shaking hands, she lit a lantern, and then delved into the darkness. Rough, crumbling steps led down. If she found a way out, she would return for a few necessary things and escape straightaway, without looking back. If nothing else, she would return to the priory from which she'd just traveled. She did not care if she had to walk there on bare and bleeding feet. She would do so and throw herself on the sisters' mercy, beg for their protection, and plead with them never to send her away again. Ah, but it was so cold, even here in this old passageway. Her breath puffed out with each breath as she took each circular turn, her hands touching the stones for support.

Perhaps she would wait until tomorrow, and make a plan with Sister Grizel. They could convince someone, a farmer or merchant, to secretly convey them away in the night. The set of knives she possessed were not worth as much as the necklace, not by far, but at least they might purchase passage for them, to get some distance away from here. She could be patient until morning, as long as she had a hope of being free.

At last she came to the end . . . and saw a faint light. Moonlight, from outside?

Setting the lantern down, she peered out through the door . . . no, an old window, with iron bars, half grown over with ivy. Curling her fingers around two of the bars, she said a prayer, and pushed. Nothing budged. She pushed again . . . then pulled, harder this time, to no avail. She touched the frame . . . searching for a latch, anything, but there was nothing. She cried out, agonized, her hopes of freedom crumbled like dust.

In the crush of her disappointment, she remembered Hugh's cruel demands, but most clearly that he would eventually command her to come to his bed. With a dread certainty, she knew if she did not escape Burnbryde, he would do just that. And even if he didn't, they'd marry her to him soon enough, and then there would be no one to save her.

A silvery glimmer caught her attention, on the ground near her feet. Taking up the lantern, she knelt and found a dagger, inscribed with an A. It was Arabel's. The one Buchan had taken from her had been the same, only engraved with a T. Her heart flooded with emotion. Sadness and grief. The blade was bent, and terribly scratched as if it had been used to strike against something repeatedly. Then she saw it.

A furrowing between the stones beside the window frame, and bits and pieces of mortar, scattered all about. In that moment, her heart shattered, imagining Arabel here, in the dark, alone and afraid, desperately trying to escape and failing.

A dark wave enveloped her then, as black as the night sea—washing away her hopes and filling her nostrils and mouth and ears with fear. Fear that she would fail as her sister had, and die here too.

A sound awakened Magnus, rendering him instantly alert.

A woman's voice, or . . . no. He listened intently. It had only been the wind. He relaxed, easing back into the warmth of his bed.

He heard it again, this time clearer. Most certainly a woman's voice, sobbing. Heartrending, choking sobs, such as he had never before heard. His heart clenched, and he pushed up from the bed, listening . . . quickly determining they came from somewhere outside his window, a small, square opening which, when opened, looked out upon a narrow, overgrown space between the castle wall and the north tower.

The north tower. The very tower that now held Tara Iverach.

He slid the bar, and pulled open the shutter, and listened a moment more.

"Who's there?" he called into the darkness, although in his heart, he already knew.

The sobs stopped.

His heart pounded faster, he was suddenly desperate for a response. Had something happened. Was she hurt?

He went to his door, and closed it against the outer chamber, where a host of snores met his ears. For whatever reason, he wanted privacy for this moment, with the young woman he had so wrongly kissed. Returning to the window, he again peered outside, seeing nothing. No light from a lantern. No hint of where she might be.

"Hello?" he said.

Silence.

"I'm here," he said. "Please answer."

"I don't want to talk to you," she answered sullenly, her voice distant.

"That hurts my feelings," he answered, a small smile turning his lips.

It was in his nature to keep things light. Perhaps that wasn't always the correct response, but humor had kept him from being eaten up by the darkness that surrounded him every day, for as long as he'd remembered.

"I *know* who you are," she replied with more fire, but she sounded as if she couldn't breathe through her nose, because she'd been crying.

He rested his forehead against the bars, listening. "Who am I, then?"

"You're the awful man who kissed me tonight. In the forest. I recognize your voice."

The awful man. Yes . . . he must claim that title. He had been awful to her, indeed, which he now regretted.

"I recognized your voice too," he answered quietly.

"I hope you're in the dungeon."

"I'm not. At least not yet. I'm standing beside my bed, talking to you."

"Well, that's a pity."

"Where are *you?*" he asked.

"Confined in this stupid tower. Held behind bars." Her voice quavered with emotion—and anger. "Locked away like a prisoner, as if I have committed a crime."

His brows gathered. Was she speaking literally or figuratively?

"What do you mean, locked away?" he asked.

He had never ventured into what had become Lady Alwyn's tower, and knew not what lay on the other side of that large wooden door. For as long as he could remember, she had ignored his existence, and he had followed suit, believing as a child that his existence offended her. They'd co-existed well in that way.

While it was true in recent years that the Lady Alwyn rarely left the tower's protective circular walls, she certainly wasn't a prisoner there. She'd withdrawn there by her own choice, establishing her own domain. She even had her own steward, Gilroy, to do her bidding.

But he'd never known the tower to be locked, or for anyone's movements to be restricted.

Mistress Iverach replied hotly. "The door to my chamber is *locked* from the outside and I do not possess the key. My traveling companion was prevented from joining me. Is this how guests are normally treated at Burnbryde?"

A strange thing indeed. He could only surmise why such a thing would be done.

He peered outward into the dark, his mind attempting to construct a face around her voice, but unsuccessfully. She sounded young, but strong, though he knew she must be afraid. They were strangers, and yet he wanted to soothe her fears, as much as he could. It was the least he could do after the wrong he'd done, in kissing her. No doubt his own actions were part of a very unpleasant day in her memory.

"Perhaps the doors were locked out of an excess of caution, and only this first night. You must know you are greatly valued. A treasured prize. You are the ward of the Alwyn's royal ally, to be married to his son. He would not want any misfortune or illness to befall you."

"Such as befell my sister." She exhaled, sounding miserable. "And yet despite all of the locks, that fate already befalls me, I fear."

If he were her, he would be none too pleased at the prospect of marrying Hugh, especially after he'd welcomed her so memorably, spilling his stomach onto her shoes. Even so, her words struck him as overly fatalistic.

"What do you mean by that?" he asked.

She did not answer, causing his mind to hone in even more intently on her last words.

"Mistress Iverach?" he queried. "Answer me. What do you mean by that?"

"I don't know you, or trust you," she answered. "I don't even know who you are."

"I am—" *Faelan Braewick of the Clan Kincaid.* "Magnus. Tell me what you meant when you said—"

"Tell me, Magnus, did you know my sister? Arabel?"

He replied, "I did not. For me to speak to her . . . to approach her . . . well, it would've been considered an affront to her betrothed."

Hugh would have gone into a rage. While Hugh had displayed no affection for the girl, Hugh made clear to all what belonged to him. He took great pride in the idea of the possession of fine things.

"Do you know anything about how she died?" she

said, her voice going husky. "Certainly people talked about her passing. The circumstances."

At hearing her question, he felt a stab of sympathy for her—and regret over his paltry response. In truth he had felt very little at hearing of Arabel Iverach's death. He had only ever seen her once, perhaps twice, and from a distance. Perhaps callously, he'd thought the girl was better off, as death had freed her from marriage to Hugh. He had not thought of her outside of this place. That she might have family. That someone might have loved her, and loved her still. In forgetting that, he'd been wrong.

"A fever, or so I heard. I'm sorry I do not know more." She sighed.

"Who *are* you, then, Magnus?" she asked. "Here, in this place. Within the Alwyn clan?"

A simple question, with a complicated answer. One he wouldn't share with her, because likewise, she was a stranger and strangers weren't to be trusted, no matter how well he liked them.

"A warrior," he replied. "That is all."

"And are you loyal to your laird?" she asked pointedly.

He straightened, intrigued by the unexpected question, which he answered carefully—and honestly. "All good and honorable warriors are loyal to their clan. To their blood."

"Well, then, Magnus," she answered in lower voice. "I'm very tired, and since this window is locked, and you are a good and loyal warrior who won't help me escape this tower or my betrothal to that buffoon, then I have no wish to discourse with you further. I am going to bed."

Escape.

She wanted to escape. Could he . . . would he help her?

Though the idea of helping the girl rebel against a common enemy held great appeal, what would the implications or benefits be? If she disappeared from Burnbryde, would Buchan respond swiftly, with an army of men to address the matter . . . or simply rage from far away, and possibly even sever his longstanding alliance the Alwyn?

Och, he must consider everything, and understand her better, before committing himself to such a plot and endangering himself on her behalf. What if, on the morrow, she changed her mind, and decided she indeed wished to be the future lady of Burnbryde? What if she told Hugh or the Lady Alwyn or a servant that he'd encouraged her to flee and offered to help her? That would be the end of him, and any vengeance he aspired to achieve for the Kincaids.

No, he could risk nothing.

"Good night then," he answered.

He heard nothing more. No shuffling. Not a breath. Was she still there? He thought so. He'd almost forgotten. There was one thing his conscience demanded he say.

"Mistress Iverach?"

"Yes."

"I am sorry I kissed you."

"Sorry?" she answered softly. "You needn't be. It was a . . . very nice kiss. My first, do you know? And likely the only nice kiss I shall ever receive."

He heard them then, her footsteps, faint and . . . distant, as they carried her away.

At dawn, Magnus stood enshrouded by fog, looking at Tara's window.

He'd never actually come to this patch of earth and stone before, to see the other side of *his* window—to know there was another one, off to the side and just above it, at the base of the north tower. There'd never been a reason to. There was nothing here, but a triangle of wasted, overgrown earth, and ivy growing up the walls that from a distance, concealed everything.

He stepped closer—not toward his small, square window, but to the larger, arched one she'd spoken through the night before, and stood on his toes to take a closer look, but it was just . . . too high, without a ladder.

Backing up, he squinted, looking as best he could . . . yes, there was something there he wished to examine more closely. Moving close again, he jumped . . . grabbed the ledge and with a curl of his muscles, pulled himself up to look.

Indeed, there was a lock, there at the base of the iron frame, and etched in the metal beneath the keyhole, the image of a crescent moon. He dropped down, landing with a thud.

If anyone were to be in possession of a key stamped with a crescent moon, it would be the Lady Alwyn's steward, Gilroy, a bull of a man who saw to his mistress's affairs outside of the north tower, and who often personally delivered word of her wishes—and demands—to the laird, to the laird's never-ending annoyance.

He'd not made a decision about whether to help her, but the information was useful to know. He backed away, looking higher, thinking perhaps to catch a glimpse of her. But no face peered out of a tower window.

That was because there were no windows.

Chapter 6

Morning arrived and with it, a brief visit from Lady Alwyn, who unlocked her chamber door and brought Grizel to her, and servants bearing breakfast.

The moment Lady Alwyn left the room—this time leaving the door unlocked—Sister Grizel closed the door, and turned toward Tara, her shoulders pressed flat against the wood.

She hissed, "What pit of vipers has your guardian fed you to?"

"I am so relieved to see you," Tara answered rushing forward, still dressed in her night rail, to embrace the old woman. "Where have you been?"

She had never embraced the sister before. On the journey here, they had only exchanged the politest of conversation. There had been no sharing of confidences or sympathies. But suddenly it seemed as if Grizel were her closest friend. Her stomach clenched, knowing that soon the old woman would leave her to return to the priory, as her only given task had been to deliver her to Burnbryde.

"There, there." The old woman patted her back comfortingly. "When I tried to enter the tower last night, I was turned away and given a place to sleep belowstairs. This morning, only after threatening God's wrath was I allowed to enter." Pulling away, she examined Tara's face. "You look as if you haven't slept."

"I couldn't," Tara answered, agonized. "Hugh came here last night when I was sleeping—"

Just speaking the words brought the unpleasantness of the moment back. The idea of seeing him again made her feel ill. She pressed a hand to her stomach.

Sister Grizel's eyes flashed fire. "Did he force himself on you—"

"No, thank God. But he is horrible." She seized Grizel's sleeves in her hands. "Sister, I cannot marry him. If I am forced to marry him . . . I don't know. I feel as if I will die."

"Just like your sister," Grizel whispered, turning away.

Tara froze, and closed her eyes. Yes, just like her sister.

Grizel shook her head. "I have a very bad feeling about this place. About these people. I can only believe my thoughts are being guided by the Lord." The nun paced, her heavy skirts *whooshing* over the carpet. "Let me think. Let me think." She let out a shaky breath, and turned, lifting a hand and fisting it in the air. "Oh, for now . . . since your new gowns were stolen by thieves, I asked the girl out there—Anna—if any of your sister's clothes remained. I was given these." She pointed to a small trunk she had brought with her. "Let us get you dressed before the lady comes looking. You are to join her for prayers after you break your fast."

Tara stared at the trunk, hesitant to touch it. Her sister's things. Seeing them would make her death seem all the more real. Grizel lifted the trunk's lid, and pulled out several gowns. "This one will do, I think."

Yes, she agreed, her gaze slipping over the sleeves, bodice, and skirts. The gown was dove gray, and plain, while the others were fashioned of the rich colors she and her sister both loved, and embellished with trim. But the gray suited her mood, and would draw no particular attention upon her. She wanted to be completely invisible to Hugh, if at all possible. She accepted the woolen kirtle from Grizel's hands, and sank her fingers into its warm softness. Perhaps Arabel had thought the same thing when she wore that gown.

Lifting the garment to her nose, she inhaled. The familiar scent struck her through . . . rose and nettle. It had been so long since they'd seen one another, but in that moment she envisioned Arabel's face as she remembered it from years ago.

"What happened to your poor dear sister?" Grizel mused, taking the gown from her and unfastening the corded ties along the arms, and the bodice. "Or like Buchan, have they already forgotten?"

The words struck her through the heart, and yet she felt immensely grateful for Grizel's understanding, and willingness to talk honestly, rather than mindlessly urging her to be happy and to submit.

"A fever, I am told." The words felt false on her tongue.

"Hmm," Grizel responded, her lips pursed.

"Indeed," she answered. "I cannot shake the feeling the truth is being concealed from me."

Her sister's memory, and death, did not deserve to be swept away like some piece of rubbish. Without answers, Tara feared her grief would never rest.

"The maid below could only say that one day Arabel was here and the next, she was not."

Tara's gaze met Grizel's. "I don't know what that means."

"Neither did the girl, it seems."

Together they worked the kirtle over her *lèine*.

After, Sister Grizel adjusted the garment along her shoulders, and in doing so, stepped closer, tightening the shoulder fastening of a sleeve.

"I know 'tis a sin for me to even speak of such things," she murmured. "But . . . did you know your guardian is rumored to have sired some forty illegitimate children?"

"Forty!" Tara exclaimed in shock. "I did *not* know. Why did no one ever tell me?"

"Because you are an innocent girl, and we wished to preserve that rare and precious state for as long as possible." Grizel took the ties of the other sleeve in hand. "But clearly, now it is in your interest to know he is a man ruled by selfish impulse, rather than wisdom or care for those around him. I would tell you, in confidence, that he is responsible for no less than five of the repudiated wives who've been left in the abbey's eternal care."

Tara's head spun, hearing the old woman's words. Why would her parents have left her and Arabel in the care of such a man?

"In my interests, yes. But why, specifically, are you telling me this now?"

"Because women must fight for one another, when they have the power to do so. And while we held out hope for your future here, Sister Agnes sent me along with you for a reason, empowered with a certain degree of discretionary authority. This because we suspected that any ally of the earl would be as equally lacking in moral judgment as he."

The sister turned her round, and grasped her by the shoulders. She peered straight into Tara's eyes.

"That suspicion has been all but confirmed, has it not?" she whispered. "I think it is true to say, we both fear for your safety."

"Yes, you speak the truth." Tara nodded, left breathless by the intensity of the moment.

Grizel squeezed her shoulders. "I will act accordingly, as Sister Agnes and I agreed that I would. Buchan's wishes be damned. We will not allow you to be sacrificed on the altar of his ambitions."

"What are you saying?" Tara asked, her pulse pounding with excitement. With hope.

The sister lifted her chin and her eyes gleamed with purpose. "I'm saying to listen carefully, child, because I have a plan."

After breaking his fast, Magnus left the great hall, intending to go straightaway toward the stables, and then on to Inverhaven as he and the laird had discussed the night before. In doing so he made it a point to pass by the laird's council chamber, for the laird had not made an early appearance in the great hall, as was his custom.

The Alwyn's voice carried into the corridor.

". . . and I again request, with all urgency, that his lordship, with full approval from the king, assist in ousting Niall Braewick, the *pretender* who falsely claims to be the dead Kincaid's eldest son, from the lands which lay north of Alwyn territory."

As always, two members of the chief's personal guard stood outside. Magnus moved closer to the door, listening.

"Already at it, is he?" he murmured to the guards.

The laird did not normally go into his chambers so early to hold council or issue correspondence.

"Since daw-day," the older man on the left, Seorais, responded.

Typically the oldest guards accompanied the laird wherever he went within the stronghold, from bedchamber to council room, or great hall, while the younger ones, like Magnus, provided escort and protection and a more impressive display of brawn outside the walls.

The muscles along his shoulders tensed. Damn. Since dawn? He cursed himself for being distracted by Mistress Iverach and her plight, when he must remain focused on his own. What had he missed? Magnus considered his absence a loss because every word, every insight, might be of use to him.

Quietly, Magnus entered the chamber, where he found the room scattered with men and hounds. Several of the older, gray-haired members of the council slept—and snored—sprawled in their chairs.

As one of the laird's personal guard, no one would question his presence here. One thing he had learned about the Alwyn was that he appreciated an audience at all times. He joined two of his younger warrior peers, who leaned against the wall near the hearth. Thus far, the missive sounded exactly like the one the laird had dispatched by courier to Buchan three days before. And the one, several days before that. Perhaps he had not missed anything at all.

"Do you have the words down, just as I've spoken them?" the Alwyn demanded.

"Yes, laird," answered his scribe. "Exactly as you've spoken them. Would you like me to read them back to you?"

"No, no, not yet," the laird rebuked. "There's more. Also add the following . . . uhhhhrrrrr . . ." He exhaled through his nose. "I should respectfully pray that his lordship will remember . . ." He paused, as if considering the composition of the words, or . . . whether to use them at all.

But he carried on, his bearing rigid and his countenance like stone. ". . . the events of *the past*. In particular, *past agreements* that were made between us, which never came to pass, in the full manner *in which they'd been promised.*"

"Go on, sir," murmured the scribe, nodding.

The Alwyn continued. "Recalling those past agreements, I beg your just and right decision that the lands seized by the imposter from the defeated Laird Mac-Claren, now be chartered by the Crown to the Alwyn clan as was most certainly intended *those many years ago.*"

Magnus had heard the words before . . . the Alwyn's claim that some portion of the Kincaid lands, intended for the Alwyn, had gone to the MacClaren. The laird even claimed to have an old map, showing that the Alwyn clan was to have been given Inverhaven, and its magnificent hilltop castle, though Magnus had never laid eyes on the map himself.

Yet now the words fell on his new Kincaid ears . . .

Past events. Past agreements.

Past promises.

Promises from the king, or from—

Buchan?

His heart paused in its beating for one moment . . . and then resumed. He had always assumed the Kincaid lands were parceled out after the treachery against his father had been carried out, and that Buchan facilitated that process on behalf of his father, who at that time had been a new king, just taking the throne.

He'd assumed that was when Alwyn had ingratiated himself to the earl, and gained him the favor that had lasted until this day.

But . . . what if his assumptions were wrong? What if the agreements and promises the laird referred to had been made with Buchan *before* his father's death?

Then . . . Buchan had been involved.

Of course he had.

The large force that had come down from the hills—bearing no identifying banners—to massacre the Kincaids had been loyal to Buchan.

His pulse hiked with excitement.

If his suspicions were true, Magnus's plotting became all the more dangerous, and his enemies all that more powerful.

But why would Buchan, a son of the king, want the Kincaid dead and his clan destroyed?

The Kincaid was known to have spoken out against David II, the *predecessor* to Buchan's father, Robert II. About what, specifically, he did not know, but he would assume the Kincaid's complaints had to do with taxation inflicted upon the Highland clans to pay for royal excesses and the general foolishness that David and his queen, Margaret, their subsequent divorce, all of which brought about a threat of a formal interdict by the Pope.

But many had opposed David's actions. Buchan himself—then without his earldom and known only as Alexander Stewart—had been accused of rebellion against that same king.

For that alleged crime, he'd even been imprisoned for a time, along with his father and brothers.

Which would seem to have made Alexander Stewart and Raghnall, the Laird of Kincaid . . . allies, of a sort.

Why would one ally conspire against the other?

It was a question he still pondered when hours later, he arrived at Inverhaven, escorted by a score of Kincaid warriors who had silently ridden alongside him after he crossed over into their lands. He had done so without stealth, so that they might see him and know he did not seek to challenge them.

He had requested an audience with the Kincaid, and from their snarls and glares, he knew his request for secrecy over his relation to the Kincaid had been respected by all those who knew the truth. On the ride to the castle, he observed that the mercenary army Niall had raised to take Inverhaven remained in place.

They appeared to be staying for the winter—if not forever. Teams of warriors worked at finishing a new barn, but he saw other structures underway, which appeared to be cottages, and even a large hall. He'd take secret pleasure watching the Alwyn losing his mind and manners over that.

It was a strange thing, riding up the road to the famed *An Caisteal Niaul*, the "Castle in the Clouds," so coveted by the Laird Alwyn. His gaze moved over the walls and towers, fashioned of light and shining stones compared to Burnbryde's sea-blasted darkness. Both were ancient bastions of highland history, each representing a long and illustrious ancestry—but only this one had ever truly been his home.

It pained him grievously that he could not remember what his life had been like here, with his family, before they'd been torn apart.

The warriors who had accompanied him thus far, dismounted, and escorted him toward the great double doors—their hands on their sword hilts, as if they would slay him at the slightest provocation. And yet before his boot touched the first stone step leading to the door—the door swung open.

Niall stood there, looking at him, with an expression he couldn't discern. The tattooed giant who accompanied him everywhere—an older, yet still fearsome warrior named Deargh—stood in the shadows behind him, along with several other men.

In the next moment, Elspeth rushed past her husband and, smiling warmly, took hold of Magnus's arm, leading him inside. "We saw you riding in, from the window above."

Her dark hair gleamed against the yellow kirtle she wore, and she looked radiant with happiness. The door closed behind him, and his warrior escort was left behind.

"Welcome, brother," said the Kincaid, reaching for his hand, and gripping it hard, his gaze scrutinizing and wary—but a warm welcome. "I had begun to suspect you'd never return."

Magnus grasped his brother's hand in both of his, and held his gaze. "I would have come sooner if able."

In so many ways they were opposites. Niall was dark-haired and impressively muscled, while Magnus was fair and while still powerfully built, more lithe and lean of stature. Magnus wondered which ancestor each of them took after.

The corner of Niall's lip turned upward with a smile. "Come as often as you can. You are always welcome here, your true home, and may stay whenever you like. But come. Let us talk."

Niall led him down a long spacious corridor to a large council chamber—one with a large rectangular table at the center, and chairs all around. At the door, only Elspeth proceeded with them inside, while the other men remained behind.

Niall gestured to a pair of chairs beside the fire. "Sit, brother, and tell me whatever it is you have come to tell me."

They were strange words to hear from a man he had viciously fought against and, for a time, mistrusted—when he'd believed himself to be an Alwyn, and Niall a mercenary, hired to protect the MacClaren borders against the Alwyns . . . as well as the savage Kincaids. Aye, he had fought for the wrong clan, the wrong chief, because the custom of the Highlands all but commanded fealty to one's own blood—and he'd believed himself to be an Alwyn, bound by duty to the betterment of that clan. Still, he'd found himself in conflict with the Alwyn's ways, and with Hugh, and had sought to make a place for himself, away from Burnbryde by trying to persuade Elspeth to marry him. This, so that he might gain possession of her *tocher* lands, not only for himself but for them both. But she had refused. Even so, their continuing friendship, and his protectiveness toward her, had put him in conflict with the warrior she now called her husband.

Though he still found it difficult to believe Niall could simply forgive what had taken place between them in the past, and accept him as a brother, that seemed very much to be true. His own heart, and the forgiveness he found there, surprised him as well.

He sat, as did the Kincaid, as Elspeth poured them both a goblet of wine.

"I do have much to share."

"Go on," his brother answered, leaning forward in the chair to look back at him.

Magnus felt a jolt of recognition. Something about Niall's face . . . its shape, the way he smiled, his manner seemed familiar, in a way he hadn't perceived before. Elspeth sat in another chair, just a space away, glowing with pleasure—as if the two of the men sitting together and conversing peacefully were her greatest wish.

"You are already aware that the Alwyn has requested the intervention of his ally, the Earl of Buchan, in ousting you from these lands."

"Aye, brother." Niall sat back in his chair, steepling his fingers together. "That I know."

"There is something else I must tell you, that may seem to have little to do with any of this."

Niall flashed a grin. "But you are telling me, so I trust that it does."

Magnus nodded. "You will recall that Hugh was betrothed to the earl's ward, and that when that marriage did not go forward—"

Elspeth interjected, "And then the Alwyn attempted to force a marriage between Hugh and me."

Niall's brows gathered, and he scowled. "I recall."

Magnus paused. "What I did not reveal at the time, because it seemed of no real consequence to the matter at hand, was that the reason the marriage did not go forward between Hugh and Buchan's ward—a girl by the name of Arabel Iverach—was that she unexpectedly died while at Burnbryde."

"Died!" Elspeth exclaimed, her hands gripping the arm rests of the chair.

"Of a fever, I was told," he said.

"So young," Elspeth murmured, her expression one of sympathy. "Poor girl."

"Iverach, you say . . ." Niall rubbed a hand over his chin, deep in thought. "The name is familiar, but I cannot recall why. Very tragic for one so young, but why are we talking about her now?"

Behind him, a large crow landed on the window ledge, and peered inward, before hopping back around, and flying away.

Magnus thought of Tara then, in the tower, and her desire to escape.

"Yesterday, her replacement arrived. A younger sister, Tara Iverach. Also Buchan's ward."

Niall's eyes narrowed. "Interesting. Buchan has provided a Highland laird with not one, but two brides for his son. What *service* could the Alwyn have *performed* or *promised* to warrant such favor?"

Magnus recognized the suspicion in his brother, for it matched his own.

"I may have the answer," he said solemnly.

Niall straightened in the chair, and leaned forward, his blue eyes ablaze with interest. "Do ye now? Then let me hear it."

Magnus told him what he'd overheard that morning, when the Alwyn had written the missive, and what he'd come to believe was true.

"But what I don't know is why?" Magnus mused. "Why would Buchan have our father murdered, if they were on the same side?"

His brother stood. He took several steps away, before turning to face him, his expression grave. "We've never talked about Buchan, you and I, but I served for several years as one of his side warriors. He had no knowledge then that I was a Kincaid. No one did. Even now, I'm not certain that he realizes that I am one and the same, and in conflict with the Alwyn. He will know soon enough, when we meet face-to-face." The firelight reflected off his features, engraving the faint lines around his eyes and his mouth. "He respects me, I think. But he can be a dangerous and vengeful man, if crossed."

"And yet you served him," said Magnus. "Why?"

Niall peered at him. "Truth be told, I was placed among his guard as a spy by his elder brother, the Earl of Carrick, who feared he lacked restraint in his exercise of influence and power."

"Buchan's own brother spied on him," Magnus murmured.

"The King wields little power now. His sons and their allies vie for control."

Magnus felt a spur of hope. "Do ye have influence with Carrick, then?"

"Perhaps." Niall rested his hands on his hips and peered at him. "If our cause aligns with his interests in some way, then aye."

Magnus rubbed his hands together. "He may be our

only hope of ever having formal justice against Buchan, through the Estates of Parliament or the King's Council. He would have influence with his father, the king."

His brother answered, "It is possible he would hear our grievances against Buchan and the Alwyn, and act on them, but I make no guarantees. These men are mercurial by nature, and serve only themselves."

"*Buchan*." Magnus, too, stood, unable to sit for the fury coursing through him. "Our father crossed him in some way. It matters not that he is the king's son. I would see him answer for what he has done."

"Do you mean you would kill him?" asked Elspeth, in a hushed voice.

"He cannot go unpunished," Magnus replied passionately. "And if neither the king nor the courts will hold him accountable, then I will."

"*We* will," said Niall, eyes flashing darkly.

"This is a dangerous and powerful man of whom you speak," she said from her chair, her tone pleading and her cheeks flushed. "The king's own son. Please proceed carefully. The both of you."

Niall nodded. "We must know for certain what occurred, before any justice can be rendered, either within— or outside—of the law. We must draw him near."

His brother's eyes reflected the same hate that he knew burned in his own.

"We won't have long to wait." Magnus replied, "Buchan promises to come for the wedding, which will take place in less than a fortnight. If Mistress Iverach does not escape by then."

"Escape. What do you mean by that?" asked Elspeth, her brows drawn together.

He felt his brother's attention grow even more intense. "Yes, what?"

His back to the fire, he looked at them. "She wants nothing more than to avoid marriage to Hugh."

"How do you know that?" Elspeth asked, her eyes alight with sudden interest.

"None of that matters," her husband gently rebuked, raising both hands in impatience, before directing his gaze once again to Magnus. "You must do everything within your power to keep her there. We can't take the chance that Buchan won't come. Understand, brother, we can only challenge him . . . defeat him *here*. In our Highlands."

"I do understand," Magnus insisted. "But I won't have her endangered."

His brother and Elspeth looked back at him in silence.

"Oh, Magnus," she said softly. "You care for her."

"I don't," he insisted. "Not in the way you imply."

"She must be very pretty," she countered.

He frowned at her. "I've never even seen her face."

"But you *have* spoken to her." She smiled impishly. "You've been charmed only by speaking to her. How powerful. How perfect!"

"Aye, Elspeth, I *have* spoken to her," he retorted, annoyed by her teasing. "And she is innocent of all this. I would not have her harmed. That is *all*."

"And she will not be harmed," said his brother. "Watch over her. Keep her safe. And if you truly believe she is in danger, bring her here in secret, and we will protect her until this thing with the Alwyn and Buchan is done."

After a long moment of inward turmoil, Magnus nodded, trusting his brother's assurances were true. "Agreed. But now I must go. I have already been here too long."

He strode forward and grasped his brother's hand. It was only then that he remembered—

"One more thing."

"Yes."

He released his brother's hand. "Last night, Mistress Iverach and her traveling party were set upon by brigands, barely a stone's throw from Burnbryde."

Niall shrugged. "They should not have traveled at night. These *are* the *hielands, after all.*"

Magnus tilted his head. "The brigands wore hoods to conceal their faces, and claimed to be Kincaids. They even accused the traveling party of venturing onto Kincaid land, when any Kincaid or Alwyn would know they did not."

Niall's eyes narrowed. "Did they, then?"

"If it is true," Magnus said, "that these men *were* Kincaids, I do not seek to question your strategy, although I find it curious. But a necklace was stolen from the girl. One that means very much to her. I would ask it be given to me so that I might return to her."

Niall's gaze intensified. "Again, this Mistress Iverach . . . arrived only yesterday, and already you put yourself forth to enter into negotiations for the return of her necklace?" His lips curled into a slow grin.

Magnus muttered through clenched teeth. "Do you have the necklace or not?"

"I don't. And your brigands weren't Kincaid men, or any of my mercenaries, I can promise you that. But I'd be interested to know who they were."

Magnus exhaled. "As would I, brother."

They all walked to the courtyard, where he said his good-byes to Niall and Elspeth. Magnus could only hope that one day soon, their days might pass differently, without mention of war or revenge. That they might forge a deeper friendship, and rebuild the bond of brotherhood that life had taken from them.

"I will return soon," he said.

"We will stand ready," Niall assured him solemnly, clasping a hand to his shoulder. "Though 'tis difficult for me to stand back, to let you face this danger alone."

"I am not alone," answered Magnus, staring into his eyes. "I carry the spirit of all the Kincaids in my blood."

Magnus reached out his hand. Niall grasped it and squeezed.

"We will either triumph—or die together," Niall said. "As brothers."

Elspeth touched a hand to both of their shoulders, tears rising in her eyes.

"You will triumph," she announced in a firm, yet tremulous, voice. "There can be no other outcome, when your cause is honorable and right."

Magnus rode away from the castle, this time without a warrior escort. Clouds burdened the sky above, and a frigid wind swept across the plain, causing his plaid to ripple and snap in the wind. Some two hours later he passed into Alwyn lands, where he spied in the distance a carriage and six outriders, which in time traveled past him at a surprising speed. He saw then that the conveyance bore the mark of the Earl of Buchan.

He waved a hand, and one of the Alwyn outriders broke away, riding closer and raising a hand in greeting.

"What is going on here?" Magnus asked. "Where are you going?"

"The Alwyn has tasked us with returning the nun to the priory. The aged sister who delivered Hugh's betrothed."

Magnus nodded. "A safe journey to you, then."

They parted, going their different ways. A short time later, Magnus encountered a party of warriors—riding fast, with Chissolm at their lead.

They slowed, and circled one another.

"What is this?" Magnus inquired, raising his hand in greeting. "Where are you going without me?"

The wind ruffling his rusty hair, Chissolm grinned back at him, his cheeks red from the cold. "It seems

Hugh's betrothed plotted a switch with the old nun who brought her here, and she's escaped."

"Escaped?" Magnus's body tensed, his heart beat faster.

"Aye, and the Alwyn has sent us tae brin' her back."

Magnus's pulse tripped, and despite his agreement with Niall to do everything in his power to keep Tara Iverach at Burnbryde, he knew a moment of indecision. Would Buchan come to Burnbryde if she were gone? Very possibly, no. But was he not selfish to use an innocent young woman for his own benefit, even if he did all he could to protect her? Did she not deserve her chance at freedom? He recalled her voice from the night before . . . the words she'd spoken. Her tears.

He looked over his shoulder, away from the men, and considered the blank landscape. He could tell them he hadn't seen the carriage—or send them off in another direction.

But one thing struck those possibilities from play.

The horses' hooves and carriage wheels had left a clear path of damp, damningly turned-up earth, making the carriage easy to follow.

If it were only himself and Chissolm. He could swear his friend to silence . . . but they were not alone. They were in the company of a score of men. Not just warriors of the Pit, who might keep his confidence, but others undoubtedly loyal to the laird.

Left with no choice, he pulled the reins of his horse and turned the animal around. "Let's go, then."

Chapter 7

He rode hard, at the forefront of them all, his heart beating with anticipation and dread. He had to get to her first.

At last he saw in the distance, the dark anomaly of the traveling party against the rust and green meadow ahead. When he drew nearer, the sound of the horses' hooves and harnesses jangling, and the carriage wheels scrabbling, drowned out any calls for them to stop, but he urged his mount faster and swept alongside, waving his arm to draw the driver's attention. At this, the carriage slowed.

He swung down from the saddle, exhaling through his nose.

"Take my horse," he said, transferring the reins to Chissolm's open hand. "I'll ride back with the lady. I don't know her state of mind, but we don't want her jumping out or harming herself in any way."

He made the excuse so that he could speak to her alone, and do what he could to calm her fears.

"Agreed. Poor lass." Chissolm nodded, and flashed a wry smile. "I wouldn't want to marry Hugh either."

Striding forward, Magnus wrenched open the wooden,

metal-banded door—which he'd expected to be locked. Bringing his booted foot up, he climbed half inside.

"Mistress—" he said in a gentle tone.

"Get out," she shouted, her slender body pushing as far away from him as she could, into the corner, turning her face away and holding her hand up so he could not see her. A nun's wimple concealed her hair. "You have no authority over me, no right to stop my carriage."

He hated her fear. Her desperation. And his part in creating it.

"Tara," he said more loudly, leaning toward her.

"Is it her?" Chissolm shouted from his horse.

Hissing through his teeth, he eased back and nodded, waving Chissolm off.

Climbing inside, he closed the door behind himself, and saw the bar lock destroyed, something which must have occurred the night before during the attack by the brigands. The carriage started roughly into motion.

"Tara, look at me—" he began.

Seating himself on the bench beside her, he reached, grasping her shoulders, bringing her around. As before, a linen veil covered her face—everything but her eyes, which remained tightly closed.

"Don't touch me," she cried, twisting away, her hands coming up to shove at his shoulder, his chest.

"*It is I, Magnus.*"

She went utterly still—then turned to him.

Two vivid green eyes flew open, shocking him through, causing his breath to stagger from his lips. Beneath them, the carriage shook, moving over the earth with greater speed.

"*Magnus?*" she gasped. A tear trickled down her cheek, to be absorbed by the linen.

Her hands, which had shoved against him, twisted,

seizing handfuls of his tunic. She slid closer, her hands moving to his shoulders.

"Please," she begged, peering up into his eyes. "*Please* release me."

'Twas not relief his presence inspired, and certainly not joy. Nay, she threw herself on his mercy, only out of the deepest desperation.

"Tara . . ." he said, his heart clenching with regret.

He could not be this close to her and not see her face. He gently pulled the veil free.

She did not flinch away but remained in place, her lips hovering near his, so close that her uneven breath brushed across his lips.

"You don't have to take me back there," she pled, looking up—her eyes flashing fire and tears. "Let me go."

"I'm sorry," he murmured, his hands coming up to hold her arms.

He *was* sorry, for what he could not do. Outside, horses' hooves sounded alongside the carriage, a reminder that a company of men surrounded them, and that there was no other possible path in this moment, but the one that returned them to Burnbryde.

"I don't have a choice."

"Do whatever you will then," she snapped.

Tara jerked back, out of his grasp, withdrawing as far away from him as she could, which was not far given the close confines of the carriage.

Her teeth snapped shut on a torrent of furious, irrational words that would accomplish nothing.

Magnus—the man whose face she'd only imagined before now—stared back at her in all of his glorious truth. Golden haired and noble featured, his vivid blue eyes scored her through, above a Viking's nose and unsmiling lips. A warrior angel, who took her breath away . . . more magnificent than any man she'd ever seen.

Yet she hated him, and more than anything she wanted him to disappear.

She wanted them *all* to disappear, so she could hie fast away to a place where she didn't feel afraid.

"Tara—" he said again, gently—as if to comfort her.

As if they were friends. As if mere sympathy could console her.

"Stop saying my name," she cried. "You don't know me. I don't know you."

"I know you are upset. I know you are afraid."

A veritable giant beside her, his body—his chest, and shoulders, and long legs—seemed to occupy every available space, making her feel even more small and helpless than before.

"You don't know *anything*," she spat.

In a fit of frustration and hopelessness she tore the wimple from her head, and threw it at him.

He clasped the veil against his chest, his long, square-knuckled fingers splayed wide. His eyes flared—then darkened, fixed on her hair.

Suddenly, he moved toward her, one booted leg coming forward, crushing against her skirt. The wimple fell to the floor, as he took hold of her shoulders. Her heartbeat raced and she gasped, overwhelmed by his swiftness, his power and his size. And though *afraid* because she was being returned to Burnbryde, to an unknown fate, she did not fear *him*. Just as she'd instinctively known in the forest he would not harm her, she knew it now.

But she knew better than to let down her guard to this man again. And if he tried to kiss her, as he had done before, she would make him duly sorry for it.

"Release me!" she insisted, trying to jerk away.

"Be still, and listen to me," he commanded.

He was *not* her friend. He was *not* her ally. He most certainly was not her protector. She had only herself to rely on.

"There is nothing you can say to me that I wish to hear—" she exclaimed, through tears.

"*Listen*," he hissed through his teeth—and gave her a firm shake.

She blinked at him, startled into silence.

He glowered down into her eyes. "I will do what I can to get you out of Burnbryde. Do you hear me? But you must trust me."

She stared at his lips.

"*Trust* you?" she repeated.

She did not feel she could trust *any* man, and it broke her heart to think it, for she wanted very desperately to trust again.

"I don't know that I can."

"Well, *try*." Exhaling through his nose, he released her, and scooted away, as if he could bear to touch her no more. "It's not as if you have any other choice."

She exhaled raggedly. That much was true.

A long moment passed before he spoke again. "If I am to endeavor to help you, you must be *patient*—and brave. Understand the position I'm in, and the danger not only for you, but for us both. There are matters of blood here. Of family and clan loyalty. They must be dealt with carefully. You must not doubt that I will do what I say, or question when I will do it. Just know I *will* get you out of that place before you are wed."

He looked away from her, his jaw rigid. His manner, tense. As if he might not trust her either. What sort of an alliance was that, with neither of them trusting the other?

"Be patient? *Brave*?" she said, her voice wavering with anger. "When Hugh has a key to the tower, and can come and go in the night, into my chamber, at will, to do as he wishes?"

His head snapped toward her.

"He did that?" he snarled, the muscles at his neck and shoulders flexing beneath his tunic.

She stared back at him, her emotions too tangled to speak. She could only nod, and peer at him through tear-blurred eyes.

He twisted toward her again on the bench, his body appearing larger and even more imposing in such close quarters, his long, muscled legs, bent at the knees, brushing against hers, but he did not come close—as if he understood that in this moment, to touch her would be wrong. His nostrils flared, and his face contorted with anger.

"It's why you were crying last night. Damn him to hell, did he . . ." He gritted out his words through clenched teeth. "You must tell me if he . . ."

"He did not." She shook her head. "But he told me when he so wishes, that I must submit. I do not know if he meant before or after we are married, but I am *afraid*—"

And afraid because she felt certain someone had hurt her sister. Only she had no proof. Only suspicion, and therefore, she couldn't speak the words to this man.

"I'll take care of it," he uttered harshly.

"Take care of it?" she answered, agonized, because the wheels of the carriage still turned, carrying her again toward shadows and darkness. "How?"

"*I will*." The scant afternoon light that permeated through the walls of the carriage illuminated his face—the tight clench of his jaw, and blue eyes gone dark and vengeful.

Fear still weighed heavy on her heart. Why should she believe him?

"You are an Alwyn," she said in a low voice. "Why would you help me?"

His gaze pinned her from across the bench.

"Don't I owe it to you? For deceiving you? For falsely claiming that which I had no right to claim?" Only his eyes touched her. And yet the intensity of that look brought the memory of their kisses blazing to life. Her cheeks burned hot.

In the next moment his gaze narrowed. "But mostly it's because I don't like Hugh that much myself, and I would do anything to thwart him."

"*The wrong eldest son*," she murmured. "Those were the words you used last night. Because you are the laird's son, too, are you not? Just not the one who bears his name."

She spoke the words softly. Even so, she all but branded him a bastard.

Neither his gaze nor his tone wavered. "So I am told."

"I can only surmise that there is a longstanding grudge between the two of you, that has nothing to do with me."

His jaw twitched. "One grudge? Nay, mistress, more like thousands."

Aye, and she could see them now, like a thousand burning candles in his eyes. Eyes that seemed to allow her a glimpse of his heart, one that bore wounds, as deep or deeper than hers.

He had promised to help her, and he seemed sincere. She did not know what to think. How to feel! She only knew he carried with him a deep unhappiness, just as she did. And yet rather than speaking words of cruelty, or trying to use her toward his own end, he had done his best to allay her fears and give her hope.

"Whatever lot life has cast you," she said. "You are a far finer man than he."

The words spilled from her lips before she could stop

them, before she could consider what reaction they might invite.

He leaned toward her suddenly, his muscled shoulders stretching the cloth of his tunic. He was handsome—dangerously so—and he looked at her mouth in a way that, despite everything, made her chest go tight with yearning. He lifted a hand, as if to touch her hair. Her breath wavered in her throat.

"Do I have your permission to speak your name again?" he asked, his voice husky.

In another time, and another place, perhaps he would chuckle when speaking those words, and she would laugh at hearing them. But there was nothing amusing or joyful about this moment. There was no teasing about his manner.

"Aye," she whispered.

Instead, with solemnity in his features, his lowered his head closer.

"Tara . . ."

Her heart pounded heavily, and heat spread out, seemingly from her soul, to filter through the rest of her body. He was going to kiss her . . . and this time, she wanted him to.

Danger surrounded her. The last thing on her mind was a rebellious warrior's kisses . . . and yet, she needed to feel something other than fear. She needed to trust another human, and to believe in the hope he offered her. She'd become so thickly tangled in this dark, shadowy place that had devoured her sister. She had to believe that somehow, some way, she'd break free. Else she too would be swallowed whole.

The sound of the wheels beneath the carriage signaled an obvious change, from earth to stone.

Closing his eyes, he exhaled through his nose . . . and lowered his hand.

"We've arrived," he said.

"Already!" she whispered, her stomach clenching with dread.

He drew back and looked out through the crack in the shutter. "The laird and Hugh are waiting." He turned his face toward her. "I would spare you these next few moments, if I could. Remember this. You are the Earl of Buchan's ward, the laird's most valuable possession. You might get a tongue lashing, but you won't be harmed. Soon, you'll be in the safety of the tower."

"I don't want to be in the tower." She closed her eyes, and clenched her hands. "It is a prison."

His gaze flared hot. "The tower will soon be the safest place for you to be."

Moments later, the carriage drew to a stop.

"*Trust me,*" he urged again, looking at her as he reached for the door. "Give me time, and I will see you safely gone from here."

She stared into his eyes, doing her best not to tremble. Not to drown in the maelstrom of fear and helplessness closed in around her. She wanted to trust him but couldn't decide . . . couldn't devote another thought to it. Already her thoughts were focused on the coming confrontation. As he said, for now she need only survive these next few moments.

She nodded jerkily.

"Are y' ready, then?"

"Aye," she whispered, knowing he could not shield her from this. That this challenge, she must face alone.

With one final glance into her eyes, he pushed open the door, and climbed out first, turning back to extend his hand. Taking it, she climbed down as well, into the path of a cold wind that tugged at the nun's habit she wore.

As she'd known he must, Magnus released her and stepped away, leaving her to face her judgment alone.

The laird descended the stairs, his face red and angry. Behind him Hugh followed, piercing her with his eyes. At the top of the steps, at either side of the door, guards were posted, two to each side.

The warriors on horseback, who had intercepted her carriage, continued on toward the stables.

Tara shored up her courage, determined not to wither. Determined to do what she could, on her own behalf, to change the path of her wayward destiny. Perhaps she had been impulsive in agreeing to Grizel's plan, and her freedom could be achieved in another, less dramatic, way.

The laird, arriving at the bottom step, approached her, appearing no less furious near, than afar.

"Mistress Iverach," he gritted. "I can only say I am shocked. You have betrayed our trust unforgivably. What could have inspired you to turn so cruelly against your betrothed—your new family—with such callous and unfeeling disregard?"

She moved toward him, trembling, but determined to speak the words. To say what she should have said late last night. This morning. All along.

"What you say is true," she answered in a clear voice. "What I've done is unforgiveable, and yet still I beg your forgiveness and your understanding. I should never have fled in such a manner. I should have come to you first, and informed you directly, and face-to-face, that I was afraid—" She glanced at Hugh, then, recalling how he had come into her room. The demands he had made. She thought of Arabel, the details of whose death everyone stuttered and stammered over. "—so afraid, I felt I had no choice but to leave Burnbryde."

"What?" barked Hugh, squinting at her, the corners of his mouth turned down into a devil's scowl.

She glanced at Hugh.

"What are you talking about?" the Alwyn demanded. "What made you afraid?"

"Ask your son," Tara replied, emphatically.

Suddenly, Sister Grizel emerged from the door behind him, accompanied by an enormous man who held her by the arm and led her along.

"Grizel!" Tara cried.

"Dear child," Grizel replied, tears dampening her aged eyes, and her short gray hair visible to all. "I hoped y'd made it far from here."

There was no opportunity to say more. The man nudged Grizel past Tara, down the steps to the carriage.

Tara took a step toward them, but a hand gripped her arm, stopping her. It was Hugh.

Off to the side, she glimpsed Magnus, tall and strong, his legs braced and his arms crossed over his chest. Though his face showed no emotion, his eyes blazed with the fire of one forced to stand by and watch.

She felt a strong connection to him, that much was true, but if he could do nothing to help her now, if he had no influence over his father or his brother, and must remain silent out of blood and clan loyalty, how would he ever be able to help her?

Turning to the laird, she implored, "Please reconsider. I throw myself on your mercy. Let her stay, please."

The laird dismissed her with a wave of his hand. "Cling not to the past. From this day forward, this clan will provide for your every need."

Without a moment's ceremony, the door of the conveyance was opened again, and Grizel hoisted inside. A servant followed, carrying her small, solitary chest, which he deposited inside at her feet. The sister's face appeared at the window for only a moment, before the carriage started into motion.

Tara watched, feeling as if her heart was being ripped out, sinking further into despair with each turn of the wheels, until the carriage disappeared through the gate.

Alone. Now she was truly alone, and without a single friend. Without anyone to witness the manner in which her days would unfold.

Behind her, the tower waited, dark and silent.

"Gilroy, escort the Mistress Iverach to her chambers," the laird instructed.

The giant who'd dispatched Grizel, moved toward her. She yanked free of Hugh's grasp. Turning, she proceeded up the steps, feeling as if her legs were encased in stone, ignoring his hard stare.

Behind her, she heard Magnus speak. "Laird, a moment please, in your chambers, if you will."

Out of the corner of her eye, she caught the turn of Hugh's face, and the hateful expression he directed toward his half-brother.

"You have been to Inverhaven?" the Alwyn answered, brusquely.

"I have," Magnus answered.

The chief nodded. "Let us go then."

Magnus added, "Hugh should come as well."

Suddenly, she feared that Magnus would betray her. That he would tell the laird that she attempted to persuade him to help her. That she had every intention of escaping again. As she preceded Gilroy inside, she looked aside at Magnus, looking for the slightest reassurance, but he did not spare her a glance.

"Is this true?" the Alwyn demanded, scowling at Hugh.

"Truly?" Hugh sneered, with a cutting glance toward Magnus. "You're going to allow your by-blow to tell tales on me?"

Hugh had always been the one person who would state

the relationship between Magnus and the laird, to his father's face, but only ever as a means to provoke.

"Answer me," the chief thundered. "*Is . . . this . . . true*?"

"What does it matter?" Hugh retorted loudly. "She is *my* betrothed. Bound to *me*, by duty and law. Not you, and certainly not him."

Magnus stood to the side, arms crossed over his chest, not wishing to be caught anywhere between them, though he'd caused the entire scene.

"*Fool*," his father bellowed. "She is far more than that. She is noble born, and Buchan's ward. The second sister of a fine family that he has seen fit to bestow unto us. One who must be treated with care and respect, so there will be no question we remain worthy of that alliance. Dolt! Do you not understand the precarious position we are in, how carefully we must tread, with the first one dead?"

"You're reveling in this, aren't you?" Hugh muttered, glaring at Magnus.

Magnus held Hugh's gaze. "I intend no malice. Your affairs, of course, are entirely your own. But in this instance, I felt it necessary to voice my concern, as it is unlikely we can defeat the Kincaid without Buchan's support."

It was crucial that he not show any glimmer of interest in Tara. That he appear as if his only concern were for the clan.

"You will surrender the key," the Alwyn barked, slamming his fists against the table. "*Now*."

He'd cast his lots, and thrown Hugh under the horse's hooves, so to speak, and for the moment, it appeared his wager had paid off, though he felt certain there'd be a price to pay later.

Hugh thrust his hand into the leather pouch he wore at his waist, and cast the key onto the table, where it *clinked* loudly, before skidding across the surface and landing with a clatter against the stone floor.

"Take the damned key, then," he uttered in a guttural tone. "Soon it won't matter, anyway."

Once he and Tara were wed, he meant. She'd be at his mercy then. Her life. Her virtue. But Magnus had already sworn that he wouldn't allow that union to take place.

"One day you will be laird of this clan," his father said. "Best you learn to act like one. It is time for your self-indulgences to end. And you will exert control over those unruly, impulsive hounds you call your *guard*. I will no longer allow them to run rampant, doing as they wish. From this moment onward, you will conduct yourself with care. Most importantly, you will devote yourself, in the coming days, to wooing that girl." He jabbed a finger upward, in the direction of the tower.

"May I go?" Hugh snarled, his jaw clenched.

Magnus spoke then. "Stay. You may be interested to hear what I have seen of the Kincaid's forces at Inverhaven."

He didn't really care if Hugh stayed, but it served his purposes to appear deferential and inclusive in the eyes of the Alwyn.

"Well, I'm not," Hugh answered in a petulant growl.

Turning on his heel, he strode from the room.

Magnus took care to keep all expression from his face of his dislike for Hugh, and of his hatred for the man who remained.

The laird stared at the empty door. "Proceed."

"Mistress," said a voice, but softly. "Mistress, awaken."

Opening her eyes, she looked up into the near identical faces of Mary and Anna, Lady Alwyn's maidservants, who wore their dark blond hair braided into neat buns on either side of their heads.

The feeling of dread returned instantly—as did her memory of the earlier hours of the day. Her failed escape. Grizel's banishment. Magnus's promise to help her. And like a recurring nightmare . . . the realization that her sister, Arabel, was dead.

Returned to her room, she'd fallen into an exhausted and anxious sleep.

The youngest of the two curtsied. "The lady has sent us to assist you in dressing for the evening meal, in the gathering hall."

The gathering hall.

She would be allowed outside of the tower? Even after her attempted escape, and her argument with the laird?

Tara sat up on the bed, shaking free of her sleep. "Yes. All right."

No, she did not wish to spend time in Lady Alwyn's company, who upon her return to the castle had greeted her with aggrieved silence, refusing even to meet her gaze, or to converse about why Tara had felt compelled to leave in subterfuge. Instead, she'd seen Tara to her chamber— and locked Tara inside.

Neither did Tara wish to see Hugh, or the laird, who would certainly treat her with contempt.

But she must take any opportunity to leave her confines, for it would allow her to better learn the world into which she'd been so forcefully thrust—and to discern opportunities for extracting herself from it, for yes, her options were again limited to escape. The laird had made it clear her wishes would not be considered, and that under no circumstances would she be allowed to end her betrothal.

She feared that her failed ruse today had considerably lessened her chances of ever breaking free. They would guard her more carefully now . . . which was exactly why she found it so curious they were now allowing her to venture from her cage.

Perhaps in the gathering hall, she would see Magnus.

Now that she knew the unfortunate truth of Hugh, she'd all but forgiven Magnus's initial deception of her in the forest. Not just because he seemed truly regretful for misrepresenting his identity to her, but because if she'd lived a lifetime with Hugh, she'd likely do anything to provoke him as well.

Now that she'd looked into Magnus's eyes, and believed she understood him better, she thought . . . *hoped* . . . she saw a hero in him. He had insisted so firmly that she trust that he would save her from this. But had he done so out of honor and goodness, or merely to best Hugh?

The truth of his heart mattered not. It was all just a game of power and control between men, and as society dictated, she would be their pawn. Or so she must allow them to believe. She would not succumb to the role of victim. No, she must be as cunning and self-serving as them. She must learn from all she heard and observed, and make use of every piece of knowledge, to her own benefit.

She would not invest the entirety of her hopes in Magnus's promises. And yet . . . after their moments together today in the carriage, just knowing he was here in the castle, gave her some small comfort.

Oh, but the heat that had flared between them when they'd kissed . . . They'd shared an undeniable attraction, the memory of which even now warmed her cheeks, and made her go breathless.

Now that she'd seen his face, and again felt the power of his warrior's body against hers, her interest in him as a man only grew. No doubt the "fires" of attraction had brought about the downfall of many a lady. She could not, under any circumstances, allow desire to affect her good judgment.

"Let us change your clothing, and dress your hair," said Anna, the younger of the two.

She still wore Grizel's rough, gray habit—a symbol of her failure, which she was eager to shed.

"Thank you both for helping me," Tara said, looking between them, seeking some glimmer of compassion or understanding.

"You are most welcome," Anna answered with a meek, yet warm smile.

Mary's eyes did not reflect the same kindness. Nor did she offer any reply.

Mary went to Tara's trunks. Opening the lid, she pulled out several kirtles.

"Your sister's clothes." Anna sighed sadly.

"Hush," warned Mary, with a sharp glance.

Anna did hush, pressing her lips together until they were thin. She avoided Tara's direct gaze after that.

"Which one," Mary asked brusquely, displaying the garments on extended arms.

"That one," said Tara, gesturing at the closest one—a blue kirtle with gold cording at the bodice and shoulders—for no particular reason, other than the room was cold and the kirtle appeared warm.

In silence, with only a murmured word here and there, they assisted her in bathing, and then donning the garment.

Anna dressed Tara's hair, smoothing out long, thick strands, and turning them into artful curls, which she pinned at either side of her head. Tara, used to simple braids, had never seen herself look so fine, and like a noble lady.

"Very pretty. Thank you, Anna. Did my sister wear her hair like this?"

Anna tilted her head, her gaze admiring. "Sometimes, but your hair is longer, and thicker and I must say, quite vivid in color." She laughed softly. "Though the style is the same, the appearance is very different."

"Anna, hush," her sister warned from the corner, where she folded Grizel's habit.

When she'd finished, Anna fastened a transparent gold head covering over her hair, which allowed an alluring glimpse of the elegant style beneath. Mary fastened an embroidered piece of linen across her bosom, tucking it artfully into the gown's bodice, where Arabel's dress, tailored for her slenderer frame, crowded Tara's bosom upward to a degree that might be considered unseemly.

"Have you any adornments to wear?" asked Mary. "Jewelry?"

Tara thought of her mother's necklace, and wondered about its present whereabouts. Had it been thrown to the bottom of a well, with other stolen prizes, or did the brigand's elderly mother or wife wear it as she darned his hose by the fire?

"I don't," she answered.

"Your sister had some things," Anna said. "Would you like to look at them?"

"I would," she responded eagerly. Her heart swelled in her chest.

She wanted to see . . . to touch . . . any object that had belonged to her sister. Perhaps Anna or Mary could tell her something about her sister's time here, and confirm the manner in which she had died, putting to rest, once and for all, the dark suspicions in her mind.

Mary left the room.

"Anna, tell me, did you know my sister?" Tara asked in a gentle tone.

"Oh, indeed." Anna nodded, smiling. "I served her, as I am serving you now."

"Can you tell me anything of her last days? Of how she died?"

The smile disappeared from her lips. "How she died . . . well, it was—a fever." A flush rose on the girl's cheeks, and she looked away, clearly uncomfortable with Tara's question.

Uncomfortable because she was telling a lie?

"So I have been told," Tara answered in what she hoped was an unsuspicious voice. "I had not seen my sister in some years, but loved her very much. I would welcome any details that might help me remember her better, even though she is gone. Did you tend to her during her illness? Were you with her when . . . when she died?"

Emotion thickened her voice, and tears blurred her vision.

"No, mistress," the girl answered softly. Her eyes, too, glimmered with tears. She turned quickly, placing the comb on the table. "For safety, Lady Alwyn forbade us from coming into the tower, so the sickness would not spread. But I wish I had been here. She was very kind to me."

She'd been kept from the tower. The words did nothing to settle Tara's doubts, for what if . . . what if the story of a fever had been a ruse, which even those in the castle had been led to believe?

Mary returned then, holding a small wooden chest. "Here are your sister's things."

Her mind still swirling with suspicions, Tara looked inside. There were several gilt brass necklaces and plated bracelets . . . various decorative hairpins and combs . . . three rings bearing inexpensive stones . . . and a locket.

None was familiar to her, and unfortunately none was valuable enough to fund a clandestine journey to Elgin. Most certainly not anywhere beyond. But while they wouldn't pay for passage on a ship or for even a horse, they might get her a goodly distance away from Burnbryde in the back of a farmer's wagon. But how to ensure she would not be intercepted again? Most importantly, she wanted no innocent person punished because of what she'd done.

"I'll wear this one," she said, lifting a delicate torc.

A sound came from the outer room . . . something like a bell tinkling.

"Oh, hurry," whispered Anna, taking the necklace and quickly fastening it at Tara's throat. "The lady is waiting. We must go."

Tara's already pensive mood tumbled. It was time to face Lady Alwyn.

Tara found Lady Alwyn waiting for her in the common room, dressed in a dark green kirtle, her throat and wrists gleaming with gold adornments.

"A word before we go down," said the older woman in a subdued tone, her expression shadowed.

"Yes," answered Tara, bracing herself for whatever chastisements the woman would issue.

Lady Alwyn nodded, sighing, clasping her hands. "I must . . . apologize."

She straightened the cuff of her sleeve.

An apology? The announcement surprised Tara. She had expected to be subjected to a lecture.

The lady continued on, speaking with obvious care. "I have been informed by my husband that . . . our son entered your room on the first night of your arrival."

"He did. Yes." Tara nodded, her back going rigid. "While I slept."

The woman's cheeks flushed. "I had . . . no idea. While he is your betrothed and will soon be your husband, there are boundaries to be observed, at least in this household. No doubt he was still in a drunken state."

"Yes. He was."

Lady Alwyn sighed. "Then of course I understand why you reacted as you did, and felt compelled to escape.

Please know that he no longer possesses a key, and his father has let him know such coarse behavior will not be tolerated."

Magnus.

Tara's heart warmed. He was responsible for this somehow. She had doubted his ability, and believed that he helplessly stood by, but this . . . this changed everything.

"I must accept my part of the blame," said Lady Alwyn. "Hugh is a spoiled boy, who has grown into an arrogant man, but I hope you will forgive him this one mistake, for which I know, deep down inside, he is truly regretful. He is just not very good at saying the words."

Tara wanted to argue. She wanted to say she knew Hugh's behavior the night before would not be a singular occurrence, and that if she were to marry him he would surely make each day of her life miserable with his cruel and controlling ways.

But mayhap it was best to remain silent, and not draw attention to her unabated discontent. Perhaps she should let Lady Alwyn believe she'd been appeased. Now that they were talking, perhaps she could broach an important subject.

"Thank you, my lady. However, it was not only Hugh's intrusion that alarmed me, but the matter of the locked doors. I am unaccustomed to being locked in my chamber, and being unable to move about as I choose."

Lady Alwyn pressed a hand to her forehead. "You are right, of course. I . . . was overzealous, as I so often am. It was only my intention to keep you safe, away from the filth and pestilence of the world below, because clearly . . ." Her eyes sparkled with tears. "Clearly I failed your sister."

Her shoulders shook with sudden tears. Despite everything, Tara could not help but feel pity for the woman.

"You didn't fail her." Tara stepped forward and touched a reassuring hand to her shoulder. After all, she couldn't condemn the woman for anything. She had no proof that Arabel's death was anything other than what she'd been told. "Oh, please don't cry."

She didn't like being so suspicious of everyone. It wasn't her nature. She would much rather know her sister had peacefully died of a fever, as was claimed. If only she had some way to know for certain.

"You're so very kind to absolve me," Lady Alwyn answered shakily, rising from her chair. "But I will forever carry that guilt. Even so . . . from this moment on, your chamber door will remain unlocked, unless you desire to lock it."

She wore a small brass ring at her waist, from which dangled several keys. Removing this, she selected one key, separating it from the others and pressed it into Tara's hand. "There you are. My gift to you. You may move about the solar as you wish. I never intended it to seem otherwise, truly I didn't."

For the first time since she'd arrived, Tara breathed a little easier. No, she would never willingly marry Hugh, but for the first time, at last, she felt as if she was having a normal conversation with someone. Even so, something the lady said repeated in her mind, that she might move about the solar. But only the solar?

"May I also come and go from the tower whenever I wish?" Tara asked hopefully.

Lady Alwyn's head tilted to the side. "Not for now, I'm afraid."

Her optimism flagged. "But . . . why?"

The lady's expression grew grave. She paced a few steps away, then turned back.

"I have no wish to frighten you, especially after all

that has happened these past two days, but you aren't a child. You're part of this clan now, and deserve to be informed."

"I want to know."

"Then, dear, I will tell you that even as we speak, warriors keep watch from Burnbryde's ramparts for any sign of an attack by the clan to our north . . . the Clan Kincaid."

Tara's heart sank, for she knew what the lady would say, that because of this rising conflict, she would be trapped here for the indeterminable future.

"The conflict between our clans goes very far back, to when Hugh was just a small child, and you, child, weren't even born. The old Kincaid laird, you see, acted in such a way as to be deemed a traitor against the king, and the Alwyns, as loyal servants of the crown, assisted their necessary defeat. Since then, the Kincaids have been landless. What a sad lot they are, all scattered to the winds. But very recently a man came forth, claiming to be the son of the Kincaid. He is, without a doubt, an imposter. And mercenary by trade, he commands a large army of similarly dangerous and untrustworthy warriors, with which he proceeded to seize lands that once belonged to the Kincaids. Lands chartered, by law, to the MacClaren laird." She shrugged. "Lands that by law they no longer had right to."

"And the Alwyns also now hold claim to what were once Kincaid lands."

"Indeed, and because of that he threatens us in much the same way."

"I see," said Tara.

"Trust that our warriors can repel any attack on the castle . . . but it is not an outright attack the laird fears most, but the infiltration of an assassin or that someone . . .

Hugh, myself, or even you, my dear, may be abducted and held for ransom or to force a certain response. We must assume that danger lurks everywhere."

"It is wise for the laird to be so careful," Tara conceded, wondering if she ought to be afraid. *Assassins?*

If only fate had not brought her to this wild and dangerous place. She wanted more than anything to leave. To live life in a large burgh like Aberdeen or Perth where there were fine houses lining wide, paved streets, and cathedrals, and most especially well-mannered people. There was nothing redeeming about Burnbryde . . . except for Anna, who had been very kind to her. And Magnus, though her thoughts of him were somewhat tangled, between trust and distrust.

"The laird has taken measures to ensure our safety. More warriors have been posted everywhere, both inside and outside the castle walls. And he has asked that we not leave the tower without escort, at least until the danger has passed." She nodded reassuringly. "We do expect that when your guardian arrives, he will bring sufficient soldiers to quell this Kincaid revolt against the Crown's authority."

Her words didn't calm Tara. Instead, they sent her thoughts into disarray. She was more a prisoner now than before. Now the tower was not only locked, but guarded.

"How fortunate that the Alwyn counts the powerful Earl of Buchan among his allies," she murmured.

"Indeed, it is. And all of this should make you feel more safe, rather than afraid," the lady said. "Again, we may move about freely, but with an escort for safety, always. Just tell me when and where you wish to go, and I shall arrange for Gilroy to accompany you."

Gilroy. The stone-faced old warrior who had ejected Grizel from Burnbryde, and on the laird's orders, returned Tara to the tower. That was exactly who she did not want following her everywhere, and observing her every move.

At that moment, Anna and Mary joined them, both dressed in finer gowns than they customarily wore, which indicated they might not be common servants, recruited from the village, but of higher birth.

Seeing them, the lady nodded. "It is time we go below stairs and join the others, which I will confide, is not my normal custom. But the laird insists that I not keep you here in the tower, all to myself."

Though she smiled, her voice bore an edge of annoyance, and Tara could only conclude the reclusive lady had been commanded by her husband, against her will, to attend dinner in the hall. Tara followed Lady Alwyn down the steps, and the two maidservants followed behind.

Gilroy met them at the bottom, where Tara observed two guards, in full armor and weaponry, posted outside the door, which he immediately secured behind them. Six male servants also waited, both older and young men who did not display the muscled brawn of the Alwyn warriors. Strangely, they carried large rectangular screens covered with gauze.

Raucous laughter emanated from the direction of the great hall—the room Tara had only seen from a distance the night before. Orange light from the hearth wavered off the walls and rippled through the shadows. Apprehension weighted her limbs at the thought of entering, because she knew Hugh and his father would be there to greet her.

Inside, the room was very dark, with only a few lanterns by which to see. Men wandered about, laughing and drinking, while others crowded on benches at long tables. In the distant corner, a young woman danced to the music of a lute. Her gown sagged off her shoulder, revealing a generous portion of her breast. She smiled, gliding around the circle of men who watched her, touching their chests, their arms, their faces—until Gilroy issued a startling shout, at which time all music and motion stopped.

"The Lady Alwyn enters," he bellowed.

At that, the male servants who had accompanied them lifted the screens, shielding them all around, from anyone's view, though she could see through the gauze enough to discern the hazy outline of faces and bodies. She'd never witnessed such a thing. Why would the lady require such privacy here, in this room intended for gathering? Such separation was more proof the lady did not intermingle often with the people of her clan. They proceeded, protected as such, to the front of the room. Tara glanced aside to see curious eyes peering through, from a respectful distance. She wondered whether Magnus was there, watching also, and she suffered disappointment at not seeing him.

At the dais, the laird waited, standing, and when they arrived, he ceremoniously led his wife to a seat. In like manner, Hugh appeared, unsmiling, his gaze locked on her. His dark eyes explored her with unfettered interest. Though dressed in fine garments, his eyes were glassy, and underscored by shadows, as if he'd already had too much to drink.

"Good evening," he said, offering his arm, which she woodenly accepted.

"Good evening," she answered, forcing the words.

She had no wish to sit beside Hugh and exchange insincere pleasantries, but in this moment there was no alternative. If she complained or refused his company, no doubt she would be portrayed as unruly and hysterical, and bring additional scrutiny upon herself.

The screens were placed in front of the table, she could only assume, so that curious eyes could not look upon Lady Alwyn and herself, though she could see wavering light and movement through them. Voices rose again in conversation. Servants approached, lowering large trenchers of food, and pouring goblets of ale, which Hugh eyed thirstily, but did not touch.

The laird, who sat on the other side of the table, leaned forward. "We are pleased to have you here tonight, as part of our family. Let us all forgive each other of our individual transgressions, and move forward from this moment on, as if this afternoon did not occur."

The words were conciliatory, yet his gaze was hard. His tone cool. His lips rigid, and unsmiling. Yet she had decided 'twas best to appear to be accepting of her fate.

She lowered her head. "Thank you, laird. I was homesick for the priory, and allowed my irrational fears to overcome my good sense."

The words were not necessarily a lie. The next time she left Burnbryde, she would proceed with more care.

"You are very young," said Lady Alwyn. "And these *hielands*—and their highlanders—can be frightening to outsiders. All is forgiven."

"But this is your home now," Hugh said firmly, staring at her with flat, inscrutable eyes. "Here, with me." Taking up the nearest trencher, Hugh selected a portion of fish for her plate. "Eat."

Tara glimpsed the look of approval on his mother and father's faces before they turned away toward their own meal. The words—which had been spoken as commands, not in welcome—weighed like chains around her neck. Hearing them, she found it difficult to breathe. They promised a future she desperately did not want. Tara focused her attention on her plate, thankful for something to look at other than his face.

And yet, it was only a brief moment before Hugh murmured near her ear.

"At first I did not find you to my liking, but that hair . . .

well, I must say I have changed my mind," he chuckled, the suggestive tone of his voice putting her on edge. "Pity they took my key."

He goaded her, daring her response. She knew that. Still, she could not keep silent.

"It wasn't right for you to come to my room uninvited," she answered.

"As if I shall require an invitation once we are married." His hand covered hers atop the table, and he stared down at her, a cruel smile on his lips. Anyone watching would believe they were simply having a private conversation. Flirting even. "Then, it will be your duty to please me. Every night . . . every morning . . . and whenever else I please. In whatever manner . . . I wish."

Heat burned her cheeks. Repulsed by his words, she looked at the fish on her plate, knowing no words would shame him. No rebuke would daunt him. He was beyond salvation.

He leaned close again, his breath on her ear sending a cold chill down her spine. "You're innocent, but you'll learn quickly. Not only from me, but from the other lovers who will share our bed."

Tara recoiled, and attempted to jerk her hand away, but Hugh held fast and moved closer, bending near.

"You disgust me," she hissed, turning her face away from him, shunning any more of his offensive words.

Except, the ones he'd already spoken still clamored inside her head, ugly and threatening. The scent of the fish, which moments before had not offended, rose up to fill her nostrils, nauseating her.

"You don't like what you hear? Well, then, you shouldn't have humiliated me by conspiring with that old nun to run away," he growled beside her. "Don't you see what you did? *Everyone* knows. *Everyone* is laughing behind my back."

She held still and silent, listening, her thoughts spiraling.

"And then you even *think* to tattle on me to my father's bastard?" he spat.

The words *I'm sorry* rose to her lips but she held them there, behind closed teeth. How could she be sorry for anything, when she suspected the man had harmed her sister?

"You don't want to make me your enemy," he said.

She turned to him suddenly, in confrontation.

"Like Arabel did?" she dared ask, hoping to provoke some telling response. Some truth.

The hate she saw there in his eyes, in his countenance, intensified. "Do not speak to me about your *whore* of a sister."

The vulgar word stunned her, along with the implication of his words.

"What do you mean by that?" she whispered.

"Do not ever mention her to me again," he ordered.

"But why would you say that?"

"Shut up." His hand tightened its grip on her arm. "Do you understand?"

Each word struck her full in the face, a dank wave of sour breath. Unwilling to inhale his breath, to share that vile intimacy, she again turned away.

In that moment her gaze happened to pierce the narrow space between the screens, and she saw him. Magnus. He sat at one of the tables, muscular and tall, surrounded by men, his pale hair gleaming bright in the firelight, making him stand out as different, as more brilliant than all the rest. His hand gripped a goblet, and his gaze blazed back into hers, alight with fury.

The connection anchored her, gave her a sudden surge of strength, knowing that someone watched, that someone cared.

"I said . . . do you understand?" Hugh repeated.

His hand bracketed her chin, turning her face toward his.

She swallowed down a sob of anger—and nodded, allowing him to believe he'd claimed his triumph.

Suddenly, the laird was there, leaning close to his son's side.

"What is going on here?" he glanced accusingly toward Hugh, and then to Tara. "Is something wrong?"

Hugh laughed, releasing her face. "Inform the kitchens. My *beloved* does not care for the fish."

"Where are you going?" Chissolm called after him.

"Do I need your permission to visit the garderobe?" Magnus replied over his shoulder.

The warrior laughed, and waved him off.

Certainly it had appeared strange to Chissolm when he'd left so abruptly—in the midst of the other warrior speaking a sentence. But he could no longer keep the expression of anger from his face. He could not sit by and watch Hugh torment Tara, without doing something about it. Without acting in some way.

What was happening with Hugh? His mind thundered with the question.

The laird's son had always been arrogant and boastful. Difficult and unpleasant. Petty and cruel. And he'd always kept terrible company, as if by encircling himself with the lowest of the low might somehow elevate him, at least in his own mind. They'd been at odds since Magnus, as a child, had come with Robina to Burnbryde. Indeed, for as long as Magnus could recall, and while he disliked Hugh intensely, he had also always felt some degree of pity toward the dark-eyed boy, because despite all the approval and attention bestowed on him, it was obvious he had never found happiness.

His mind thundered with questions. Was this Tara's mother's necklace? If so, why did Gilroy have it? Had Gilroy been involved in the attack on Tara's traveling party?

Had he done so at the behest of Lady Alwyn?

The necklace still clenched in hand, he closed the lid and returned the trunk to its place.

The door creaked. He froze, and closed his eyes. Several heavy footsteps sounded on the floor.

Hell.

"What are ye doing here?" Gilroy's voice said, rough and startled, from behind him.

Magnus turned on the heel of his boot, his heart beating wild and fast. Perhaps faster than his heart had ever beaten before. Gilroy's enormous frame blocked his only path to escape.

Was this it? Had he lost everything by coming here? Would he be forced to fight for his life, to flee Burnbryde in the night, without ever claiming the confession he so desperately desired, and his revenge?

Tara . . . what of her?

Gilroy needed only to take one step back to shout an alarm to the guards.

But Gilroy did not sound an alarm. Instead, he looked at Magnus in silence, his face blanked out by the shadows.

Suddenly, the old giant moved stepped inside, and closed the door. He continued forward, brushing roughly past and took up the chest Magnus had held only a moment before. Only to turn again to face him.

"Ah said, what are ye doing here?" he snarled. "No-around in me things?"

But the outrage in the man's voice rang false and ed.

Magnus considered every lie he could possibly tell,

But after tonight, Magnus could no longer deny that something in Hugh had changed, and threatened to spiral out of control. First, he had attacked Elspeth at the Festival of the Cearcal. Now, he behaved so lecherously toward Tara that Magnus feared for her safety.

For the first time, the death of her sister, Arabel, prodded, like a sharp-tipped dagger at his conscience. A fever, he'd heard. But was that truly what had occurred? Had Hugh harmed the girl? Had some crime occurred, to which he and the rest of the Alwyn clan had remained oblivious?

Something did not sit well in his mind, in his soul. If something terrible and secret had occurred, did that not make him part of the crime? That he had not noticed, that he had not asked questions until he discovered the truth. That he'd been so consumed with himself and his own affairs that her passing had gone unmarked, when that young woman had deserved to be protected, just as much as her younger sister did.

Tara. She had been so brave upon their return to the castle, facing the Alwyn and Hugh. But she would not be able to save herself. This was the Highlands, and whether right or wrong, men most often decided and women had little choice but to comply, unless another strong man defended the woman's decisions, her rightful choice.

Though he did not wish to examine his motivations too closely, he must be that man for Tara. He would go again to Niall, voice his concerns, and make a plan to take her to Inverhaven. There, she could spend her days with Elspeth, and when all this was done, if he lived, he would see her again and perhaps . . . persuade her to stay. Beyond that, he could not involve his heart, for he must remain singularly angry and full of hate for his enemies, if he were to do what he had to do, without fear or regret.

His gaze shifted across the room, searching for, and

finding Gilroy. The Lady Alwyn's steward conversed and ate at his customary table, his enormous shoulders hunched over his food. Backing into the darker shadows, he proceeded away from the great hall, toward the tower, where he observed the guards that had been posted laughing with other warriors, a short distance away, in the entrance hall.

He did not go to the large doors that would lead to Lady Alwyn's domain. Instead he followed the shadowed corridor around the base of the tower, to a small room tucked beneath the stairs.

Chapter 8

He closed the door behind him, and crossed the narrow chamber, lit only by the red coals of a dying fire on small hearth. Other than that, there was a narrow be table and two stools. Gilroy carried the key to the to on a brass keyring at his belt. Perhaps he also had session of the others, such as the one to Tara's secret dow, which would not oft, if ever, be used. On th near the bed, he found three small chests, and flip lid to the first one, peering inside. Coins. The one . . . yes. Keys. A score of them—and other could not discern. He lifted the chest, taking it the fire, and scrutinized them as best he coul one. One key bore the image of the sun. Anot The third one . . . he did not discern, but it wa cent moon.

Just then . . . something else caught his glimmering, and a circular sort of shine stopped beating as he lifted a necklace fro

A very fine, very expensive . . . ruby and p

and decided he wasn't a very good liar. He wanted to know the truth, and he wanted it now.

He held up the necklace, so that the glittering gold chain dropped to swing from his hand. "Where did you get this necklace?"

Gilroy blinked several times. "It belongs to me."

Was it possible there was more than one very fine, very expensive pearl and ruby necklace in existence in this rugged corner of the highlands? He supposed there might be. But would such an item belong to an old warrior? Likely not.

Instinct—and his memory of that night in the forest—told him otherwise.

"The necklace belongs to Mistress Iverach," Magnus asserted forcefully. "It was taken from her the night she arrived here, by a masked brigand. A very tall masked brigand claiming to be a Kincaid. Tell me, Gilroy, what do you know about that?"

Gilroy stared at him in silence for a very long moment. With a sudden roar, he threw the chest to the ground—

And with the force of a rampaging bull, shoved Magnus aside, slamming him violently against the stone wall. Magnus's vision blurred.

The man stormed past, but Magnus righted himself, and twisted . . . *lunging*, seizing Gilroy around his chest. Only to be wrenched free and trampled as Gilroy barreled past, shoving a chair down atop Magnus as he fled through the door.

Magnus blinked, stunned by the force exerted by the man, then pushed the chair off himself, quickly rising to his feet. What the hell had just happened? Still clenching the necklace, he went to the door, and peered outward. The man was nowhere to be seen.

Magnus stood there on the threshold, his chest tight, the blood pounding in his temples, for the first time in a long while, indecisive . . . uncertain of what to do. Was Gilroy, at this very moment, informing the Lady Alwyn, or even the laird of the confrontation that had just occurred? Should he go straightaway to the stables for a horse, and ride toward Kincaid lands before any confrontation or capture could take place?

He clenched his teeth, agonized, his head filled with clashing thoughts and the silence of the corridor.

He couldn't do it. He couldn't just leave. If there was any chance he could still succeed at drawing the truth from the Alwyn, of knowing the why and the how of the plot that had brought about the destruction of his family and his clan and his life, then he must take it.

There was also Tara. He had made a vow to her, one he wouldn't break.

Still breathing heavily, he secured the necklace inside the small leather pouch attached to the inside of his belt, and with care, entered the corridor.

His shoulders tight with tension and readiness, he made his return to the smoky din of the hall, all the while trying to fashion some reasonable explanation for being caught rummaging about in Gilroy's room. All the while expecting to be confronted by Gilroy, with a company of guards. But that didn't happen.

But *why?* Where had Gilroy gone?

Little had changed since he'd departed the room a short time earlier. Conversation still flowed. The musicians still played.

Tara sat alone, her shoulders straight. Not moving. Not eating or conversing with those around her. And Hugh? Magnus found him in the corner, leering at the dancing girl along with Ferchar and his customary companions, a goblet in his hand, which gave him some relief, as his attention was no longer on Tara.

He saw Gilroy nowhere.

Cautiously, Magnus returned to the company of Chissolm and the others, and took his seat. There, the conversation rose up around him, as he watched and waited.

It was not long before Lady Alwyn lifted a hand, signaling her intention to leave. He watched, riveted at the unfolding commotion, as voices called out for Gilroy. At any moment he might be forced to fight or flee. Several of the laird's men stood and walked between the rows of tables, searching the room, but returned to the laird's table shaking their heads. One of the other servants stepped in, directing the men to lift the screens, and provide escort to the ladies as they departed.

When Tara stood, everything male inside him came alive and aware, the danger of the moment heightening his response. She no longer wore the shapeless garb of a nun, but a blue kirtle that sheathed her body, making apparent the high, round fullness of her breasts, her slender torso and the flare of her hips. Her braids glinted beneath her sheer head covering, the color of a midnight flame. He wondered how her hair would look free and tumbling down her back . . . or draped across a pillow. His pillow.

He could not help but think it.

He had risked so much for her. Because of that he could not help but feel *more*, as he looked upon her. The animal part of him wanted to lay claim, in exchange for his sacrifice, even while his rational mind told him he had no right.

For a momentary instant as she passed by his table, she went unprotected by the screen. She turned her head, and their eyes met. Though the connection lasted only a second . . . perhaps two, it electrified him through, taking him back to the moment in the carriage where they'd looked into one another's eyes, and breathed each other's breath, more intense, even, than when they'd kissed.

When she disappeared from his view, his abdomen clenched with apprehension, because even with Hugh divested of his key, he did not know if she would be safe in that tower.

Tara turned the key, locking her chamber door after Mary and Anna, who had helped her prepare for bed.

Alone, again. A prisoner, again.

And yet she took some comfort in knowing the locked door would protect her from Hugh . . . although the troubling thought struck her that someone still had possession of his forfeited key. The laird, no doubt. She prayed he kept it hidden, where her dull-eyed, dull-toned betrothed would not find it again.

Whore.

The word had been a vicious affront against the gentle sister she'd known, and whom she held so dear in her memory. *Why* had he used such a word to describe her? Could it be possible that her sister had been in love with someone else, either here, or before she'd arrived at Burnbryde, and he'd found out about it?

The anger she'd heard in Hugh's voice had been palpable, and only gave more life to her suspicions that he had harmed Arabel . . . and might find cause to harm her too.

Perhaps, however, she was safe as long as she did not draw his attention. He did not seem to care for her, as a person, overmuch. Only the idea of possessing and keeping her, as an object of pride. He had lost interest in her soon after making his threats. The dancing girl had held far more allure for him. She had not missed the moment when the dark-haired young woman had danced closer to Hugh, seemingly familiar with him. He had grabbed the dancer's hand and pressed it hard against his groin. The brunette had laughed gaily and smiled as Tara's betrothed had filled her other hand with what she could only assume were coins, and spoken into her ear, no doubt making arrangements to meet with her later. If the lady or laird had noticed, they'd given no indication.

She, herself, did not care one small bit that he found entertainment elsewhere, other than to feel a deep pity for the girl, who no doubt feigned her interest in exchange for money.

She crossed the floor, shivering as the chill crept beneath her night rail. Earlier that evening, while sitting at the laird's table observing everything, she'd concealed her rather sturdy eating knife in her bell sleeve. Whilst Anna and Mary had been distracted with turning down her bed linens and tending to the fire, she had managed to discreetly drop the blade into her open trunk. Returning now, she lifted her folded garments and found the long-handled blade there along the interior wall of the trunk, and took her new tool in hand.

Less than a fortnight . . . she had less than a fortnight to determine another means of escape. Time already passed too quickly, hurtling her forward, toward a destiny she refused to accept. How she would succeed in getting out of here, she did not know, but she would not simply lay abed each night, praying that someone else would save her. Someone like Magnus.

After all, how could he possibly help her, with all the *screens* and *locked doors* and *stone walls* and *guards* and *iron bars* between them? It wasn't his fault he could not perform a miracle. She did not hold it against him. She would only hold it against herself if she did not try.

Slipping on her shoes, she drew her cloak onto her shoulders, remembering the numbing cold of the night before. Knife and lantern in hand, she pushed the tapestry aside and opened the secret passageway. A wall of darkness and cold met her, as if to ward her away. But despite her heart clenching in dread and fear, she passed through and secured the wooden panel behind her and descended the dark stairs . . . assuring herself it was only the whisper of her garments against the stones that she heard, and not the warnings of long-dead ghosts . . . *Arabel?* . . . as she delved downward.

Her breath puffed out in front of her, as she turned one corner, and then another. At last she came to the barred window. Breathing unevenly, she set the lantern on the steps, so that its light would not shine too brightly out from the window and draw attention from the outside.

It was frightening here, alone in the dark and the silence.

Frightening also, knowing that Arabel had stood in this same exact place, desperate for a freedom she would never find. As she had the night before, Tara sent up a prayer that her fate would not be the same. She touched her finger to the mortar, and raised the knife. Perhaps chipping away here for hours, until her hands throbbed, wouldn't set her free, but she had to try.

"Tara," a man's voice called from the darkness.

Not realizing exactly where the voice came from, she gasped, and shrank back.

And yet in the next moment, she recognized the voice as belonging to Magnus. The closest thing she had to an ally at Burnbryde. Her heartbeat jumped.

"*Tara?*" he said again, from outside the window, she now discerned. "It's me."

She moved closer to the bars, and peered out into the night.

No moonlight reached this narrow crevice, between the tower and the castle wall. She did not call his name for fear she was wrong, that she had been mistaken. She would not want anyone to know he sympathized with her, if indeed he did sympathize with her. She would not want to bring him to harm in any way.

But there . . . yes. She could just make out his shape in the darkness below, approaching the window, tall, rangy and male, and impressively broad at the shoulders.

"Yes," she answered, her chest tight with emotions she didn't understand, emotions so strong that tears flooded her eyes.

She only knew she'd been afraid, and so very sad and alone, and that the sound of his voice speaking her name . . . his presence here, lifted her up somehow.

"May I come up there, to speak to you?" he asked, looking up, although she could not discern any aspect of his face. "I have a ladder."

"Of course," she answered, blinking away her tears. She forced normality to her voice because she did not want him to know how much his presence meant to her, how much relief it gave her, because . . . because she didn't trust him still. She couldn't. Not completely. To do so wouldn't be smart. Though she didn't *distrust* him, either.

Nearing the window, he momentarily disappeared. There came the sound of wood striking dully against the stone, then creaking as he climbed up.

A certain eagerness quickened her blood. Soon, she would see his familiar face. A face that was not yet so familiar, that she could recall every detail, because she had only ever looked upon him in times of duress. But she recalled that his eyes were blue. Blazingly . . . startlingly blue.

He appeared, his head and shoulders rising above the ledge. His silver-blond hair gleamed in the lamplight, pushed back from his face and falling loose behind his ears—a face so attractive . . . and yes, so welcome . . .

her blood and her bones seemed to surge forward to greet him.

"Hello there," he said, his lips sweeping into a crooked smile. His breath clouded in the cold night air. "Again."

Something felt different now, in the way they talked to one another. There was a gentleness to not only his gaze, but his voice. A reverence that calmed her.

"Hello again," she repeated. Suddenly, she forgot all about the cold.

He climbed up a few more steps.

"Determined to chisel yourself out of there, are you?" he said, his gaze dropping to her hand.

She realized then that she still clenched the knife. She set it onto the ledge, and pushed it aside. "If I must."

Moving with ease and no apparent fear of falling, he climbed off the ladder, his shoulders flexing beneath his tunic. He lowered himself onto the deep outer ledge, deftly turning crosswise to sit. This positioned him almost face-to-face with her as she stood looking out. He bent his long, booted legs, settling one foot flat against the ledge. The other he pressed against the larger, raised stones of the outer arch. Confined as such, in a space akin to a normal doorway, his large body filled the space.

He turned his face, leveling a look upon her, between the bars, so direct and powerful, that he took her breath away all over again. She thought to step away, to put more space between them, but she didn't. Instead she remained close, so close she felt the warmth radiating off him, drawing reassurance from his size, his strength and most importantly, his sense of calm.

"I'm sorry you feel you must do that," he said. "But I understand why you would, after watching Hugh to-night."

He had watched, angrily. She had known that.

"I said it before, and I will say it again . . . I will not

marry him," she said, looking into his eyes, her rising emotions causing her throat to close on the words.

"He's a beast," he murmured coldly. "More now than before, though why I don't know. I cannot help but hold myself responsible for your plight. That first night . . . I should have told you to go." He shook his head, his lips drawn into a thin line. "I should have turned your carriage around and told you to return from whence you came."

His jaw tightened as he spoke the words, and his eyes flashed with regret.

"You did not know me, then," she said.

"Should that matter?" he replied.

"'Twould have done no good," she answered softly. "Even with the outriders gone, the driver would have refused. He would not disobey Buchan's orders. I believe even Sister Grizel would have insisted on finishing our journey and seeing for herself what awaited us."

"If only my regrets ended there," he muttered.

"What regrets?" she answered.

He shifted on the stones, turning toward her. His hand came between the bars. Though spaced too closely together for a child to squeeze through, they were wide enough for his arm to pass—but only his arm, for the bulk of his shoulder prevented any further trespass. His hand found hers and tightened around it. Her heartbeat increased at the touch. She felt no desire to pull away.

His blue eyes pierced her through. "When I saw him acting so roughly toward you tonight, I wanted to bludgeon him with his own damn fists, right there, in front of everyone. And believe me, I did so in my mind." He gritted the words out, before exhaling in frustration. "But Tara, I sat and watched, as still as a statue. All I could think was that if I were thrown into the dungeon for crimes against the laird's heir, his *ceann-cath*, I could do nothing more to help you escape this marriage to him."

His words fell on her ears. Her *eager* ears. Her heart opened to him a fragment more, her gaze sweeping over his face, memorizing his features. His strong shoulders and arms.

"But I understand why," she answered, turning her hand inside his, so she could hold his just as tight. She did understand. The words he spoke were true. She would not see him imprisoned for recklessly defending her. "I am no fool. I do not expect you to endanger yourself for me."

"But I *would* . . . endanger myself," he growled, his gaze snapping, seizing her hand upward, against his chest. "To keep him from hurting you. If he hurt you, I would never forgive myself for standing by."

She felt the powerful beat of his heart, there against the back of her hand. Her own pulse raced, hearing his words, at being this close to him, so familiarly touched.

He closed his eyes for a moment, and shook his head slowly before opening them again. "If he hurt *any* woman—"

"I do not think he will hurt me," she replied. "Not if I pretend to fear and obey him. Not if I assure him that I am resigned now to marrying him and being the subservient betrothed that he demands I be."

"How can you be so certain?" he demanded, his brows drawing together, making him look fierce.

"I don't believe he is compelled by lust," she answered, the word bringing a blush into her cheeks. "But rather by the desire to control me. He seems to look upon me as a possession. As a symbol of his connection to the earl—a connection which pleases his father. As long as I acquiesce, and acknowledge his power over me, I believe I will be safe . . . at least until the wedding."

"A wedding that will not take place," he answered resolutely.

Still, Tara's fears rose in her throat, suspicions on which she could no longer keep silent. She prayed she did not make a mistake in confiding to him, in making such a dangerous accusation when she had no proof.

"But I do think he hurt my sister," she whispered, tears filling her eyes. "I know they say 'twas a fever. Everyone does. But something is *wrong*, Magnus." Her hands found the front of his tunic, and she seized hold of him there. He stared back into her eyes, listening. "Something isn't right. No one seems to be able to say they saw her ill, other than the Lady Alwyn, who kept everyone else away, save for a priest she did not name. I don't believe I'm being told the truth—"

He turned, shifting onto his hip, as she remained standing on the other side of the window.

A tear trickled down her cheek, and the cold chilled its path on her skin.

His hand came up to cradle her jaw. She sighed, taking comfort in his touch, his concern, his gentleness. Although the thick iron bars separated them, their bodies pressed closer, in what was almost an embrace.

"I'm *sorry*," he murmured. His face coming between the bars, he pressed a fervent kiss to her temple. "I'm sorry Arabel is gone."

Tilting her face in his hands, he kissed her closed eyelids. A tremor went through her at the sensation. She'd never been touched thusly. So comfortingly. So tenderly. So when he drew her arms, slenderer than his, through the bars, and brought them about his shoulders, she allowed it. She wanted to be close to him—to touch like this. He made her feel stronger. Less alone. Less afraid.

"I'm sorry I was here, all the while," he murmured, his mouth on her cheek, "and did not ask questions that might have saved her life. That I did not know she needed protection."

She closed her eyes, wholly focused on the sound of his voice, rumbling in her ear, the vibration of his chest, when he spoke, against her breasts. They were the exact words she needed to hear. She needed to know that someone cared, that someone else felt regret. That Arabel had meant something, and that she did too.

She tilted her face, looking up, wanting . . .

His lips touched hers, grazing slowly, tentatively across her mouth—a kiss . . . yet not a kiss at all.

A fire blazed to life in her heart, a hunger she hadn't known existed. She wanted nothing more than for him to press his mouth against hers, for him to claim her in that way. She wanted to disappear into his touch, his body . . . his kiss. She wanted to forget everything else. She could not breathe for wanting it so badly.

But he let out a long, uneven breath, and pulled back.

"And I am sorry for that," he said, still holding her, one hand splayed at her back, the other gripping her hip. "I should not have kissed you. 'Twas wrong for me to do so, like this, when you are afraid." His voiced lowered. "In truth, it makes me no better than him."

One hand came up to touch her hair. Her face. And then he released her, pulling his arms back through to his side of the bars.

She swayed, set free.

"That's not true," she answered, hating that he likened himself to Hugh in any way, for no two men could be any more different.

"I wanted you to kiss me," she confessed softly, her hands coming up to grasp the bars.

And she still did—but no, she couldn't be so bold as to say it.

He stared at her, his gaze darkening to smoldering.

"Oh, I intend to kiss you again," he replied, his voice

low and smoky. "Once I get you out of here. When you are a free woman, free to choose."

Her cheeks flushed darker, hearing the promise in his words.

"What if I get my own self out of here?"

"I'll kiss ye then too." A momentary smile touched his lips, before falling away. "Because in truth, you may be the only one who can get yourself out of that tower."

Her heartbeat jumped. "Tell me how, and I will do it."

God, she was sweet—and strong.

And every time he saw her, she seemed to grow even more beautiful. She looked back at him, with the lamplight at her back, her red hair gleaming like a halo around her pale, lovely face.

Aye, he was besotted, as he'd never been before in his life. It took all his willpower to keep his hands and his mouth on this side of the bars. But she didn't belong to him.

She didn't belong to Hugh either, and he'd make sure that didn't change.

But for now, there were words to be said. "Tonight in the gathering hall, I was so . . . displeased at being forced to do stand by and do nothing, that I left the gathering hall, but with a purpose."

It made him furious, just to remember everything he saw, how Hugh had touched her so roughly.

"I saw you go," she whispered.

He wondered if she'd felt abandoned.

"What did he say to you?" he asked, his eyes narrowing.

She leaned forward again, her hands wrapping around two bars and peered at him in between. "That I humiliated him by running away. That I don't want to make an enemy of him. And some other vile things that I won't repeat."

The sheen of tears returned to her eyes.

He nodded, and lifted a hand, grazed his knuckles against hers.

"I thought as much. So I went to Gilroy's room."

"Gilroy's room." Her eyes widened, underneath her slender brows. "Why?"

"To see if I could find the key to this window," he answered. "To get you out of here. *Tonight*."

"You didn't find it though," she answered. "I know you didn't, or you'd have told me already."

"I didn't. But I found something else."

"Something else?"

Touching his hands to his belt, he tugged open the leather pouch. With care, he removed the necklace, allowing it to fall its full length from his fingers, and swing free. The rubies and pearls shone in the lamplight.

She gasped. "Oh, Magnus."

"Your mother's necklace?"

"Yes," she exclaimed, reaching.

For the first time, he saw her smile. Truly smile. His mind went dizzy from the beauty of it. His soul, happy and warm. How could he not smile too?

He reached through the window, and lowered the necklace over her head. "I repaired the clasp as best I could."

She touched the necklace where it lay on the alluring swell of her breast, and peered down at the glittering chain through damp eyes. She moved suddenly, then, pressing herself to the bars, reaching for him with her empty hand, pulling him by the tunic, closer.

He allowed it, his blood thumping heavily in his veins.

"Thank you," she whispered. And with her hand at his neck, she pulled him down. Her eyes closed, and she kissed him full and hard on the mouth.

There was something distinctly different about kissing a woman—and having a woman kiss you. He liked both very much, but Tara's innocent kiss was a pleasure such as he'd never known. He inhaled, savoring the painfully pure, sensual rush that struck through him, to his core.

Her fingers moved higher, into his hair, and her face tilted . . . her lips moving against his as she renewed the kiss again. He lost himself to the sensation of responding to her willing, seeking lips . . . soft and warm and perfect. Just as he imagined the rest of her would feel. His shoulders, his abdomen, his groin—all seized tight in response. Wanting, anticipating more. Desire grew, deep in his abdomen, until he felt consumed. All the hunger he'd felt moments before and reined in, returned, and he kissed her back with a passion that came straight from his heart.

The wolf in him cursed the bars between them. The honorable man he wished to be gave thanks for them.

She dropped her hand away, and ended the kiss, leaving him no less than stunned.

"Thank you," she repeated breathlessly, her cheeks flushed and her lips dark in the shadows. "You don't know what this necklace means to me. It's the only thing I have of my mother's, and . . . I was going to use it to pay for my escape from here. I felt so helpless when it was taken from me. I feel so much better now, so relieved, as if my hopes of freedom are not as futile, having it back in my possession."

He heard her talking, but as if from the end of a long tunnel. His body remained completely aroused. Even his cheeks burned. He couldn't recall ever reacting to a kiss like that before. He blinked and shook his head.

"It was your mother's, and you will keep it," he said, huskily. "You won't need it to pay for your escape. I will see to that."

Her eyes shone up at him filled with gratefulness, and yet he sensed that still, she doubted.

It was all right. Despite the newfound closeness between them, and the kisses, he was still very much a stranger to her. He did not take it personally, given her predicament. He'd doubt everyone and everything too. Indeed, she was smart to do so.

"But why would Gilroy have my necklace?" she asked. "Was it he who led the band of brigands against my traveling party?"

"Yes," Magnus answered. "I just don't know why, and I can't make him answer for it, because he's gone."

He recounted what had occurred in Gilroy's room. Their struggle, and the man's disappearance.

"What if he returns?" she whispered, her upward turn of mood instantly muted. "You'll be in danger if he tells anyone."

Magnus answered. "I can only believe that he ran away, so the laird would not learn of his thieving. Perhaps he's done it before? The laird would be furious to know he attacked and terrified Buchan's ward. I don't know. None of it really makes sense to me, but let me worry about him, if he comes back. It is you who are in danger if the Lady Alwyn had anything to do with this."

Tara shook her head. "I can't imagine that she does. She is a peculiar woman, but not a cruel or scheming one. I don't believe she'd want to hurt or frighten me."

"She wants you to marry Hugh," he said, his voice edged with sarcasm.

He felt no love for the Lady Alwyn. But neither did he feel hate. She felt the same way toward him, he knew, from years of living in the castle together.

Tara replied, "Like all mothers, she believes in her child's goodness."

He could not help but wonder what his mother would have thought about him. Would she have believed he could do no wrong? Would she have only seen the angel in him, and none of the devil?

The devil that was looking at Tara's rosy lips right now. Her bare collarbone, visible between the gap in her night rail and her cloak.

"It is very late," he said, feeling the desire to touch her, to kiss her again, all the way to his bones.

But she was vulnerable. A captive in an unhappy place, desperate to be free. To kiss her now, again, somehow felt wrong. As if he was only helping her because he expected something in return, when he did not.

"Aye," she answered softly. " 'Tis. But I'd rather stay here with you, than go back to that room alone."

"Well, ye can't stay here."

"Why not?"

"Because all I can think of is kissing you, and touching you, Tara," he confessed, his groin tight with desire, even now. "And I've already vowed I won't do that again, so truly it's just cruel of ye to stay in my company a moment more, tempting me with your pretty mouth, isn't it?"

"I don't want to be cruel," she answered in a quiet voice. "I shouldn't have kissed you, then—"

"I wouldn't say that," he answered, chuckling wryly.

She sighed. "I feel like I'm a different person here. One I don't really know anymore. I don't know if that's good or bad."

Which was exactly why he couldn't kiss her again. Not until she was free of Hugh. Free to decide if she wanted him to kiss her. To claim her. To make love to her.

He suspected she'd flee Burnbryde the moment she had the chance, and never look back, which was why he best not allow himself to care too deeply.

"You're all good, Tara." He dared to take her hand in his own again.

How strange that he liked the feel of her slender hand, held in his, almost as much as the kissing.

"That's plain and clear to me, and never doubt it. Don't let this place change you." He dropped his hand away, too tempted still. "Ye'll not be chiseling your way out of the tower tonight. Now take your necklace, and your lantern, and your knife, and go to bed. And when it is safe, look wherever ye can for a key stamped with a crescent moon. If Gilroy doesn't have it, then I can only believe the lady does. If ye don't find it, don't fear, we'll make something else work. Go now, Tara. I'll watch until you're gone."

She took up the knife, and backed away from the window. Taking up the lantern, she went to the stairs, but turned back to peer at him through the darkness.

"But you'll come back here, to the window, again, won't you, Magnus?"

"Aye, Tara. I will."

"Good morning, mistress," said a female voice in the darkness. Tara opened her eyes to find Anna standing over her. "I have come to dress you for morning prayers."

Her heart started. Magnus. The necklace.

She touched the front of her night rail, between her breasts, and felt the hard outline of the jeweled chain, which proved their time together had not been a dream.

Oh, but it felt like a dream, in so many ways. Would another man's kisses ever make her feel like that? She couldn't imagine so.

He had returned her necklace to her, and in doing so, returned a degree of power to her hands. She could bribe her way out of Burnbryde, if that became necessary. She must only find the key to the locked tower window. Most importantly, she had Magnus's vow that he would help her—and she believed that he would try.

For the first time in days, she felt some small bit of hope.

She pushed up, and she touched her feet to the floor, her mind filled with the image of his face—his arresting blue eyes. His kiss. The strong warrior arms that had held her so close, against his muscular warrior's body. Just remembering sent a surge of warmth through her, all the way to her toes. Though he was not here with her, in her chamber, it felt as if he protected her still.

But . . . certainly he had ambitions of his own. No doubt he wished to become more powerful within his clan.

What *did* he expect in exchange for helping her?

Was it truly that he only welcomed the opportunity to undermine Hugh, his hateful younger half-brother, in something? Anything? Perhaps at the start. But now . . . was it wrong to believe he cared for her in some way? Was it possible that he wanted her for himself? Did she want him too?

Or did she, in her innocence, make too much of it all? Had she allowed herself to become too impressed by him?

Be careful, her heart warned. She could not be the only young woman he had ever held. Ever consoled. Ever kissed.

It mattered not what had occurred between them, she told herself. Not the words, not the kisses. He did not belong to her, and she did not belong to him. She would be wise to guard her heart, and next time they spoke, in the darkened shadow of her tower window, not be so free with her kisses and embraces.

After all, if they were successful, she would leave

here, and she would never see him again. It wasn't as if he would run away with her. He was an Alwyn, and even though he might despise his half-brother, blood and duty bound him here.

That truth troubled her more deeply than she wished to admit.

Although Anna had lit a fire, the room was still cold—because the door had been left open, and a draft carried through. The girl knelt, placing slippers on her feet—and as she did so, Tara removed the necklace, concealing it in her hand. A moment later, she discreetly secured the jeweled chain in her wooden chest. Soon she was dressed, and sitting in the chair, as the maid braided and pinned her hair.

"You have such pretty hair," Anna said softly. Shyly. "So different than your sister's."

"*Tapadh leat*," Tara answered. "My sister took after my mother, and I was always told I look very much like my father's grandmother. Anna, may I ask you something in confidence?"

"Yes," she answered softly, but an expression of doubt crossed her face, as if she knew she should not agree.

"Did my sister love someone?" Given the open door, she asked the question quietly. "Not Hugh. Someone else?"

The girl's gaze lowered.

"Please," urged Tara, reaching up to squeeze the girl's hand. "She was my sister. I deserve to know."

Anna nodded jerkily. "I knew . . . almost from the start, but I swear, I did not tell Lady Alwyn." Her gaze shifted to the door. "I liked your sister very much. She was very sweet natured, but also . . . sad."

Tara's heart constricted, hearing the word. "Sad? Oh, please tell me what you mean. I had not seen her in years.

I had only letters, as a glimpse into her life, but she never mentioned anyone."

Anna nodded. "I do believe when she arrived here, she was suffering from a broken heart."

Tara exhaled, and pressed a curled fist against her lips. "Because . . . because she'd been separated from the man she loved, and sent here to marry Hugh."

"At least that's what I believed."

"Who was he?" Tara looked up into Anna's eyes. "Did she ever say?"

She paused, holding a comb aloft. "No, mistress. But . . . I believe the answer is there." She lifted her chin toward the jewelry chest on the table beside them.

Her heart pounding in anticipation, Tara lifted the chest, and placed it onto her lap. Looking inside, she lifted a ring and examined it, then—

"The brooch," whispered Anna. "Don't you see, it's fashioned in the shape of a heart. She spent a lot of time looking at it, and would often pin it to her *léine*, where it would not be seen."

Tara held the brooch to the light. Fashioned of gold, the filigreed badge was indeed shaped like a heart, though that was not so apparent at first glance. A narrow sword divided its center. Turning it over, she saw that the back of the piece had been inscribed. She squinted. "Love never dies."

"Is that what it says?" said Anna, with interest. "I wondered, but I can't read."

Tara nodded. "It is Latin. *Amor numquam moritur.* There's also letters. An A for Arabel . . . and . . . I can't tell what the other one is. A P . . . or an R?" The flourishes were simply too hard to read. She sighed in disappointment. She needed no mysteries now. Only answers to her questions. "Most certainly though, it is not an H."

"No, it wouldn't be," Anna murmured beneath her breath, glancing toward the open door. "Your sister had no fondness for the laird's son. I don't see how you would, either."

"I do not," Tara whispered, returning the brooch to the box.

Her stomach spasmed at the thought of seeing Hugh again, especially after the time she had spent with Magnus the night before. What twist of fate made one man kind and caring, and another one cruel? No matter what legal document or agreement declared her to belong to Hugh, her heart did not agree.

When Anna was finished, and had secured a veil over her hair, she left her room, her cloak over her shoulders because of the cold that permeated everything. As in previous days, Lady Alwyn awaited her in the common room. This time, rather than standing, she held a needle, and threaded it through a large square of linen, stretched on a wooden frame.

"There you are." Lady Alwyn said, glancing up from her work, her expression fretful, her eyes damp with tears. "Good. Let us go downstairs to the chapel. I have much to pray about."

Tara's replied with genuine concern. "Is everything well, my lady?"

"No, it is not. Everything is very wrong." She lifted her hands into the air. "Gilroy, it appears, is gone. Truly gone. Perhaps forever."

"Your steward?" Tara answered, now forced to feign ignorance. "What do you mean, he is gone?"

Tara felt nothing but relief. If Gilroy was still gone, then she had no need to fear him, and Magnus's presence in the steward's room would continue to go unmentioned—and most importantly, unquestioned.

"I do not know." The lady sighed heavily. "As you

know, he disappeared from last night's meal, which is not like him at all, and worse, he has not returned. I am very aggrieved! He has always been very loyal. Who will do my bidding now, with such care as he?"

"Does he have family?" Tara inquired in a gentle tone. "Perhaps he received word of some illness or desperate need and departed in haste?"

Her intentions were true. She really did want to calm the lady, who appeared very upset.

"He has never left without permission. Without explanation. What if something happened to him?" The lady reached for a nearby cloth, and pressed it to her eyes.

"I'm certain he will return very soon, and with a good explanation."

Although she prayed, most fervently, that he would not. Even so, no doubt Gilroy was alive and well *somewhere*.

"I pray you are right." Lady Alwyn stood from her embroidery. "Regarding another matter . . . *you*, my dear. The laird has sent me a missive just this morning, reminding me not to smother you with my attentions, so that you will not want to run away again."

"You were not the foremost reason I fled," said Tara, before sharply reminding herself to just stay quiet. She must appear dutiful and resigned to the marriage.

"Forgiveness!" warbled the lady, not meeting her gaze. "We must always forgive, just as Hugh has forgiven you."

Tara flinched inwardly at the idea that she had done anything Hugh needed to forgive. The lady, of course, had not heard the terrible things her son had said to her last night. She *could* tell her . . . but she suspected she would only be encouraged, once more, to forgive.

Indeed, she would strive to forgive and forget all, once she was far from here. She'd forget everything but Magnus, that is. She knew of a certain, he'd be impossible to forget.

For now, best she remained focused on finding the key. She'd already counted half a dozen little wooden chests about the room, and no doubt there were more in the lady's chambers. If the key were even to be found in a chest! It might be on the very ring she wore at her waist.

She narrowed her gaze on the keys in question, swinging on their ring, as the lady tucked her embroidery away. "This morning after prayers, you may walk about the castle grounds, with Anna, as Mary prefers to remain with me. Dear girl. I rely on her so."

Tara's mood lifted again. She would be allowed to go outside. To see the sky and the sea, and the rest of Burnbryde. To inform herself on her surroundings.

Lady Alwyn continued on. "I've been assured by the laird there are enough warriors posted about to ensure your safety. Our afternoons, from this day on, will be very busy. I assume you have no wedding garments."

"I assumed I would wear something I already owned."

And all she owned were her dead sister's gowns. What did it matter? She would be gone by then.

Mary appeared, with a shawl, which she draped over the lady's shoulders.

"Nonsense," Lady Alwyn replied with a scowl. "I will summon my tailor for the gown and my seamstress for your undergarments, and an appropriate wedding costume will be made, befitting the ward of the Earl of Buchan in her marriage to my handsome and important son. We will simply advise them all to hurry, as the wedding will take place in a matter of days. And of course, we must see that the chambers you will share with Hugh are properly fitted with linens and furnishings suitable for the laird's married son and heir."

Tara's throat seized closed, at simply imagining being left alone in a room with Hugh, let alone being married to him. She nodded, fearing she could not rely upon her voice to offer a steady reply.

But something else the lady had said caused Tara's heartbeat to skitter nervously. *A matter of days.*

"We need not be in such a rush," Tara reassured the lady, softly. "We have at least a fortnight to prepare. Perhaps just a few days less. So said the earl himself, when we parted ways."

"Perhaps, perhaps not," the older woman responded, brows gathered. "We must be prepared, in the event he arrives sooner than that."

Sooner than a fortnight? She prayed not. Already the moments passed by, tolling like a bell in her head, bringing her closer to a marriage she could not, under any circumstances, abide.

Lady Alwyn touched her neck, and looked toward her chamber. "Mary. Oh, Mary. I wish to wear my cross." Looking at Tara, she said, "Just a moment more and we'll go down." She swept toward her room, and disappeared within.

Tara moved quickly, going to the largest of the wooden chests, situated near what appeared to be the lady's favorite chair. Flipping open the lid, she quickly sorted through the clutter of notions and thread, her ears alert for any sound of returning footsteps. At the bottom, there were coins . . . a small key, yes, but not the one she needed.

"Oh, mistress," said a voice. Anna's. "Step away, before she sees you."

She had been caught. Her heart pounded in panic. Numb with fear, Tara closed the lid, and turning quickly, moved away, returning to the place where she'd stood before.

She looked at Anna, who looked back at her.

"Please don't tell her," she begged.

The girl blinked, and lifted a hand to her mouth, before answering. "What are you looking for?"

Tara held silent.

"*Tell me, mistress*," Anna urged, her face pale with tension. "I shall try to help you."

"There is a concealed passage in my room that leads to a window, down below. I want the key. It is marked with a crescent moon."

Anna stared back at her, her lips set into a fine line.

Lady Alwyn returned then, a gleaming cross at her throat, and Mary followed, looking as stern as usual.

Tara waited . . . uncertain whether Anna truly wanted to help her, or whether she would feel obligated to inform the lady of the castle what she'd observed Tara doing, and what Tara had confessed to be looking for. But Anna remained silent.

Tara descended the stairs behind the lady, followed by Mary and Anna. Once Lady Alwyn unlocked the door, they emerged into the company of several warriors, who provided them with an escort. Lanterns, fixed to the wall, lit their way until they arrived at a narrow chapel at the back of the castle. Dim morning light illuminated narrow windows. The laird's warriors filled the room, their breath clouding the cold morning air.

Her heart stopped, seeing Hugh at the center of the nave. He looked at her, glassy-eyed and unsmiling, and extended his hand to her. Dark shadows underscored his eyes, and he wore his dark hair wet, and slicked back from his face.

She glanced at Lady Alwyn, who smiled encouragingly. "Yes, go. Stand beside your betrothed, here, in the presence of God, where soon, you shall be joined together forever."

It was an edict with which she had no choice but to comply. She forced herself forward, filled with dread.

"You look . . . lovely this morning," he said in a thick, hollow voice. His eyes flared with a predatory light that made her want to recoil. "Almost too beautiful to touch."

But he did touch her, as she knew he would. Rather than taking her by the hand, he caught her by the wrist. His palm moist and cool against her skin, he led her to the front of the church. Her heart pounded harder . . . and harder . . . she overtaken by a sudden terror that she had been tricked, and that they would be married, here and now.

It was then she saw Magnus, standing with a row of warriors, his face turned toward her. His blue eyes seared her through and dropped to fix upon Hugh's hand, where it claimed her.

Thankfully, Hugh did *not* take her to the chancel. Instead . . . he led her directly to where Magnus stood, standing directly in front of him. It was then that she saw the laird there as well.

He greeted her with raised eyebrows and a scowl. "At long last. The ladies have emerged from the tower."

His gaze shifted to his wife, who had followed. He met her, and taking her hand, placed it on his arm.

Tara wanted nothing more than to look at Magnus again—to take comfort from his presence, but she could only look straight forward. Even so, her body reacted, tortured by his nearness—and at the same time, repulsed by Hugh's.

Heat burned her cheeks, and she prayed the chapel was dim enough that no one would notice. She let out a low, quavering breath.

Tara heard Hugh speak beside her, in a low hiss. "Are you staring at my betrothed for some reason?" He had turned, and looked behind her.

Tara stiffened, alarmed, but did not look back.

"She is standing right in front of me," Magnus answered in a cool voice. "It's not as if I can help it."

"Watch yourself, cur," Hugh muttered.

Three priests appeared, dressed in holy vestments, one swinging a smoking thurible.

"Hugh," the Alwyn growled, in a low voice. "This is not the time, or the place."

"Bastard," muttered Hugh, his lips drawing back into a sneer.

Tara stiffened and attempted to pull her wrist free—infuriated that he should behave so, in this sacred place. But he held her fast, gripping her so hard she gasped from the sudden pain.

"I merely wish to pray," she gritted, though it was a blasphemous lie. The truth was that she could not bear his touch one moment more.

Hugh looked back at her, his eyes as black and empty as an adder's.

"You are devout, then?" he murmured, his lip drawn back to reveal his teeth. "A pity."

A hand clapped onto his shoulder, and she saw Magnus out of the corner of her eye.

"You're hurting her," he uttered in a guttural tone. "Let her go."

Hugh wrenched his shoulder free, and stared with outright hatred into Magnus's eyes.

"Hugh," his mother warned sharply, glaring out at him from beneath her veil.

Hugh let out a huff of air from between his lips, and turned to face forward, his hand still on her arm, but less of a vise now.

Tara stood numb . . . *trembling*, hardly hearing the prayers spoken. For all her thoughts of escape, she feared she would not be successful and that she'd be forced to marry this beast and live her life with him.

When they were finished, the priests ceremoniously left the room. The Alwyn led his wife after them, up the side aisle. Hugh, still leading Tara by the wrist, followed, with a withering look toward Magnus.

The Alwyn waited in the corridor. His glance fell darkly on Hugh, but moved just as quickly to his wife. "Will you join us for the morning meal?"

The lady shook her head, glancing warily around, throwing a distancing look to the nearest man as if he had ventured too close. "All this has tired me. As has my son's behavior. We shall return to our chambers."

The chief's lips thinned, and he nodded, giving Tara the impression it was an answer he often received.

He glanced to her. "Mistress Iverach?"

"I am not hungry," she said, prying her arm free of Hugh's grip, agitated and flustered—trying her best to remain calm. "Lady Alwyn, you said I could go for a walk with Anna. I would like to do that, please, and see the castle from the outside. The ocean. I'd like to breathe some air."

It was all she could think of. Being outside these thick, stone walls. Seeing what lay beyond.

"I will accompany you," said Hugh.

Her heart froze in her chest.

"Why don't you come with *us* instead?" said a voice behind him. Magnus drew alongside them, staring coldly at Hugh.

In the shadows of the corridor, he took her breath away. Standing a head taller than Hugh, he stared down his nose, his gleaming eyes and clenched jaw issuing a clear challenge to the man who had called him a cur just a short time ago.

Behind him stood some seven men, looking at Hugh with much the same expression—men clearly loyal to Magnus.

Looking at the two of them, standing face-to-face as they were, only confirmed their differences. There was no comparison. Magnus was a finer warrior, a finer man. He glowed, radiant and golden, from inside and without, while Hugh, in comparison, was a dull, spiteful lump of coal.

"Go with you. What for?" said Hugh, dismissively. He squinted suspiciously.

Magnus answered. "For our customary morning weapons practice."

"That you usually sleep through," the laird chuckled, and yet no smile lit his eyes. "A fine idea. With the earl arriving soon, you will want to be in your best form. I will come along as well."

He clasped a hand to his son's shoulder, and led him away, followed by the others. Only Magnus held back. No words were spoken. Barely even a glance passed between them, but she felt his claiming of her just as certainly as if he'd kissed her there on the stones, in full sight of everyone. Then, he was gone with the others.

She, Anna, and Mary walked with Lady Alwyn to the tower stairs. At the bottom, the older woman peered up, her cheeks pale, and her stance, suddenly unsteady.

"Oh . . ." she murmured thickly.

Despite everything, concern welled up inside Tara. She reached out to take her arm. "My lady, are you unwell?"

The older shook her head. "Just . . . unsteady, as I have been of late."

Mary stepped closer. "She sometimes has these spells. I will help her up the stairs." She turned and called to a nearby male servant, who rushed to assist.

"Should a healer be called?" Tara inquired.

Mary answered. "If she does not improve. Go on. It is likely nothing, and she will improve once rested."

The three of them made their way up the steps. Tara watched until they safely reached the top, before turning to Anna. "How long has she suffered the spells?"

"Since last winter. Excitement seems to bring them on. Emotion. And anyone can see she was very displeased by Hugh's behavior. She has a very strong respect for the church." She gave a small smile. "She is always threatening to leave Burnbryde, and put herself away in a nunnery."

They walked out of the doors, between guards that were posted there, into the courtyard. It was early morning still, and very cold, and she was thankful she'd worn her cloak, in addition to layers of wool.

"Why is she so unhappy here?"

Anna answered in a hushed voice. "I can only surmise it is because the men in her life have disappointed her greatly, though she would never confess it to anyone but her priest. Certainly not you or I. But I know her heart is broken a little more each time she discovers the laird has another mistress. And every time her son . . . behaves as he does." Anna's eyes widened and she shrugged. "But I talk too much. I'd be sent away if she knew. And most especially if she found out I knew, and did not tell her, that you were looking for the key to that window."

"Let's talk about something else then," said Tara, her heart beating faster.

She liked Anna very much, and did not want to overly test her loyalties.

"Yes, let us do that." Anna nodded, smiling—her cheeks bright from the frigid wind. "You said you wished to see the ocean?"

"Yes. As you yourself know, there are no windows in the tower, and it was too dark the night of my arrival to see."

Even now she could hear it crashing against the rocks.

They walked, still inside the castle walls, meandering

through a myriad of smaller, wattle-and-daub cottages and work structures. She could not help but notice Alwyn warriors, stationed everywhere. They stood on the walls above. At the gates, and it seemed, everywhere in between. But her importance within the castle was already established, apparently. None met her gaze, and if they did, a polite nod was offered, before the man in question quickly looked away.

Other, common people moved about—women with wash baskets, and men with rakes and hoes—nodding in greeting as they passed. Children chased one another, screaming happily.

Tara realized, in that moment, that Burnbryde was not so terrible or frightening a place. Under other circumstances, she thought she might be happy here. She allowed herself a moment's fantasy, that there was no Laird or Lady Alwyn, and certainly no Hugh. There was only Magnus, who would be a natural leader, she thought, as well as a fine husband . . . and lover.

The cold air cooled her heated cheeks, and tugged at her cloak, causing it to snap in the wind.

Anna lifted a hand. "We'll just continue on this way. There is a gate at the back wall." She paused, and smiled. "Oh, but look, it's the whitesmith."

Tara looked in the same direction and observed a tiny little man standing beside a wagon, covered with all manner of shiny things. Spoons and cups and crosses, and many other household items. Together they walked to the wagon.

Anna smiled brightly. "He had the most beautiful hair combs when he visited last." Walking forward, she waved a greeting and called out to him. "Have y' come to repair all the broken things in the kitchen?"

He bent his head. "'at I 'ave! It's guid fur me 'at the

cook likes throwin' and breakin' things. Lass, I've got yer hair combs 'ere that ye liked th' last time."

"And me with no coin to buy them with," she declared. She held up her empty hands.

"Nor I," added Tara, thinking that she would treat them both to a pair of the hair combs, and Mary as well—and even Lady Alwyn, just to be nice. "How long will you be here?"

"Oh, lass, I'll be here and there, and all around for at least a sennecht," he answered. "Until th' festival in Rackamoor is dain."

She and Anna promised to return for the combs, and said good-bye. They continued on toward the back of the castle.

"A festival," said Tara. "That sounds wonderful. I've not been to one since I was a child, before my parents died. Where is Rackamoor?"

"Not far. It's a village just north of here, less than an hour's ride away. You might have traveled past it on your journey to Burnbryde. If you blinked you would have missed it, but once a year, they have festival, where you can purchase all sorts of wares. It's just country folk who come out, and some from the castle here. It is nothing grand, like the great festival of the Cearcal, but there is dancing and a bonfire!"

"Is Rackamoor on Kincaid land, or Alwyn?" Tara mused, working to get her bearings. "The Kincaid lands also lie north of here, do they not?"

"Most certainly on Alwyn lands!" Anna exclaimed, as they passed through two large gates, and emerged onto the cliffs that overlooked the sea. "No one of sound mind would venture onto that of the Kincaids."

For a moment, Tara could only stare in silence at the impressive sight of the enormous waves rising and falling in the distance. Her heart sank, seeing the jagged shore-line, that spread like an endless expanse of rotten teeth. No ships would seek harbor here, for the shore was nonexistent, and any vessel daring to venture close would certainly be dashed to bits.

That only left land as a possibility for flight.

She broke her gaze away and looked again to Anna, for she had a reason for asking about Rackamoor and the Kincaids. "Why do you say it like that? Are the Kincaids so fearsome?"

They meandered along in the shadow of the salt black-ened castle, looking out over the ocean. Both wrapping their arms around themselves against the chill.

"I only know what I have heard," Anna answered, her brows gathering. "I've never actually seen a Kincaid my-self. For the longest time . . . all my life, really . . . I heard they were savages living in the hills, having surrendered their lands, by order of David the Second, to the Alwyn and another laird who was once our ally, the MacClaren. It's something no one at Burnbryde seems to want to talk about. Once, they all lived in peace, but now, all are sworn enemies."

"Lady Alwyn told me of an imposter. A man claim-ing to be the Kincaid's son."

"Aye, there were three sons, but all of them slain. You'll hear ghost stories and sad songs about it, from time to time. But yes, a man claiming to be the eldest son of the old Kincaid laird seized back the castle, which until just a fortnight ago had been in the possession of the MacClaren. Whether his claim is true, many doubt, but he is in residence there now, with an army of merce-naries." She leaned close, and murmured, "I hear he even forced marriage upon the MacClaren's daughter, the poor girl. Can you imagine? I pray we have nothing to fear."

Tara's heart beat a pace faster, and what had seemed

at first a simple plan in theory now became, in reality, more complicated. If she were to escape to Kincaid lands, and ask for shelter there, would she be safe, or place herself in even greater danger?

"Well, then, I shall be certain never to wander onto their lands," Tara declared, although . . . if left with no choice, she would and soon. "Just where are . . . their lands, in case I am ever placed in the position of having to avoid them?"

"Straight north, out of the front gate." Anna pointed. "Just beyond Rackamoor, the last village on the Alwyn side of the border."

If she truly intended to escape, she must not be afraid. If she needed protection from Hugh, there would be no better place to take it than behind the castle walls of the Alwyn's greatest enemy.

She wondered, if she fled there, if Magnus would follow—or worse, if he would be sent by the Alwyn to bring her back.

They reached the distant end of the castle, and stood on a high berm, overlooking the stables and fields.

A sound arose—the voices of men, roaring.

"Look," said Anna. "There, there are the men. The laird, and Hugh."

She spied Magnus instantly. She took a step forward . . . drawn by the sight of him, at the center of a large circle of cheering warriors.

Magnus stood with his back to her, naked to the waist and wearing only a short plaid, clenching a sword. Here, in the light of day, there were no shadows to hide his masculine beauty. Muscles corded his arms, and defined his back and torso. His legs were long, and powerfully formed. Her knees went weak, just remembering his impassioned kisses on her mouth and her skin, the night before.

"Is he not the most magnificent thing?" Anna whispered. "All the ladies think so, but thus far, no one has claimed his interest or his heart."

Tara's heartbeat stalled in her chest, realizing he faced Hugh . . . who knelt, gasping and red-faced, in the dirt of the practice yard, also holding a sword, but point down in the ground as he leaned upon it for support.

Magnus circled him, as alert and agile as a hunting lion assessing his weaker opponent. Hugh attempted to stand . . . but collapsed back to his knees. The men cheered loudly, some of them leaning in and shouting encouragements, or perhaps taunts.

The Alwyn did not cheer, but watched with several older, gray-haired men, off to the side.

Another man, wearing armor—perhaps the weapons master—stepped into the ring, and waved his arms, ending the contest. The circle of men shifted, closing around another pair of men who faced one another, raising swords.

Yet she still watched Magnus, transfixed by the sight of his body, her mouth gone dry, and Anna forgotten.

At that moment he turned toward her, striding away from Hugh, who crouched on the ground, defeated.

His gaze lifted just then, and their eyes met, and he stopped. She felt the heat in his gaze, even from that distance. She knew in that moment that he had defeated Hugh not only for himself, but for her.

Behind him, she saw a blur of movement.

Hugh standing, lifting his sword, and *lurching toward Magnus*—

Tara gasped. Pointed—and s*creamed*.

Chapter 10

Magnus spun round—and seeing Hugh, slashing—twisted away. The blade *whooshed* across his torso.

He stared into Hugh's hate-filled eyes, and bellowed in rage.

"You want to kill me?" he shouted, stalking toward him—only half aware of the men gathering round . . . the faces watching . . . the voices shouting. "Kill me now then, face-to-face. Not with a blade to my back."

"I *will* kill you." Hugh lifted his sword with both hands, and swung the blade.

Magnus repelled the attack with a shattering series of counterblows, beating Hugh *back*, *back and back again* . . . and with the last powerful blow, forcing him to the ground.

Hugh lay panting on his side, his sword at a useless angle beside him.

"Coward," Magnus shouted at him. "*Cheat*."

The Alwyn stepped into his line of view, his gaze sharp and steady. "That is all. The contest is done. You have won, Magnus, and rightfully so." He glared down at Hugh contemptuously. "What were you thinking?"

Magnus exhaled deeply, backing away. Only then did he realize he was bleeding from his side. Touching the wound, he judged it to be nothing serious. No deeper than other wounds he'd suffered before. He turned and strode from the field.

The Alwyn called after him. "Magnus, I wish to see you in my counsel room. As soon as you tend to your wound."

Magnus heard the words, but his eyes were fixed on Tara, who looked at him, her eyes wide with fear and concern, over her shoulder as another young woman led her toward the castle.

He wished he could go to her. Talk to her. Make sure she was all right. And most of all, thank her for warning him of Hugh's attack, but he couldn't, not with everyone watching.

"Aye, laird. As you wish."

He found his discarded tunic at the edge of the field, and taking it in hand, set off toward the castle.

A short time later, he lay on the large wooden table at the center of the kitchen while Lorna stitched him up. He gritted his teeth at each pinch of her needle, and tug of the thread, but he had suffered worse. When she was done, he sat up and patiently allowed Kyla and Laire and a score of other young women to flutter about him, wrapping his waist with unnecessary bandages, and dabbing his forehead with damp cloths, the point of which, he did not understand because he'd suffered no injuries there and had no fever.

"Thank you all," he said. "But I really must go."

Kyla tilted her head and looked at him sympathetically. "Someone should stay with y' tonight. I don't mind at all. Your bandages will need changing."

Bandages he planned to remove as soon as he could get away.

"I can tend to myself," he replied.

Laire's gaze moved to his bloodstained plaid. "If y' give me that now, I can wash it, straightaway."

What, and stand naked here in the kitchen, with all of them ogling him? He was tempted to drop the garment just to watch their reactions.

"Thank ye, Laire, but no."

Lorna turned from the hearth holding an enormous steaming pot. "You'll need ta eat, ta keep yer strength up. Sit down, and I'll serve y' some of my stew."

Well, then. The stew did tempt.

"All this extra care, while appreciated, is not necessary," he said, extracting himself from their midst. "'Twas merely a flesh wound, no different than others I've suffered before. Lorna, I'll return for stew later. Have no doubt of that. For now I must go."

After all, why delay? If he was going to receive a tongue-lashing and punishment from the laird for taking down Hugh before God and everyone, then he preferred to get that out of the way now. He knew of a certain, that there would be no apology issued to him, no acknowledgement that Hugh had unfairly attacked him.

He entered the laird's council room. Three elder council members sat at a table, in earnest discussions over something. They lifted their hands in greeting when he entered. The Alwyn stood beside the hearth, his hands clasped behind his back.

For Magnus, it had gotten easier each day, to conceal his hate. To act normally when in the man's presence. But now, looking at the man he once believed to be his father—a distant father who had never shown any desire to acknowledge him as a son—he wished more than anything, his true father was still alive, and that it was he who he came to visit, rather than the conspirator who had plotted his death.

"Magnus," the Alwyn said. "There you are."

The clan's leader had changed tunics since returning indoors, this one made of deep blue, while Magnus remained clad in a blood-stained plaid, his legs and boots spattered with mud. Magnus strode closer.

"I came as soon as I could," said Magnus.

The laird tilted his head, scrutinizing him. "I have wanted to speak to you for some time now."

Then they met to discuss something other than the public humility he had just inflicted upon Hugh.

"Have you?" answered Magnus. "About what?"

"Aye . . . as you know, very soon, Buchan will arrive. I am certain that when he does, he and his forces will support us in taking the necessary actions against the false Kincaid, and his army."

"It is what you want," Magnus replied, even as the fires of rebellion flared hot inside his chest.

"Indeed it is. And . . . I have made a decision . . ." The Alwyn's gaze burned with the delight of a secret held, and he smiled.

Magnus stood tense, and listening. "Yes, laird?"

"I want you to stand at my side, to represent the clan as the Alwyn war-captain."

The words echoed in his ears. Words he'd never expected to hear.

"Me?" Magnus answered, stunned. "But . . . there are other warriors who have served you far longer."

And also Hugh, who by Alwyn tradition, would normally hold the honor.

"But *you*—" the laird said, pointing at his chest. "You are the best."

Despite his hate for the man . . . pride rose up through

Magnus's chest. Aye, he knew he was the best. He had striven endlessly to become so, and praise from this man's lips was rare. But the pride he felt was that of a Kincaid, who would one day soon use his lethal talents to defeat the man into whose eyes he presently stared.

Turning, the Alwyn paced several steps, appearing deep in thought, before shifting on his heels, and looking back. "You know as well as I, our lowland rulers and their governments believe us to be barbaric savages in need of transformation." He spoke with an edge of sarcasm, holding his hands upward, toward the Heavens. "Since I was a boy, they have been trying to . . . change us. Our language, the way we possess these lands and our very way of life. While I, like every highlander, find this gravely offensive, if we are to survive, we must look forward, and change. Others have refused, and paid the price."

"Such as the Kincaid clan?" His heart pounded.

The Alwyn dipped his head in agreement, his gaze darkening. "Such as the Kincaid clan, indeed."

He looked away a moment, before turning back.

"Hugh is my son, and my *ceann-cath*. But you are. . . . deserving in other ways. The council is in full agreement. We want you here, taking part in the meetings of the council, as a leader of this clan, and of our warriors. It is important for me—for all of us—that Buchan understand that the Alwyns, as a clan, are far more civilized as men and skilled as warriors than those who surround us. He is a powerful ally we must impress and keep. You are the man who will represent us best. Not only that, but the men respect you. They will follow your order. Your example."

For most of his life, he'd lived at Burnbryde, just hoping for the slightest scrap of recognition from this man. And now that he, as a secret son of the murdered Kincaid, plotted the Alwyn's demise . . . that he should be chosen to lead forces against the Kincaid clan . . .

Well, how perfect.

Indeed, he could not imagine any circumstance more perfect than this.

"I am honored," he answered. "And I accept."

"Very good." The Alwyn clapped a hand on his shoulder. "There are chambers, upstairs. A fine set of rooms, befitting your new position."

"Thank you, laird, but I prefer to remain with the men of the Pit."

"Somehow I knew you would say that," the laird answered. "Because you're a warrior, through and through. Whatever you prefer. Just make ready. New garments. A finer horse. They are yours for the asking. Make ready, as you will." The laird tapped his shoulder with his fist. "Just know that Buchan arrives in less than a fortnight."

The council members rose from the nearby table. Coming nearer, they congratulated him, and voiced their agreement with the laird's choice. He could not help but wonder if any of them had been present when his father was murdered. Likely, all of them—and he felt pleasure knowing they would remember this moment, and realize they themselves had given him the power to defeat them.

The Alwyn walked him to the door. "As for this thing between Hugh and yourself . . . try not to kill him. I would never hear the end of it from his mother."

"I will do my best." Magnus nodded, assuming the chief was jesting, and took his leave.

In the corridor, he exhaled, still in disbelief. He had been appointed clan war-chief. It was a clear sign the laird had lost hope that his true son would prove worthy to lead.

And yet the decision would be the laird's downfall—the key to his own destruction.

Returning to his chamber, he found the men of the Pit already there, some washing and some resting, but all in a state of anger and disbelief over Hugh's cowardly act on the practice field. They gathered around him as soon as he stepped into the room.

"The craven fool!" growled Finlay.

"'e would have killed you," Walter muttered, fire in his eyes.

"'e'll go ta the dewill, by God," Quentin snarled.

Magnus lifted a hand and all grew quiet.

"I met with the laird," he said.

He told them what had taken place, and within moments grinning male faces surrounded him, and hands clapped on his back.

"Well deserved!" Chissolm shouted.

"Our leader!"

Adam pushed in close, smiling. "We will follow you anywhere."

Would they, if they knew? It felt wrong to keep the truth from them, but he must for a while longer. He sought the solitude of his room, and after removing his blood-stained plaid, and boots, he washed and wearing only linen *braies*, stretched out on his bed.

Whereas before, his plan for revenge had been a vague plot in his mind and utterly reliant on the chance that he—a warrior of the guard, without authority or command, could bring the Alwyn and Buchan together, and elicit the testimony necessary to condemn them both, he now held the necessary position and status to do just that.

As war-chief of the clan, and thereby a leader of the council, all he needed to do was summon the two men when he was ready . . . and they would appear.

Only . . . should he pursue justice by his blade, or take

both men prisoner, and petition the Estates of Parliament?

If he killed Buchan—the king's son—he would be a wanted man forever. He would never be able to speak his true name, for fear of royal reprisals against the Kincaids. He would have no choice but to leave Scotland, and allow everyone to believe the Alwyn's bastard had inexplicably committed murder, and seek a life of anonymity abroad.

He was willing to sacrifice himself in that way, but not before he talked to Niall. Together they could decide what must be done.

And yet as soon as he closed his eyes, he thought of her. She lit up his mind like a flame.

Less than a fortnight and the earl would be here. Any wedding would take place quickly, he had no doubt, in order to solidify the alliance that would then march against the Kincaids.

His hand moved to the wound on his side. An inch deeper . . .

His heart beat faster and sweat broke out on his skin, as he allowed the truth to settle over him. An inch deeper and he would either be grievously wounded or dead. Hugh *had* intended to kill him. Tara had saved his life.

Now he must save hers.

That meant, saying good-bye to her.

Restless, his skin drawn tight, and his mind swarming with thoughts of her face, her voice, her lips, her hands, Magnus sat up, planting bare feet on the ground. Bending, scoring his fingers through his hair, he groaned in agony.

He would not rest until he saw her again.

Tara stood to the side, as servants poured steaming buckets of water into the tub.

"Anna, you are too kind to me."

But it wasn't the bath for which she thanked her.

Rather it was the key the girl had furtively pressed into her hands some two hours before, as she'd lay on the bed, awash in devastated tears. A key stamped with the shape of a crescent moon.

Anna poured a goblet of wine and set it on the table, very near to the tub's edge.

"You suffered a terrible shock today."

"You saw it too," Tara answered quietly. "So where is your bath?"

"It is different for me," the maid answered. "I am not betrothed to Hugh."

Anna referred, of course, to the shameful thing Hugh had done. *Tara's betrothed*. It had replayed in her mind all day, until she felt ill from it. She could never marry a man who attacked his own half-brother when his back was turned. She had never witnessed such cowardice and in truth he had dishonored her beyond forgiveness, being that they were betrothed.

But they weren't betrothed. Not in her heart. She would never consent.

And Magnus . . .

As much as she had cautioned herself not to care for him, not to form an attachment to a man she would perhaps never see again after leaving this place . . . when she had seen the blood fall from the wound in his side, and spill down to stain his plaid, she had nearly fainted out of fear that he would die.

She could deny her feelings for him no more. Yes, they'd formed quickly, but without a doubt, they were real.

She had sent Anna out into the castle to confirm the wound had been tended to and that he lived, but concern for him had left Tara in a state of agitation for the rest of the day. It was not only the wound!

How he must feel. His own half-brother had tried to

kill him, in full view of everyone, in the most cowardly of ways. Her heart hurt for him. She had not even been able to see him at the evening meal, as Lady Alwyn still felt unwell, and they had supped in the tower. Had he even been well enough to attend? She wanted nothing more than to see him.

Even now, she did not know how she would sleep. She wouldn't sleep. As soon as her door was locked for the night, and she was left alone, she would descend the secret passageway in hopes he might be waiting for her below. Hours earlier, when she'd been left alone to rest, she had even dared to leave the bars unlocked for him. She just needed to hear words from his lips, to know he was all right.

Mary appeared then, at the door. "Anna, can you help me with the lady?"

Anna hesitated, looking toward Tara.

"I can tend to myself, Anna. Actually, I prefer to do so. Thank you."

Mary withdrew and her footsteps faded.

"Thank you, Mistress," Anna answered. "The lady continues to feel so poorly. I'll return shortly."

The girl turned, her hand on the door . . . but then paused and looked back.

"Yes, Anna," she said quietly. "I will be here when you return."

Anna exhaled, appearing reassured. "I'll pull this closed, so you won't feel the draft."

She sighed, grateful to be alone at last. It had been difficult, concealing the true depth of her concern for Magnus all this time, pretending that the only reason for her tears was her disappointment with Hugh's character. She wanted to be alone, and think about Magnus without worrying everyone would read her feelings on her face.

Now alone, Tara undressed beside the fire, and shivering . . . sank into the bath.

There were also decisions she must make. She now had her necklace. She had a key. She must think about what to do from here. Was it possible that Magnus would leave this place, and start a new life with her far away from here?

What foolishness was this—these wild, reckless thoughts arising inside her mind? They had spent only moments alone in one another's company. Shared only one brief kiss. And she was ready to run away with him? Her mind said no. But her heart . . . her heart demanded otherwise. There was something about the darkness of Castle Burnbryde. The danger to not only her life, but his, that magnified . . . clarified her feelings for him. Aye, the feelings were new, but they were real and powerful, and when she'd feared he'd been harmed . . . that she might lose him forever, her soul had grieved to a degree that stunned her.

She would not lose him again. She would claim him—and his warrior's heart—if she could, and take whatever happiness she could from this life, rather than allow it to slip through her fingers. But did he feel the same?

She did not know. Perhaps despite his dislike for Hugh, too much blood, too much clan loyalty bound him here, and she must prepare herself for that. With or without him, she would leave this place.

An escape, alone, would be no simple child's game. There was danger everywhere, for a woman alone, traveling without protection and she would not simply jump from one perilous situation into another under the pretense of being free. She could not simply run headlong into the night, and offer her necklace to the first stranger with a wagon or horse that she came upon, in exchange

for whisking her away from here. That lack of caution
would just as likely bring about another theft of the
necklace—or even her murder, rather than her escape.

She must find someone to trust, and that might take
days. If not Magnus, then the traveling whitesmith, perhaps. He had seemed kind enough, and trustworthy. No
formal introduction had been made, so he did not know
anything about who she was. If she could find him again,
and convince him to take her away from Burnbryde inside his traveling wagon of wares, certainly he would
know others who could be trusted to take her even far-
ther away.

A few days, in which to make preparations . . . she
could survive that. She had to. In that time, she would
press to find out the truth of what had happened to Arabel, because without knowing, she would never truly be
free.

The water, though thoroughly heated, did nothing to
warm the chill in her heart. She sipped the wine, and
eased back, her hair falling over the high edge of the tub,
savoring the intoxicating, numbing sensation that crept
through her veins. Again, she saw Magnus's face in
her mind. Remembered the night before, and being held
in his arms and comforted with such gentle care. How
he'd looked standing over Hugh today—like a conqueror.
The way the men had gathered around *him* afterward,
because he was their champion, their leader, all but shunning Hugh.

The thoughts awakened a fever in her blood, and what
the water could not warm, thoughts of Magnus did. She
ached for him, body and soul. Wished he was here with
her now, so that he could hold and kiss her again, this
time without bars separating them.

It was then she heard it . . . the quiet opening of the

secret door behind her. Or had it only been a fantasy created of her own mind?

"Tara," he said, his voice ragged.

Footsteps. The sound of him kneeling behind her.

She felt two hands sink into her hair, lifting it. He inhaled, and she knew he buried his face in the long, curling mass.

"Forgive me for coming here," he rasped. "I know it is wrong, but when I found the bars unlocked, I thought you were gone. Fled. That you were out there somewhere, unsafe and unprotected. That I would never find you again."

Her heart—her lungs, expanded with relief, that he was safe and well, and pleasure that he had come to her.

He dared much. She was naked, in her bath. The door was unlocked and Anna could return at any moment. Her skin flushed hot, and her heart raced, knowing everything about their meeting like this was forbidden. Each moment they passed together meant danger. She did not care. This stranger had, like a strike of lightning, taken possession of her heart and soul. He was here, and she did not want him to go. Her breasts swelled with excitement, nipples tightening, and she crossed her arms over herself in modesty.

His arm came round, cradling her head from behind.

"I needed to see you," he murmured, his voice deep, and harsh. His warm lips pressed fervent kisses to her cheek . . . her jaw . . . her neck . . . leaving her more drunk than any wine. "To thank you for saving my life."

Pleasure rushed through her, like a tidal wave. Her emotions, which had been snarled—a tight tangle in her chest all day—released.

"I thought he would kill you," she answered all in a rush, through tears.

"Never," he said softly—so softly she hardly heard the words.

He shifted, coming round on his knee, the other leg extended in half a crouch, wearing an open throated tunic and a plaid at his waist, blocking the firelight with his broad shoulders, casting them both into shadows. In the flickering shadow and light, his countenance was drawn and stark.

"You found the key."

"Anna gave it to me."

"Then you're a free woman now," he said, his gaze glittering.

"I am."

He caught her face, his palms and fingers caging her jaw and cheeks, strong and sure, and he kissed her in a way that said power and possession and care.

"I'll get you out of here, then. As soon as I know I can do so safely."

He kissed her again, the urgency of his lips conveying his hunger. As if he could not stop. Deep inside, she felt an awakening. A rush of emotion and sensations that overpowered all caution . . . all rational sense. She moaned into his mouth, her arms going around his shoulders, streaming water . . . and felt him tremble. She trembled too.

He broke away, murmuring near her ear. "I want you to be free and safe, but God, Tara—at the same time, I don't want to let y' go."

"Then come with me," she whispered, clinging to him. Drawing back, he went completely still, staring into her eyes, one hand cradling her head, the other gripping her shoulder.

The words . . . the confession of her feelings startled even her, but she did not regret saying them and would not take them back.

Distantly, she heard footsteps. Her heart started in fear—

Already he stood, eyes dark and passion-filled— backing between the bed frame and the stone wall, to stand concealed by the long curtains and dark shadows.

Her blood pounding, she strove to clear all emotion— all *passion* from her face.

"Here we are." Anna entered, carrying a small basket of folded linens. Mary followed her, and went directly to her trunk, where she selected a night rail.

"I beg your forgiveness for not returning before now," Anna said, setting the linen on the table, and taking the topmost one in hand. "The water must be cooling by now. Let's get you out and dry before you catch a chill."

She unfurled a swath of linen and held it wide, and waited for Tara to stand.

In the darkness, she saw Magnus. Just the barest, almost imperceptible outline of his shoulder, and above that, the angular cut of his jaw. Her breath hitched in her throat, and her heart beat wildly. Perhaps she dared too much. Perhaps it was wrong . . . perhaps it was a *sin*, but she wanted him there. She wanted him to see that there would be nothing hidden between them. That she would hold nothing back. She had seen more of a hero in him, in this short span of time, than any other man she'd ever known—and her heart refused to let him go.

Placing her hands on the rim of the tub, she exhaled through parted lips . . . and stood.

Magnus stood in the shadows, unable to tear his gaze away, unable to breathe, as water sluiced down Tara's skin, the firelight painting her gold like some ancient river goddess.

He had known her body would be beautiful. He had felt her soft curves pressed against him when he'd kissed her, glimpsed her tempting loveliness hidden by her night rail the night before.

But seeing her now, the full magnitude of her perfection bared to his gaze, caused his blood to catch fire and his sex to stiffen with such suddenness, he gasped from the pain. A most exquisite pain, that shattered him, all the way to his soul, for it was not mere desire he felt for Tara, but something far deeper.

Thankfully the fire shifted and cracked at that moment, so his spontaneous exhalation went unheard.

Her attendants circled her—one buffing her skin with the linen, while the other poured oil from a small pitcher, and rubbed it over her shoulders, arms, and back as Tara stood, her lips parted and her shoulders back.

She knew that he was there . . . that he watched, and yet she did not attempt to hide herself with her hands, or snatch at the linen to cover herself.

Instead, her stare fixed on the secret place where he stood as she stepped from the tub, and lifted her arms above her head. His hungry gaze devoured her full, high breasts, with their small, pink nipples . . . a smooth torso that descended to a pinched waist . . . her gleaming hips, thighs, and the shadowed place between her legs.

His scalp tightened, and his palms burned. Desire surged through him, rampant and all consuming. His hand gripped the wooden column of the bed post. Arousal clouded his mind so thickly he feared no danger. Suffered no concern for future regrets. There was only her, and a consuming need to claim her for his own, not just for this one night, but forever.

His cock hung heavy and tight, jutting agonizingly against the wool of his plaid. One maid lifted the gown above Tara's head, and slipping it onto her arms, let the linen fall, covering her.

She was no less lovely for it. Her nipples tantalized

against the soft bodice. The other maid pulled her hair from under the neck of her gown and combed the long tresses so that they shone like copper fire, before fashioning one long braid that hung down her back.

The attendants—hell, he did not even know what they looked like, so rapt was his attention on Tara—set about tidying the area of the bath, and at a word, two more female servants appeared and lugged the tub away, sloshing between them. Tara's garments were returned to their trunk. Then, at last, there was only one maid—who paused on the threshold.

"Be sure to lock the door," she announced. "Lady Alwyn continues to insist."

His heartbeat hitched faster.

"I will," Tara answered in a whisper, moving to stand at the corner of the bed. "Good night."

The door closed. Tara took several steps, and took up a key from the table, she moved forward, and turned the key in the lock. Footsteps on the other side, faded into the distance.

He approached her from behind, every muscle alive and tight, his breaths weighted by the grave import of the moment, which seemed to unfold like a dream.

"I told you I wouldn't kiss you again until you were free. And one moment in your company, and I've already broken that vow."

"I have the key to the tower window," she whispered. "Does that not make me free?"

Tara . . . did not move. She stood, with her shoulders straight . . . awaiting his touch.

Her hair had, from the first moment he'd seen it, enchanted him. He tugged the cord from the end of her braid, and slowly, from the bottom up, freed the rippling, silken mass from its confines, allowing it to slip across his fingertips, his palms. Scoring his fingers through, he grazed his nails against her scalp, lifting the soft curls high. Tara sighed and tilted her head, welcoming his touch.

Hungry for her, he pressed his open mouth against the curve of her neck, tasting her skin with his tongue, inhaling the intoxicating fragrance of the scented oil into his nostrils, floral . . . sensual . . . woman.

"Come with me, Magnus," she whispered. "Leave this place with me. Please say yes. I choose you."

His soul shook at the import of her words.

"Yes," he answered. "I will."

After he had his revenge.

She pressed her back to him, sighing in surrender.

"I want to make love to you," he murmured, his voice raspy with passion. "I *need* to make love to you."

It was no lie. Considering the state of his arousal, he thought he just might die if he didn't, and now, more than ever, he wanted to live. He wanted to live for himself and Tara, and the future they could have together.

"Yes," she answered, growing still in his arms. "I want that too."

"You'll be mine," he murmured near her ear.

They were not simple words of seduction, spoken without meaning. They were a promise, solemnly made. She would never be Hugh's. He would do anything to protect her, from this moment on. She belonged to him.

"And you will be mine," she answered, reaching back to touch his face, to graze her knuckles, her palm, against his beard roughened jaw.

He took pleasure in her words, and he felt no regret, no shame for what he did, because it felt right. Turning her, holding her within the tight band of his arm, he kissed her mouth, voracious, taking her deeply with his tongue.

His woman. Only his. Forever.

From behind he slipped his arms around her waist, one coming upward and crosswise so that his hand might cage the full softness of her breast. She gasped, her hands fisting in his plaid at his thighs, her nipple jutting against his palm. Spreading his hand wide, he grazed her there, in a slow, circular caress, teasing . . . awakening her body and submitting himself to the most exquisite torment he had ever known.

God, she was an enchantment. So slight and feminine compared to his brutish size. Desire, instinctive and primal, blurred all rational thought. Hooking his thumb into the neck of her shift, he tugged the linen down, kissing her neck again, nuzzling the place behind her ear, while drinking in the sight of her bare breast, plump and pink-tipped, in his hand.

He urged her backward, against the bed post, his hands sliding up the sides of her torso. He bent, catching her tight nipple in his mouth, teasing it with his tongue. She moaned, smoothing her hands over his head, into his hair.

"You're the most beautiful thing I've ever seen. Ever touched. I can't get enough of you," he murmured against her skin. "I want to see you. I want to taste you. All of you."

"Magnus," she whispered, moving restlessly, shifting her thighs together.

Her gown hung from her hips. He pushed it lower so that it dropped with a whisper to the floor, and she stood naked. Her movements equally urgent, she pushed his tunic up, sliding her hands over his skin, grazing his stitched wound. He hissed—not from pain, but from pleasure—and wrenched the garment over his head and tossed it aside.

She leaned forward, hazy eyed, and pressed her mouth

against the skin of his collarbone, but drawing back to look again at the place where Hugh's craven sword had split his skin. Her fingertips brushed near, and a quavering breath left her lips.

"Tell me what to do," she said.

Chapter 11

He gripped her slender wrists, breathing hard—reminding himself he must take care. "What do you know of a man's body? Of a man's desire?"

"A little," she whispered. "Very . . . little."

"There is nothing little about mine," he replied, then clenched his teeth in immediate regret, for he intended nothing vulgar or bawdy. Not with her, an innocent. "What I'm saying is that I don't want to frighten you."

"I won't be frightened," she asserted softly. "Not by you. I am only amazed, and . . ."

She blushed so deeply, he could do nothing but kiss her mouth.

"And what?" he murmured against her lips, tracing her jaw with his thumb.

"Wanting more," she whispered, demurely turning her face aside.

He caught her chin, and lifting her face, kissed her hard.

"And I . . . want . . . more," he said.

Heart pounding, he guided her hand to the front of his plaid, to press against his hard sex.

Through clenched teeth he uttered, "This is what being alone with you . . . kissing you . . . seeing your body . . . wanting to be inside you . . . does to me."

With a quavering breath, she slowly slid her palm against him, gauging his shape and his size until he groaned.

"You don't know what you do to me, touching me like that."

"Then show me," she said, a wide-eyed temptress in the firelight. "I want to see you. To touch you, as you are touching me."

"I'll die if you don't," he growled.

Fisting a hand in his plaid, he seized the garment upward and pressed her hand to his bare, hot flesh, turning her palm, curling her fingers so that she gripped him tight.

She showed no fear or shock . . . instead she stared down at his sex in her small, pale hand, her lips parted. *He* stared down at his sex in her hand, knowing he would remember the erotic sight forever.

"I think I understand now." She relaxed her hold, and let out a shallow breath. She smoothed the fingertips of her other hand along his length, grazing his crown with her thumb—drawing a gasp from deep in his throat. "Although I'm not sure how we shall manage it." A frown tugged at her lips. "We seem to be . . ."

"What?" he groaned, throbbing, half blinded by need.

"Unsuited," she said, eyebrows raised, her expression crestfallen. "You are far too . . . well, it won't work, I fear."

"I *promise* it will," he countered, in a rasp. "It's rather amazing, how it happens."

She looked into his eyes.

THE REBEL OF CLAN KINCAID   207

"Truly?" she asked, her expression doubtful but . . . interested.

"I'll show you." Kissing her, he *carefully* removed her hand, and pressed her again to the bedpost, guiding her arms upward, to encircle the wood column above her head. "Stay . . . like that. Don't move."

Asserting control over his almost out-of-control passion, he inhaled deeply, kissing her forehead . . . her eyes, her nose . . . and languidly worked his way lower . . . squeezing, kissing and licking her breasts. Her warm, fragrant skin.

"Oh, Magnus . . . I . . ." she pled softly, her back arching, her body moving restlessly. "*Please.*"

"Please . . . what?" he murmured, caressing her waist, savoring the perfect torment of prolonging their passion, knowing he must heighten her arousal, so that she would be ready.

"I . . . I don't know," she answered.

"Tara?"

"Yes?"

"Don't let go of the post."

Sinking to his knees, he pressed his face against the tight seam of her thighs, and above, into her soft curls. He breathed in the scent of her—lavender and woman—kissing her there, urging her with his hands and his thumbs to open to him, which she did, murmuring his name and emitting sweet, urgent sighs until at last he pressed deeper, plunging his tongue deep into her softness.

Desire coursing like fire in his veins, he made love to her with his mouth, indulging in a deep, rhythmic spearing of his tongue until she responded, panting and moving her hips urgently against him, her hands coming down at last, to seize handfuls of his hair.

"Magnus!" she cried, her knees buckling.

"Shhhh." He stood, lifting her up, off the floor, his hands beneath her soft, sweet bottom. He guided her legs around his waist and held her suspended against him. She clung to him, kissing his face. He loved the feel of her hair falling down over his arms as he held her. "Quiet, love."

He lay her on the bed, and paused a moment, crouched above her. He'd grown to care for her in such a short time. His desire for her came from his heart, running soul deep. He did not want to hurt her—but nor did he want to let her go.

"Are you certain?" he asked. "Once it is done, there's no going back."

He took her breath away, looking as he did in the firelight. Magnus with his warrior's body, taut and powerful above her, the firelight playing off the flexed muscles of his shoulders. They were very much strangers still, she knew . . . and yet she felt as if from the first moment her soul had somehow recognized him. As if this had been intended forever.

"I'm certain," she whispered. She did not want to go back. Whatever happened tomorrow, or the next day, without question—she wanted this now.

"You want me . . . *inside* you . . ." he said provocatively, his eyes glittering with arousal.

Her cheeks flamed at the boldness of his words, but she understood . . . he wanted her to know the truth of what would happen between them.

But she also knew this was no simple seduction, based on lust alone. Gravity underscored his words. His every touch. From the moment they'd met in the forest, their hearts and their destinies had been entwined.

"Yes," she answered, without qualm.

Always, before now, others had made decisions for

her. This decision—this most *important* decision, she made for herself, and she knew set the course for the rest of her life. She would give her loyalty to this remarkable man—and he would give his loyalty to her. She knew not what the coming days would bring—her escape or . . . her doom. She did not know if he could save her— perhaps she could only save herself, but she could face tomorrow more bravely just knowing he cared.

He backed out from the shadows of the bed. She lifted up to sit, to watch him, not wanting to miss a moment. He was a magnificent sight, all long limbs and corded muscle. Lifting his foot to the edge of a stool, he dispatched one leather boot, and then the other. His gaze pinned to hers, he straightened, his hands going to his plaid, which he unfastened and unwound, the shadows defining the chiseled indentions defining his chest, his arms and his abdomen and at last . . . his sex, which jutted out from his body, rigidly aroused.

She stared at it, exhaling unevenly, fearing again that they would only meet with frustration, for despite his assurances, she could not imagine how this thing between them would be accomplished.

He returned to the bed, his eyes burning on her. She went up on her knees, meeting him for a kiss—wanting to be woman enough for this warrior.

"You are . . . extraordinary," he murmured against her skin. His hand fisted in her hair. Pulling her head back, he pressed kisses along her neck and lower, onto the upper swells of her breasts. "More than extraordinary."

"You make me feel that way." The barest touch of his hand awakened her passion anew. Each kiss thrilled more than the last.

"Tara . . ." He let out a deep, rough sound, bringing his knee up, pushing her gently down onto the pillows, spreading her hair across the linens. Kissing her. Smothering her. Overwhelming her with his mouth and his touch until she succumbed to delirium. She lay on her back, him sprawled beside her, the both of them tangled in linen, the firelight playing off their bodies.

Slowly, he stroked her between her legs, pressing his thumb to the exact place where she felt so painfully tight and aroused. Aye, the man clearly knew a woman's body and that caused her both consternation and pride, though she would make sure he never needed another woman for as long as he lived. He stroked slower . . . and deeper . . . and deeper still, until she moaned with want for something else. Her arms went round his neck, her hands into his hair, she hanging on, lest she be swept away.

"Beautiful," he murmured, his gaze searing over her.

Yes, beautiful—the way he made her body respond. But the pull of pleasure between her legs was too much, and coaxed her close to the edge of some pleasurable oblivion. She arched, her head thrown back—

And gasped as his long, square-tipped finger sank inside her, only to ease away, and enter her body again, joined by a second, stretching her . . . shocking her with an even more satisfying sensation than she'd known before. She cried his name against his throat.

"Yes, love," he soothed. "Shhh. Quiet."

Suddenly he was there, his hard legs . . . his knees, parting her thighs, his hips . . . his weight coming down between. His hand came between them, and she looked down, watching . . . spellbound by the sight of him, in shadows and firelight, holding his swollen member. She felt . . . and *watched* the hard, steely prod of his sex against her damp and needful flesh, and the rounded, swarthy crown pushed just inside. She closed her eyes in ecstasy and her heartbeat quickened, knowing he would take her now.

"Yes," she whispered, lifting her hips.

Bracing above her, his stomach taut, he gave a thrust of his hips, stabbing deep.

"Ah . . ." he gritted out.

He stretched her tight. She groaned in discomfort, seizing his shoulders, and widening her legs, digging her heels into the backs of his muscled thighs.

"Almost . . ." He moved slowly . . . rocking deeper, and deeper. "Almost . . . perfect."

Yes . . . perfect.

She went suddenly still, as everything changed in an instant. His thickness, moving inside her, no longer gave her pain, but pleasure.

Gasping deep, she moved, matching each of his movements with her hips. Intensifying pleasure and heat spiraled through her, but concentrated *there*, at the place where their bodies joined, with such intensity, she felt the need to cry out, but she knew she could not. She had never imagined making love would feel like this. So ethereal—so divine.

"I could die here now, inside you, Tara." He hissed, peering down at her through passion glazed eyes, his cheeks ruddy. "You feel that good. But I need more, and I fear I will hurt you."

His words gave her just as much pleasure as his body. She had never felt so close to anyone, in all her life.

"I'm yours," she whispered feverishly, gripping his forearms. "Do as you will."

With a sudden thrust, he buried his face in her neck. Pain streaked through her womb, a powerful renting from within. Tears glazed her eyes and she let out a shocked cry—which he smothered with his mouth. His body went still.

"I'm sorry," he murmured against her lips.

Aye, there was pain. She nearly cried out from it, but the pain made her his, and she took a different kind of pleasure from that. They belonged to each other now.

"I'm all right," she whispered, stroking her hands down his back. "Don't stop."

She kissed his neck, and slowly, he moved inside her, each time deeper, until at last, his body coaxed the same response from her as before, only this time more powerful. Her breasts felt swollen with it, and her nipples grazed tantalizingly against his chest as they moved together, panting and gasping and groaning. And yet she felt desperate and greedy for more. More of his hands on her, more his mouth on hers, more his sex inside her. She squeezed her thighs at his hips, demanding all from him and receiving it—

And suddenly her womb seized *tight*. She gasped, holding him close, as pleasure wracked her body, through and through.

"Oh, Magnus," she half-sobbed.

"My beautiful love," he murmured.

His muscles shuddered beneath her hands . . . and she felt his sex pulse larger, again and again, deep inside her womb.

He kissed her deeply, gasping into her mouth. After a long moment, he rolled to his side and gathered her close against his hard chest, laying face-to-face, as he breathed heavily into her hair.

"Tara," he rasped, kissing her temple. "God . . . I never imagined it could be that way."

She clung to him, feeling . . . changed forever.

She thought of Arabel then, and her broken heart. Had she been abandoned by a lover who cared nothing for her, or torn from the man she loved and who loved her in return? But just as quickly she closed her mind to those thoughts. Not because she wanted to forget her sister, but because she had to believe her life would not end in tragedy as well. Everything felt so perfect in this moment, she feared the slightest strike or crack would shatter it.

"Careful not to stain the linen," he said softly. "The servants will see."

She left him, to go to the basin, dropping the cloth, afterward, onto the fire. Afterward, he did the same. Together, they returned to the bed, where he smothered her with kisses, leaving her breathless, and eager for the next time they would make love.

"Where will we go?" Tara whispered, holding him tight.

"Where you will be safe." He pressed her back onto the pillow, and peered down with a dark glimmer of intensity in his eyes. "With people I trust."

"What do you mean, where *I* will be safe. What about you?"

"I must return to Burnbryde," Magnus said.

Her eyes widened, flashing with sudden fire. "Return to Burnbryde?"

"There are matters at hand of which I cannot speak. Matters which must be concluded."

She opened her mouth as if to argue, but he cut in.

"I will tell you everything, Tara, but not until you are safe and far from here."

She pushed out of his arms, and moved to sit at the edge of the bed, the blaze of her hair falling down her naked back, then twisted back to glare at him . . . presenting him with a beguiling profile of one perfectly round breast and its lovely, pink tip.

"Either we both leave, or neither of us do."

He let out a breath. "This from the woman who has talked of nothing but escape since the moment she arrived."

Her gaze intensified. "Things are different now. I have a key to get out of this tower, whenever I wish. And most importantly, I have you. Because of that I am not afraid. At least not as afraid as before and Magnus, before I go I *must* find out what happened to my sister."

He considered her words—but after a half-moment's contemplation, shook his head. "Tara, I could hardly bear to see Hugh touch you before. Now, I'll kill him, which could get me killed. No. You'll go where I know he can't get you."

"I am not a child, Magnus, or a stupid girl."

"I know you aren't."

"If you think I'm so fragile that I can't survive his . . . grabbing my arm or . . . speaking vile words to me then you're wrong. You'll get me out of here before any wedding can take place. I know you will. That is all that matters. That and that I find out the truth of what happened to Arabel."

He admired the stubbornness, the bravery he saw in her eyes. But he wouldn't risk her being hurt. No matter what she demanded. He just wasn't going to argue with her right now, while they were both naked, and still in the bed. He would take her to Inverhaven at the first sign Hugh grew out of hand, or at the first sign of Buchan's impending arrival, whether she'd learned the truth about her sister or not.

"If you insist," he said.

"I do insist," she said seriously.

"I insist on kissing you." With one hand, he pulled her down, so that she lay flat on her back, her breasts and her torso and legs aglow in the firelight, and he kissed her lips from upside down.

"Yes, do that." She sighed, her hands coming up into his hair, and kissed him back. "Again, and again."

"Come here," he murmured. "Lay beside me. I want to hold you while you sleep."

She did fall asleep in his arms. Hours passed, but he remained awake. Aware. Vigilant. He did not regret making love to her—taking her innocence for his own. He had not done so out of selfishness, but because he could not convince his soul there was any other answer but being with her.

He would change nothing. And yet . . .

Damn if his life had not become infinitely more complicated in doing so, for now he must live for her and not only for himself. If he died, he must make sure she would be safe and protected, without him. What if they'd made a child tonight?

He gently eased her to the pillow and left the bed to stand naked in front of the dwindling fire, allowing the night chill to claim his skin. He had no doubt his cause against the Alwyn, and certainly also Buchan, was right. And yet now . . . beneath all the righteous certainty there existed a heavy thread of guilt. Guilt that to satisfy his desire for her, he'd made her *his* prisoner, just as certainly as any other villain in their story. She hated Burnbryde. Would she hate Inverhaven too? Yes, they were truly different places and different clans, but at present, this corner of the highlands was a place of constant turmoil and danger. If he truly cared for her, more than he cared for himself, would he not have found some way to let her go to some safe haven? Some other place?

There came a rustling from the bed. Looking there, he could just make out the pale gleam of her shoulders, and the titian glimmer of her long hair as she sat up, peering out from the curtains at him. She held the coverlet against her breasts. "Magnus?"

He felt the blood and heat rush through his body, and

into his groin. That was all it took, one glimpse of her . . . her sleepy-eyed and speaking his name to make him forget his conscience.

He neared the bed. Her gaze dropped—sweeping over his naked body, inflaming his arousal further.

"Come back to me." She lay back and drew aside the bed linens in invitation. He took in the sight of her perfect skin, her pillow-soft breasts and slender waist. "I want you to make love to me again."

A laugh emitted from deep in his throat, a raspy, needful sound and desire took over. He climbed between the curtains, covering her soft, pliant body with his, kissing her, loving her scent in his nostrils. Her hands and her mouth, eager, on his skin.

"Like this," he murmured.

He turned her onto her stomach so that she lay raised on her elbows as he placed slow, teasing kisses, assisted by his tongue and his fingertips, down her spine until she gasped and sighed, arching her back.

He had been with other women before, but they all seemed so far away and forever ago. Forgotten. With her, everything felt new.

"Your body . . . is so lovely. As lovely as your face, and your heart." He paused, grazing his lips over the small, enchanting indentations just above her buttocks, and made his way back up to the place between her shoulders. He smoothed a hand down her back, to her hip, pulling her smaller, slenderer body against the length of his, so that she lay on her side.

Pressed against her softness, his arousal grew. Her arm came back, and she touched his face. He bent, testing the skin of her neck with his teeth, and skimmed his fingertips up, over her ribs. She responded with a soft giggle, and squirmed against him, in a way that made him lose all patience to be inside her again.

"I want you like this," he whispered, taking hold of the inside of her knee, and lifting . . . widening her legs, bringing her hips toward him. Stroking her, he found her slick and ready.

"Hurry," she whispered, her thighs clenching against his hand.

Grasping hold of his cock, he guided himself . . . tilted his hips and thrust, entering her.

"Ah . . ." she gasped, tossing her head, her hair back.

She was so narrow, so tight. His mind went hazy with lust. Another thrust, and he was fully ensheathed.

"Like this," he murmured, moving inside her. Pleasure tightened his every muscle. Awakened every inch of his skin. Making love to her was better than any fantasy his mind had ever conjured.

He rose onto one elbow, aligning her against him so that they both lay on their sides, her upper leg lifted and bent so that her foot rested on the outside of his calf.

With his hand on her waist . . . sliding down over her stomach to stroke between her legs . . . he guided her into a slow rhythm. Drawing her hair aside, he kissed her neck, her cheek. Squeezed her breast. Oh, god, yes. Perfect.

But it wasn't enough. Clenching his teeth, he pulled out and rolled her to her back.

"I need to see your face," he rasped.

He kissed her, hard and earnestly. Because even now, he almost couldn't believe it was her. That they were here making love in her bed. Tonight couldn't last long enough. Spreading her legs, he exerted every fragment of his control, and slowly entered her again.

"Mmm." She sighed. "Oh . . . Magnus."

Buried inside her, he lowered his head and caught her nipple in his mouth, and sucked and licked until her hips came off the bed, hitching higher and harder to match each pull and push of his rigid sex.

The muscles of his abdomen flexed with each thrust. His stitched wound stung, but the pain only heightened his pleasure.

"I'm not hurting you?" he rasped.

"No . . ." she whispered through swollen lips.

Unable to hold back, to control his desire, he rose up on his knees, and seized her buttocks high against him. He sank into her, deep and hard, watching the beautiful sight of her breasts bouncing, nipples hard as diamonds, as he thrust into her, again and again. Too hard and too rough, he feared, but he couldn't seem to stop. It wasn't enough. It would never be enough.

A ragged sound broke from her lips, but peering down, he saw ecstasy on her face, her lips curled into a dazed smile.

"*Magnus.*" Her nails gouged the backs of his thighs, where she clenched him tight.

She felt so good. So hot. So tight. The bed frame creaked and groaned, and he prayed the stone walls would silence the sound to outside ears.

Just when he thought he would explode, her womb clenched him tight, and pulsed in climax around him. His bollocks seized tight and he saw stars at the back of his eyes. His body fractured and he drove deep, his cock throbbing so powerfully he groaned in combined bliss and agony, feeling in that moment, illuminated, as if he'd ventured inside heaven. For the second time that night, he spent himself inside her.

Gasping, kissing . . . their bodies relaxed into a tangle of arms and legs.

Breathing hard, he pressed his forehead to hers, and kissed her mouth. "Did I hurt you? I know I did."

She half-chuckled, half-groaned. "It felt wonderful at the time, but now . . ."

Carefully, he withdrew from her body. "I'm sorry."

"Don't be." She peered at him steadily, her cheeks pink. "Give me a moment, and I know I will want to do it again."

"I fear that we have almost certainly created a child tonight. It is my fault. I should have been more careful. I should have shown more control—"

"Shhhh," she whispered, her eyes bright, kissing him. "I'm not sorry. Whatever happens."

They lay together, embracing, for a long while, until their breathing slowed.

"I must go," he said, his chest tight with regret. "It is almost dawn."

"I don't want you to leave." She squeezed him tight, burying her face in his neck. "But I know you must."

He turned her face and pressed a kiss to her mouth, drawing his knuckle down her cheek. "I could kiss you a thousand times, and it wouldn't be enough." He peered at her solemnly. "They aren't just words. I hope you know that. I'm sworn to you, heart and soul."

She squeezed his hand, tears welling in her eyes. "And I to you."

"I meant what I said." His gaze fixed on hers. "You are mine now. I would die to protect you. Do not doubt that."

She nodded. "I do believe you."

"And do not risk drawing attention to yourself, asking questions all about. I will find out what I can about your sister." He kissed her once more, slow and lingeringly, and stood. Retrieving her gown, he helped clothe her before dressing himself.

"Stay here, where it is warm," he said, kissing her forehead. "Sleep."

"I will, but here." She went to a wooden chest, and a moment later turned. "Lock the window behind you when you go." She pressed a key into his hand.

"You should keep the key," he said.

"I told you. I'm not leaving without you, so I don't need it."

At the secret door, he looked over his shoulder at her once more.

She did not smile, but lifted a hand. She looked small and fragile and so very alone. His chest tightened, already aching for her.

Hell. He strode across the room, framed her face in his hand and kissed her once more.

Backing away, saying nothing, he returned to the door, and passed through, securing it behind him. He descended into darkness, his mood growing surlier and surlier with each step he took away from her.

Leaving through the window, he locked it behind him, and jumped down, because he'd kicked the ladder down where it wouldn't be seen by anyone who might happen to wander by. He made his way around the wall of the tower, to enter the castle. The guards greeted him with knowing smiles, allowing him to pass without question. He would not be the only warrior who crept in at early-morning hours, after having spent the night in a woman's arms. On silent steps he passed through the Pit, his ears met on all sides by deep snores.

"So . . . who is she?" said a voice off to the side.

He looked there, and saw Chissolm pushing up onto his elbow, his face darkened by his beard, bleary-eyed.

"What are you talking about," he answered, doing his best to keep his manner easy.

"Y'er a man who values his sleep. And you aren't one to stay out until dawn *reitheachas* around with just anyone."

Chissolm was his friend, but Magnus flinched inwardly at the vulgarity, because it hadn't been like that with Tara.

But Magnus had never been one to share stories of his exploits, so it would not seem strange that he answered over his shoulder, as he disappeared into his chamber.

"No one you know."

Tara walked along the cliffs, looking out over the ocean, with Anna walking beside her. A cold wind lifted her cloak and veil, but inside she felt warmed through, re-membering the night she had spent in Magnus's arms. She counted the hours until night fell once more, when she knew he would come to her and make love to her again . . . and again.

Where was he now, she wondered? Safe, she prayed. He would be on his guard, she reassured herself, and Hugh would not be able to make such a cowardly attack on him again. He was an exceptional warrior and could protect himself, of that she had no doubt, but she too must know how to survive. She would have not only his heart, but his respect. They had not talked of marriage, but even now she might carry his child. If she was to be the wife of a highlander, either here or abroad, then she must be strong as well, and not simply exist as a woman in peril, in constant need of protection and defense.

She could not help but wonder where he intended to take them when they left this place, or who the people were that he trusted so greatly, above the people of his own clan. As much as he held her heart, he remained very much a mystery to her, and she wondered if that would ever change.

Last night he had urged her not to draw attention to herself by asking questions about Arabel's death, that he would find out what he could, but she had walked this way for a reason this morning, because yesterday, before Hugh had attacked Magnus, she had seen the castle cem-etery in the distance, along with a church.

A short time later, she and Anna entered through the stone gate. Though they'd not requested any escort, a warrior had followed them from the castle, no doubt dispatched to keep watch over them, even though they remained in sight of the castle. Together, she and her maid walked the rows of markers . . . and then walked them again, this time more slowly.

"She isn't here," said Tara, her body gone numb with shock and sadness.

Not only did she not know of a certainty how her sister had died, but she didn't even know where her body had been buried.

"I don't understand it," Anna replied. "I don't even see any new graves, awaiting markers."

"Neither do I. Lady Alwyn told me there was a priest present when she died."

"Where else would they have buried her?" the girl murmured. "There *is* nowhere else. They wouldn't have placed her in the village cemetery with the common folk. Not the ward of the Earl of Buchan."

"Come, let us return to the castle," Tara said, blinking away tears. "There is no need for us to remain here."

Together they climbed the hillside, and made their way along the cliffs again.

"The days grow colder now," Anna said. "Let us go inside, where there is a fire, and it is warm."

Tara nodded. There, she would ask the lady where her sister was buried.

"Mistress," said a male voice from behind them.

Tara turned to find Hugh standing very close.

She let out a startled breath.

Chapter 12

"May we talk?" he said, reaching a hand for her.

Instinctively, she stepped back so that he would not touch her.

"Perhaps there," he said. "Inside the garden wall, where the wind is not so bothersome?"

He smiled, a courtier's smile, and the thought flitted across her mind that he would be handsome if he had a soul, but she had never seen any light in his eyes, only darkness.

And she could not forget the repugnant thing he had done in attacking Magnus.

"We are very cold from our walk," she replied, unable to infuse warmth into her voice. "Perhaps you would like to join us in the tower, where you can also visit with your mother, who is still not feeling well. I know she would enjoy your visit."

He shook his head slowly, never taking his eyes off her. "She has a tendency to talk overly long, and at present I have no time for that, I am afraid."

She had no wish to be alone with him, but she could

not refuse his request. He had proven himself a coward, and so she would not fear him anymore. At least not here, in the open and daylight, with others about.

"As you wish," she answered, and joined him, but she pretended not to see the hand he offered, so he instead touched the center of her back as they walked.

Anna followed them at a distance, which gave her some comfort.

Entering through a narrow back gate, he led her to a space inside the castle wall where there was no real garden to speak of, but several benches, statuaries, and alcoves fashioned of sea-weathered stone.

He looked at her for a long moment. "I fear I shocked you yesterday when I struck out against that man."

Remembering the blood that had spilled from Magnus's side, as a result of Hugh's craven act, sent a tremor moving through her.

"That man. Do you mean Magnus, your half-brother?" She spoke calmly, refusing to let him unnerve her. "It did not seem fair or honorable, striking him from behind. But 'tis none of my concern—you may do all things, as you wish. After all, you are the laird's son."

She mocked him, but he seemed not to know.

He let out a dark laugh. "You must know there is much more to the story. I am only repaying him in kind, for all he has done to me."

"What has he done to you, so that you would want to harm him in such a way?"

Harm him. No, he'd attempted to murder Magnus, plain and simple.

"What has he done to me? He was born. That's what." Hugh gave a cold smile. "He is nothing but a baseborn cur. One day, when my father is dead, I will not suffer his presence in this place."

She would hear no more of his hate for Magnus. Soon,

she and Magnus would be gone from this place, never to return. There were other matters to discuss.

"Hugh, I know you did not care for my sister, but she is part of my family and I wish to visit her grave. Can you tell me where she is buried?"

She scrutinized his face, watchful for any clue. His face went slack, and a full moment later, he shrugged.

"In the cemetery, of course."

"I went there, and I was unable to find her grave. There is . . . no marker bearing her name."

His thick eyebrows went up. "That is because . . . the marker I chose for her, has not yet been completed by the mason. Very soon, I think. I will send a servant to ask after it later today, if it pleases you."

She was not convinced by his words. She and Anna had both seen there were no new graves without markers. She felt just as certain as before that her sister's remains did not lie in the hallowed ground of the cemetery.

"It would please me," she answered, because she knew not what else to say.

"Mistress Iverach . . . *Tara* . . ." he said.

It was the first time he'd spoken her given name, and she did not like it. It felt too personal, too close, when she had already sworn herself to another. Just being here with him felt wrong.

"Yes," she answered tersely.

"You and I have had a bad start, but we will be married in a matter of days."

"Hmmm," she answered in a whisper, glancing away.

No, they would not be. She could promise him that.

"Don't you agree that we should learn to get along? To know one another better." He came toward her, but she moved aside, pretending to look at a statue of a lion.

Her heartbeat hitched. "'Tis true. We barely know one another. You should come to the tower for the midday meal with your mother, and we can talk, and learn more about each other."

He did not give up the chase, but came close to stand behind her.

"That isn't what I mean, and I think you know it."

Tara shivered. She hated him being this close to her, and speaking to her in that tone. His behavior made a mockery of everything real and meaningful between a man and a woman.

She turned to face him. "I do not understand why, from the first moment, you have felt the need to torment me. Did my sister do something to anger you? If so, tell me what she did."

Like lightning, his hand moved to snare her wrist with bruising strength, and he seized her close. "Tell me, have you ever been with a man before?"

Anna's voice sounded from behind him, soft and fearful. "Mistress. I do believe the lady will be expecting our return."

Hugh snarled over his shoulder. "Get away, *peasant*, lest you wish me to punish you for your impudence."

Magnus watched them from the window of the laird's counsel chamber, a snarl hovering at the back of his throat. Tara had insisted she was strong enough to withstand Hugh's aggressions, and perhaps she was, but he could not simply stand and watch as Hugh laid hands on his woman.

He answered the question put forth to him by the laird. "Aye, each warrior, as of yesterday, has in their possession both a short and longsword."

Tara.

"And horses?" the Alwyn asked.

Hugh was touching Tara.

He forced a calmness to his voice, which he did not

feel. "We have added twelve to our stable. I suspect the Kincaid boasts more, but with our skill—and the backing of Buchan's forces—I have no doubt we can best him and his mercenaries on the field of battle."

If Hugh hurt her, he'd kill him.

At this pause in the conversation, Magnus moved forward, forcing calm over his demeanor, his manner. "Laird, were is Hugh? As your son, should he not be included in these discussions?"

"Indeed," he answered, with a lift of his eyebrows, looking around the room as if he only now noticed the absence of his son. "Was he informed the council would be meeting?"

He sounded tired, where the subject of Hugh was concerned. Put out. Annoyed.

"Indeed," answered one of the older council members. "Within the last hour."

The Alwyn scowled. "Perhaps he was waylaid by other matters."

His statement carried a tone of derision that Magnus had not heard in the laird's voice before, when speaking of his son.

But Magnus did not care at the moment . . . because *Tara*. His heart pounded in his chest.

"Perhaps so," Magnus responded, impatient . . . worried, to the point of being breathless. "If you will excuse me for a moment, I will go find and inform Hugh. I know also he will wish to be here, to have a voice in this meeting, as your heir should so rightly do."

"Very good," the Alwyn answered, and walked with him to the door, clasping his shoulder. In a quieter voice, he murmured, "Your efforts to bring Hugh into the fold are most welcome. He has drifted of late. You of all people, after the events of yesterday, know that. Your forgiveness . . . your *example* means everything."

Once, the words might have meant something to him, but they were forgotten the moment he stepped across the threshold.

"I pray so, laird." He moved to step away.

The laird's hand gripped his arm. "As you know, Hugh will be married as soon as Buchan arrives. As is custom, let us take him to the High Lodge for a wedding hunt, to provide meat for the nuptial feast. Two days is all we can spare, I think, given this thing with the Kincaids. You will come, of course, and others whom I will choose."

Leave Burnbryde, now? But a hunting trip would keep Hugh away from Tara, at least for a few days, and perhaps there, away from the stronghold, the laird would talk of times past . . .

"Aye, laird. As you wish."

Heart thumping heavily, he set off alone down the corridor, and when he turned the corner—he ran, straining the muscles of his legs, out of the castle, and along the wall until he arrived at the garden, where he passed Tara's stricken-faced maid looking inward.

Entering, Magnus's gaze pinpointed to the far corner of the garden, where Hugh attempted to corner Tara into an alcove. He saw the dark glint of Tara's hair in the clouded morning light.

Magnus moved swiftly toward them, close enough to hear.

Hugh muttered. "If you are anything like your slut of a sister—"

The word offended Magnus to his core. His stride picked up pace.

"I said *no*." Tara shoved the flat of her palm against his chin, forcing his face away from hers.

Fury splintered through Magnus, and he saw red.

"Hugh," he barked.

Hugh froze. Turning, he glared at Magnus, his lip drawn back in a snarl. "What?"

"The council . . . we are all waiting for you. Did you forget your father had called a meeting?"

Hugh sneered. "Go along, messenger boy. Tell them to proceed without me. I'll be there in due time."

Magnus stepped closer. "I'm afraid he is waiting. We are . . . *all* waiting for you. There is much to be decided in these last days before Buchan arrives, and your father, of course, wishes for you to be part of the planning."

Hugh let out a groan of annoyance, sounding more like a petulant boy than a grown man. "I'm sure you don't want me there. What a coincidence. I don't want you there either. In fact, I'd rather you were dead."

Though he stared hard at Hugh, he was fully aware of Tara, pressed against the stone wall, breathing hard, her eyes wide with fear.

Magnus tilted his head. "It is time for us to move past our differences. We both want what is best for the clan, do we not?"

Hugh looked upward, toward the clouded sky, his arms dropping to his sides. "You are so tiresome, Magnus. All your constant displays of valor, loyalty, and goodness." He snorted sarcastically, and looked straight into his eyes. "Tell them I am coming."

Magnus answered in a low voice of command. "You will come with me now."

Hugh turned, eyes narrowing, visibly bristling. "What did you say to me?"

"*Hugh*," a voice thundered from above.

Looking over his shoulder and up, Magnus saw the laird standing at the same window he'd stood at just a short time before.

"*Inside*," the laird shouted angrily. "Now."

"Damn you all," Hugh muttered, brushing past Magnus.

As he stormed off, Magnus looked at Tara, feeling as if his heart were torn open and bleeding.

"Wait here," he mouthed, before turning on his heel and following Hugh.

He followed Hugh to the stairs, where he paused to talk to a warrior passing by. When Hugh was out of sight, he quickly broke the conversation off, and returned to the garden.

The maidservant was gone now . . . he found her inside the garden with Tara. Her eyes widened at seeing him.

"Leave us," he said, and she fled once again outside the gate.

Looking upward, he made sure no one stood at the window as he had done just a short time before. Grasping Tara's hand, he pulled her behind him toward the far wall, where they would be hidden from view. In the blur of emotion and fury that he felt, he did not know if he reached first for her, or she for him, but in a moment, they were in each other's arms, their bodies, their garments, tangled tight.

"Are you all right?" he growled, his face in her fragrant hair. His boots crunched heavily against the earth.

One night. One night and already she had grown so precious to him. Already he knew . . . he *knew* that nothing would ever satisfy his soul more than holding her like this. Holding her tight and keeping her safe from all worry and harm.

"Yes!" For a moment she clung to him—but then she balled her fists against his chest and pushed hard, and looked up at him with bright green eyes—her pale face ethereal in the morning light, made more vivid by the bright spots of color on her cheeks. "But you cannot run to my aid every time he glances my way."

He still held her tight. "He was not only *looking* at you. Damn him. Damn this place to hell. I knew I should have taken you from here last night but like the selfish bastard that I am, instead I took you straight to bed."

"And anyone who saw us now would certainly know that," she retorted, eyes flashing. "What Anna must think. I know you want to protect me, but it is my choice to be here, for just a while longer. Just as you have chosen to be."

"You may never know what happened to your sister. You must make peace with that and keep yourself safe. You must keep to the tower from this moment on, so that your paths do not cross again. If anyone asks, tell them you don't wish to be seen before the wedding."

She shook her head, her expression one of stubbornness. "I wouldn't have learned that Arabel doesn't have a grave if I hadn't ventured out of the tower."

"What do you mean, she has no grave?"

She informed him of her and Anna's search, and that her sister's remains did not lie in the cemetery, despite Hugh's assertion that they did.

"But where would her body be?" he murmured.

"I must find out." She embraced him, bringing his head down and pressed her mouth to his. "I must know what happened to her. Now go, before we are discovered together. You've already stayed too long."

He kissed her back. One day, and one day soon, he vowed, he would kiss her for all to see, and hide from no one.

He peered down, hating to leave her. "I will be gone with Hugh and the laird for two days."

"Gone?" she exclaimed, her hands seizing his tight.

He raised her mittened hands and kissed their knuckles.

"To hunt at the High Lodge, to provide for a wedding feast that I vow will never take place. You must keep yourself safe while I am gone."

She looked vulnerable—her small, pale face looking out from her dark, hooded cloak.

But she nodded. "Do not fear for me."

He remembered the way she had looked the night before, brave and fearless with a fire in her eyes, as they had made love. He wanted, more than anything, to make the world a place where each day would bring her only smiles and happiness.

He pulled the key to her window, which he wore at a cord at his throat, and pressed it into her hand. "Here. Take this back. Use it if you are in danger. If you must flee, go into the village and ask for a woman named Robina."

"Robina?" she queried, her gaze going dark—as if, perhaps, he spoke of a lover.

"My mother."

She sighed, and nodded.

He kissed her once more, then left her, wanting more than anything to turn around, and sweep her in his arms and carry her out of this place forever. But he could not. Not yet.

At the gate, he paused to speak to the maidservant, whom he had no doubt had peered into the garden and seen him and Tara embracing.

"You will tell no one that you have seen us together," he said to her forcefully, but not unkindly. "Do you understand?"

The girl nodded.

"I wish only happiness for her," she answered. "I will tell no one."

* * *

Magnus held true to his word. Tara did not see him that night, nor Hugh. As she had for the past several evenings, she took her meal with Lady Alwyn, who continued to complain of weariness and an overly rapid beating of her heart. They conversed little, and when they did it was to discuss the wedding.

Perhaps she should feel burdened by guilt, living here, in the home of a laird whose son—her legally betrothed— she had betrayed for another man. But try as she might, she could find no regret within her heart. She had not come here by choice, and had made clear to them her wish to sever the betrothal agreement, that any marriage would be by force. She loved Magnus with every ounce of her being, and impatiently waited for him to return to her, though . . . with a certain degree of foreboding about whatever matters at hand kept Magnus at Burnbryde rather than fleeing straightaway with her.

Most certainly, danger would be involved. If he intended some sort of rebellion against his father, he could be defeated. He could be killed, and she feared if he died, her spirit would die with him, and she would be left on this earth, an empty shell of a woman, married to a cruel man she would forever despise.

She forced herself to put those fears from her mind. Magnus would meet any challenge like the hero he was, and she had to believe he would prevail. Even if his triumph meant leaving Burnbryde forever, with no possessions of which to speak, she would go with him. She would rather live in love and light with Magnus, even if that meant existing in poverty, than here in this castle in endless darkness with Hugh.

Aye, she had some fortune of her own, and land, but Buchan controlled everything. She feared she would forfeit all by disobeying him.

For the first time . . . she wondered if that was what the earl wanted.

The next four days were a mirror of each other. There were morning prayers in the tower with Lady Alwyn. A walk along the cliffs with Anna. The rest of the day she spent confined to the tower, being fitted for a wedding gown she never intended to wear, and meeting with the cook about the upcoming feast and sweets to be served to the guests. She listened to Lady Alwyn go on and on about which guests should be greeted with enthusiasm, and which should all but be ignored. Each night seemed to last forever, as she did not sleep well. It was in those dark hours, she remembered Hugh's craven attack on Magnus, and his plainspoken wish that his bastard brother was dead. She prayed that Magnus would remain always on his guard because if Hugh had tried to murder him once, would he not attempt to kill him again? And would not a hunting trip be the perfect opportunity?

At last, as the evening of the fourth day darkened into night, Anna appeared to summon Tara for dinner with Lady Alwyn.

"The men have returned from their hunt."

Tara's heart leapt with happiness, for she knew she would see Magnus again soon.

"Thank you for telling me," she said.

"I knew you would want to know."

Anna, blessedly, had said nothing of her private meeting in the garden with Magnus, asked no curious or demanding questions, but had remained just as kind and caring as before.

That night Tara bathed and prepared for bed, waiting at every moment to hear the sound of him at the secret door, because she'd left the window unlocked . . . but he did not come.

Certainly, he would, as soon as he could break away

from the Alwyn or his men. Yet the night grew later and later. Eventually she drifted into sleep.

The great room echoed with minstrel song and laughter. The hunt had been successful, and the mood was much like a celebration. The laird and Hugh, and the older men of the council had already partaken of their meal. Magnus sat at his customary table, along with his men. Gaily dressed female servants with ribbons streaming from their hair, including Kyla and Laire, brought out their food and poured their cups full of ale.

For four days he had thought of little else but Tara, and seeing her again. He had focused all his frustration at being separated from her into the hunt, and at last, now that it was done and he was here, he impatiently counted the moments until he could be with her again. Yes, he had kept Hugh away from her, but he would not be satisfied that she was out of harm until she was safely ensconced at Inverhaven behind the impenetrable wall of the Kincaid mercenary army.

A shout went up from beside the laird's table, a captain shouting for all to be silent. The Alwyn stood, holding a goblet and leveling his gaze outward, across the room.

"Listen, one and all," he said. Firelight illuminated the prominent arch of his nose. "The coming days will be one of our greatest challenges, to oust the pretender who calls himself the Kincaid, along with his army of mercenaries. Hired men with no loyalty to clan or king, only to the man who will pay them the most coins. I ask that you stand ready to answer the call of your kinsmen at any moment, to stand with them in what will be a legendary day on the field of battle."

A cheer went up.

"Aye, we will suffer losses, as always occur among the

most brave and valiant of men. But our allies are watching and will see that we are rewarded, just as we have been rewarded in the past."

The cheers grew louder.

"There will also be more cause for celebration. My son, my *ceann-cath,* will marry the ward of the Earl of Buchan. In his honor, the warriors of our clan have hunted these past four days, to provide a feast worthy of the king himself." He raised his goblet high to a rousing round of cheers. "Thank you all."

Then, to Magnus's surprise, the laird's gaze settled on him.

"But most of all you, Magnus." He raised the goblet higher. Looking around the room, he announced, "There is no huntsman, no warrior more skilled among the ranks of the Alwyns and we thank you for your contribution to the coming days' celebrations, a true gift to the man who will be your future laird."

The warriors of the Pit rose up around him, clapping their hands on his shoulders.

"Y' Braggart!"

"I still can't believe how you stood that devil of a boar down."

"You've made us all proud."

Kyla poured his goblet full, and pressed a kiss to his cheek, while Laire kissed the other.

Suddenly Hugh was there, pressing forward, a goblet raised high in his hand, his gaze fixed glassily on Magnus.

"Yes, all hail Magnus. The finest warrior and hunter this clan has ever known. Protector of all. Shining star of God. The finest son a man ever had."

"I did not say that," shouted his father from where stood on the dais.

Turning, Hugh spat, "You did not have to."

Twisting back around, he lunged drunkenly toward Magnus, fists swinging, but the men of the Pit converged on him, and carried him away.

The laird waved his hand, laughing. "Yes, throw him in a trough. He is drunk and more than ready to be wed. He will have forgotten all of this tomorrow, as shall we." He raised his goblet again. "Music. More music. More ale."

The tension between him and Hugh had simmered all through the hunt, more than once nearly culminating in violence. Magnus ceded that he was much to blame. Even though he knew he'd claimed Tara's heart, by the laws of Scotland, she belonged to Hugh and it tormented him.

Because of that, he could not help but take every opportunity to best Hugh at everything, and rub his hateful nose in it, just as he could not wait for the moment Hugh realized that Tara belonged to him.

Tara . . . he wanted her. Could think of nothing but her soft skin, and her passionate kisses.

His men returned, without Hugh. He bided his time, long past midnight, until at last he felt he could slip away from the revelry unnoticed. He pushed through the crowd toward the door, and strode down the darkened corridor, his blood pulsing with anticipation, thinking only of her—

"Magnus," called a woman's voice from behind him, frantic and strained.

He turned to find Kyla, her hair wild. Tears streamed over her cheeks.

"It's Ferchar," she cried. "He's got Laire."

Tara started awake. She sat up, wondering how long she'd slept. She suspected it was early morning.

But . . . why hadn't Magnus come in the night?

Her heart clenched in her chest, and suddenly she

feared the worst. Suddenly, in her mind she was a young girl again, confined to her chambers with Arabel, waiting for word of her ill parents and how they had passed the night, and no one came. No one came for so long and when they did, it was with the most devastating, heartbreaking news that had changed their lives forever, sending them out from the home they'd loved, into the care of others. Others who did not love them as their mother and father had.

Was it possible that Magnus had been hurt? It was, of course. If he had been, there would be no one to come and tell her.

Now that she was awake, with her mind filled with such fears, she would not sleep again.

Not until she saw him . . . spoke to him . . . assured herself he was unharmed.

She touched the key where it hung from a cord, between her breasts. In the darkness, she shivered from the cold, and dressed quickly. A moment later, she descended the secret stairway, lantern in hand. It took her several attempts to insert the key inside the lock, but once she did it turned easily. Leaving the lantern on the floor, she pushed open the bars, and crawled to the end of the ledge, and peered over. She could just see the edge of Magnus's window from this spot.

"Magnus," she called.

Her voice sounded shockingly loud in the darkness.

"Magnus," she said again, this time louder.

She heard no movement of the shutter, no response.

It was not *that* far of a drop to the ground. She pushed off . . . landing harder than she expected. Her ankles and knees gave out, and she landed on her bottom with a teeth-jarring jolt. Pushing up, she walked a few steps, gingerly at first, to see if she'd injured herself, but she had not.

Standing here, outside of the stone walls, surrounded by darkness, she suddenly felt very vulnerable.

Not only was it frightening here, but what if one of the night guards passed by, and thought to peer inside the crevice? What if one of Magnus's companions answered at his window, instead of him? Searching along the edge of the wall, she found the ladder Magnus had used before. Hoisting it up, she set it into place so that she could return quickly to her window if needed, and kick the ladder down where it would not be seen at first glance.

Returning to his window, she tapped on the shutter.

"Magnus," she said quietly. "Are you there?"

Again, no one answered. Her stomach clenched with anxiety. If he wasn't there, where was he? Had he even returned from the hunt?

She tried once more, knocking harder. "Magnus."

The shutter jerked open, startling her.

Chapter 13

"Who is there?" queried a young woman, her voice soft and sleepy. "Hello?"

The voice sent a jagged shock through Tara's heart. Tara's lips went numb. *Everything* went numb.

It was not the voice she'd expected to hear.

Quickly, she pressed herself against the wall, so she would not be seen. The cold stones, against her back, chilled her through.

She didn't understand. There were no other windows in sight. *This* was the window he'd spoken from that night, just below and to the side of hers. The one he'd told her to come to if she needed him.

It was the place where he slept.

"I'm so sorry for waking you," Tara said, speaking toward the window. "I . . . must be mistaken. I was looking for Magnus."

"He's here, but he's asleep," the voice answered.

"*Who* is asking?" demanded *another* woman's voice, sounding bleary and annoyed.

There was not one woman, but *two* in Magnus's bed.

With Magnus?

The night was silent, save for the crash of the ocean waves, and yet it seemed as if as if a thousand cymbals smashed against one another inside her head.

It couldn't be true.

But it was.

"I don't know who it is," the other one answered quietly. "I can't see her. She is hiding against the wall where I can't see her."

Hiding. Yes—she was hiding. How pitiable. How sad.

"Well, tell her to go away," the one insisted sharply.

"That's not very nice," the gentler one whispered.

"Then *I shall*," the other one said. "Hello? *Hello there*?" she said in a loud, provocative voice. "He's not interested in you. He's already got more than he can handle with the two of us in his bed."

The words stabbed through her heart. Tara did not respond. She stood frozen against the wall, her eyes wide and tear-filled. Her heart clenched in her chest. She covered her mouth with her hand, to keep from making a sound.

"Oh you, shush!" chastised the other. "You're going to wake him."

"Wake *who*?" It was *his* voice, thick with sleep. Magnus *was* there. "Go back to sleep."

The two women giggled, and the shutters slammed closed.

She backed away from the window, staring at the shutters, waiting for them to fly open, for his face to appear. For him to smile and laugh, in that easy, gregarious way of his, and provide some completely plausible explanation for what she'd just seen and heard.

But there was nothing. Only the cold and the darkness, pressing all around her.

She gasped, smothered by a sudden wave of loneliness

that barreled through her, and *shame* that she had placed all her trust in him. It wasn't even that she had expected him to save her. She feared that wasn't possible. But she had let him make love to her. Imagined him to be the one—the only one. Her soul's match. Her one true . . . love.

It all seemed so foolish now. She'd been overly trusting. So stupid!

She backed away, her slippers scraping over the uneven earth, and bumped into the ladder.

Turning, she grasped the sides, and attempted three times to set her foot on the bottom rung before she found purchase and climbed.

Magnus did not see Tara the next day—or the next night, because he had no key to the barred window, so had no way to enter her room as he'd done before—and when he'd gone there in the dark, he'd found the bars locked. He could only think that perhaps news of the hunting party's return had not reached the occupants of the tower.

On the morning of the next day, he emerged from the Pit, his stomach in knots, having gone too long without seeing her. Tension pulled at the muscles between his shoulders. Agitation interrupted his every thought. He'd barely slept, kept awake by memories of her body . . . of their lovemaking, and his desire for more.

But other, more concerning questions interfered with his rest. Was she all right? God, he missed her. Until he saw her for himself, he felt as if he'd exist with some sort of a hole in his heart.

Then suddenly, she was there, standing beside the Lady Alwyn in the chapel during prayers, her head covered with a veil, revealing only the barest outline of her face.

He hadn't realized how miserable he'd been, kept apart

from her, until that moment, as relief filtered through him. At the same time, heat warmed his blood with the pleasure of seeing her again.

Thankfully, Hugh was nowhere to be seen. He had sulked in his chambers in protest after Magnus had formally petitioned the laird to imprison Ferchar and two of his companions in the castle's dungeon for the next fortnight for their attempted assault of Kyla and Laire. Though Magnus had intervened before any true harm could be done, they and the other young women who worked in the castle had come to live in fear of the same three men. To his satisfaction, his new position as war-chief gave his opinions weight. The laird listened and the men had been straightaway summoned and escorted to their new homes below the castle floors.

When prayers were done, he followed at a distance behind the women, and observed as Tara and her maidservant broke away, as if to go for a walk. He followed them along the cliffs, to the cemetery, where peering through the trees, he saw her standing above a grave—a grave bearing a marker carved with her sister's name.

When he came closer, the maid quickly moved away, leaving them together.

"Tara?" he said.

"Hugh told me that Arabel's stone had not yet been completed by the mason, and that's why I couldn't find it before."

"Do you believe him?"

"No."

There was something distant about her manner.

He moved to stand beside her, and glanced down to find her staring straight ahead at the stone.

"I have missed you," he said, puzzled by her demeanor, when before, everything had felt so natural between them.

". . . Have you?" she asked.

Taking her by the arms, he turned her toward him. "I have. I have wanted nothing more than to see you, but it seems everything has worked against me since I have returned from the hunt."

She said nothing. She only looked at him in silence, her expression inscrutable. He saw then, the paleness of her skin. The shadows beneath her eyes.

"Tara, are you well?" His heart tripped a beat. "Is everything all right? Did something happen while I was gone?"

"No, nothing happened while you were gone." She exhaled, avoiding his gaze. "It's just . . . that I have spent the last four days in that tower, and even now, I feel as if I am a prisoner. Buchan will arrive soon. Any day. I cannot help but feel . . . apprehensive."

"I understand," he answered. "But you must not fear."

"I just want to know what happened to my sister."

She stood rigidly, and he could not help but feel that she was a thousand miles away. To embrace her now . . . to kiss her, seemed an intrusion. The astounding closeness they'd shared before seemed to have been lost. Was it possible she regretted what had happened between them four nights ago? He must remember that she was an innocent, and that he had taken something from her she could never have back. Something precious. And then he'd left her alone, in this unhappy place, with nothing but her thoughts and fears. He must take care, and give her any assurances she needed.

"I could come for you tonight," he suggested. "And take you for a ride, away from here."

She lifted a hand touched it to the center of his chest. The movement seemed careful, without true familiarity or ease.

"I have heard there is a celebration taking place in a village near to here. With dancing and a bonfire. I would so very much like to go. Just to see. Just to feel free again."

"Rackamoor." He nodded, relieved that she wanted him to take her anywhere because just a moment before, he'd thought with some certainty she would tell him that they must never speak to one another again. "It is not far from Burnbryde. I will take you there. Tonight."

There would be others there from Burnbryde, but he knew from times past, the night would be dark, and ale flowing. He felt certain they could enjoy the revelry in secret and chase away the shadows he saw in her eyes. Best of all, it would be the perfect excuse to get her away from the castle—and take her to Inverhaven. He would not tell her until tonight at Rackamoor, for fear she would refuse to go. She would see once she was there. She would adore Elspeth, as he did, and she would be safe until he could return to her, his vengeful destiny fulfilled.

She nodded. "I will wait for you at the window until you come."

Already she was gone from his embrace, without a kiss, without so much as a squeeze of her hand on his arm. She joined her companion and together they made their way up the stony incline, their cloaks snapping in the ocean wind.

Something felt distinctly off kilter, but he felt certain that when they were alone, she would confide her fears or whatever was wrong. Still, he wondered what had changed between those passionate hours in her chambers, and now.

That evening, in the smoky darkness of the great hall, he sat among Chissolm and Adam and the others, once again, waiting for the time when he could break away un-noticed to see Tara again. The castle had undergone a thorough cleaning, and gleaming banners had been hung in expectation of the Earl of Buchan's arrival in the coming days.

Tonight, while delivering Tara to the care of the Kincaids, Magnus would meet with his brother to finalize his plan. As a member of the laird's inner circle, he would be privy to meetings with Buchan.

He must harness every bit of his fury, of his cunning, and elicit . . . provoke . . . compel explanations from the Alwyn and Buchan, their confessions of whatever plotting against the Kincaids they'd done, and then he would join Niall on the battlefield to defeat them, with the understanding the Alwyn and Hugh, as battle opponents, belonged to him alone. Because of his love for Tara . . . his wish for them to have a future, and children . . . he would not slay the men, but seek justice to the courts, which meant capturing and imprisoning them in the tower at Inverhaven, and demanding their trial by the Estates of Parliament. Based on the history of the land as he knew it, he could not expect that he and his brother would be punished for presenting true evidence and testimony, even against the son of the king. The process would either result in punishment—or their freedom, but he must live with that, and be satisfied that their shameful crimes had been revealed to all, if he expected to live himself and have a long life with Tara.

There was so much that could go awry. Uncertainty over how events would unfold kept his nerves drawn tight, and yet he must proceed forward observing *everything* and reacting decisively, believing the righteous and true cause of the Kincaids would prevail.

And that Tara, in the end, would be his.

Kyla and Laire hovered about, tending to his every need. Though he had insisted they did not need to show him any gratitude beyond simple thanks, he knew they remained fearful of being caught alone by Hugh and kept close to his side at all times. It was not that any other warrior of the Pit would not defend them, just as fiercely as he, but any other man would be punished severely by the laird for challenging and humiliating his son in such a public place, in full view of the gathered clan, while everyone knew that Magnus, in recent days, had found increased favor and in the eyes of the Alwyn, and a respected position within the clan.

But he also noticed, with no amusement, that they vied for his attention, more now than ever before. He feared there were hopes . . . expectations . . . that he might show a preference for one of them, but he had never felt for either woman to that degree. He loved them, aye, but he would never be *in love* with either. Never feel for either as he felt for Tara. Had he known that first moment in the forest? Perhaps. He wasn't exactly certain when his soul had sworn itself to her, and no other, but it was done, and now every other woman seemed invisible to him, at least where his passions were concerned.

When their duties were done in the kitchen, the young women returned, sinking down on either side of his legs, for there was no room on the bench. Kyla rested her head on his bent knee, while Laire propped her elbows on the opposite leg, chattering into her friend's ear. He allowed it for only the briefest moment, then stood, moving to the end of the table to speak with Chissolm.

It was then that he saw Tara passing along the edge of the room, accompanied by one of Lady Alwyn's tower guards, making her way toward the kitchen. Her gaze already shifted away from him. The room grew silent, as others took note of her.

When she emerged from the kitchen—still accompanied by the guard, carrying an earthenware crock in her hands—she did not so much as glance in his direction.

Instead, she looked rigidly forward, until with a bewitching swirl of her kirtle's long skirt, she disappeared into the outer corridor.

An hour later, he was relieved to find her waiting on the ledge when he approached in the darkness, drawing his horse behind him. She perched there, watching him approach in silence, her body enveloped in a hood and cloak, with only the pale moon of her face to draw his eye in the darkness.

"Do you still wish to go to Rackamoor?"

"If you still wish to take me." Her voice, smooth and soft, made his groin go warm and tight. It seemed even the smallest thing about her aroused a passion inside him.

"That, I do."

He reached for her, helping her from the ledge. Her hands rested on his shoulders as he brought her down. Her body brushed heavily against his, all softness and mystery. When her feet touched the ground, he lifted her chin, and kissed her. When she did not respond, he held her chin, and kissed her again, slowly and with seductive intent.

At first she did not move, but then, he felt it. Desire flared up between them, as real and magnificent as before.

She exhaled unevenly, and curled her fingers against his shoulders. His mouth slanted on hers, opening, and he stepped closer . . . pulled her closer.

She stepped back, her hands pushing gently at his chest—putting distance between them. "If you start that now, we'll never get to Rackamoor, and I want more than anything to see a bonfire tonight."

He watched as she moved directly to his horse, his heart beating in his chest. Standing there, she made no attempt to climb into the saddle. Instead she stood, her back straight, staring ahead as if she were thinking very hard over some thought, or . . . gathering her emotions.

In the distance, ocean waves crashed against the cliffs. His boots crunched on the earth under his feet.

"Tara, something is wrong. Something has happened to upset you. Tell me."

"There is nothing." She turned to him, and he thought, in the darkness, that he saw tears in her eyes. "I am only eager to be gone from this place. Will you take me to Rackamoor?"

Something *was* wrong. He was certain of it. But now was not the time to press her, here where someone might pass by and see or overhear them. He would take her to Rackamoor and there, in the light of the fire, coax out the truth about whatever troubled her then. And, perhaps before going on to Inverhaven, he would make love to her on some dark piece of earth, on a bed made of his plaid . . . and reclaim the closeness that seemed to have been lost between them.

"Let us go then," he said, knowing he must be understanding and patient.

She rode astride on the saddle before him, which satisfied, at least in some small way, his need to hold her. Though nearly midnight, there were still people about, and Magnus kept to the shadows so that no one they passed along the way would see her face. The guards at the gate did not dare question him about who his female companion was for the night.

He urged his horse into a run, and they traveled under a dark blue sky, dotted by distant stars. It was a pleasure, holding her smaller body against his larger one, within the circle of his arms, groin, and thighs. The nearness only brought to mind, in a heated rush of memories, the night they'd shared, visions emblazoned upon his mind, which he could not help but replay over again. Each night of the hunt he'd passed in torment, assailed with memories of her bare skin, of how it had felt to be inside her. He could not help but think the same thoughts now.

Though she wore her hooded cloak against the cold, he gave into temptation more than once as they rode, to press a kiss on her cheek. When he did so, she closed her eyes and breathed heavily, her slender hands, covered with woolen mittens, clenching his thighs, proof his kisses still affected her just as much as they did him.

But at last a large fire appeared in the night, a radiant ember in the dark. Drumbeats and the wild trill of flutes carried on the wind. A raucous multitude danced and shouted and laughed, illuminated only by torches planted in the ground, here and there, a scene both pagan and wild.

Magnus pulled a stake from its leather band at the back of his saddle, and drove it into the ground, tying his mount so he would not wander.

"Come." Taking Tara's hand, he drew her along the edge of the crowd, before turning toward her . . . leading her by both hands into the midst of the dance, where the hooded cloaks they wore, and the dense throng of revelers and shadows concealed their faces.

He had never been one to dance—not without much cajoling by a pretty face. But this was different. This was Tara. He took her into his arms, holding her tight and spun her around, again, and again, circling . . . moving through the crowd.

At last, she smiled the smile he had been waiting to see, and even laughed, looking delighted and dizzied.

His heartbeat hitched in his chest, and in that moment he felt far more than desire for her. More than the need to possess her.

"I'm glad we came," he said.

He kissed her, his arm coming round her, as he held the other one out to protect her from being bumped by those spinning around them. It was a perfect moment. A magical moment. She sighed into his mouth, as her hands gripped the front of his tunic.

Backing away, her shadowed face peering up at him from her cowl, she shouted over the noise.

"I must talk to you," she said.

Talk. Yes. About the awkwardness between them. He had to know why, and he hoped she would tell him now. He must also make a successful argument for taking her to Inverhaven now, even though she still did not know the truth of her sister's death. He would tell her everything— who he was, and about his plan to punish the men who had murdered his father. He would need all of his concentration in the coming days, and could not afford to lose half his mind every time he saw her in Hugh's company.

He led the way, making a path through the throng drawing her along by the hand, behind the bulwark of his body. He was thankful for the darkness that concealed them, but one day . . . one day he would take pleasure in walking with her like this in the daylight, for all eyes to see.

"Magnus!" a female voice shouted from behind them. He stiffened—then brought her quickly around, and turned, so as to shelter her behind his back, shielding her from being seen by whoever approached.

It was Kyla and Laire, waving and smiling back at him. At some distance followed Chissolm and Adam, and several others.

Hell.

He turned aside to Tara, shielding her with the wall of his body. "Go to my horse and wait for me. I'll join you as soon as I can."

He did not like sending her away alone in the night, not even for a moment. Indeed, tension pulled between his shoulders as she nodded, and pulling her hood closer around her face, backed away. But he could not under any circumstances allow anyone to see them together, even these men he trusted. He turned, and went to them.

"Is that her?" Chissolm grinned, leaning aside, trying to peer around Magnus.

"Her who?" asked Adam, his eyebrows going up. "Is there something . . . someone I don't know about?"

"What's this?" exclaimed Quentin, dramatically pressing his hand to his heart. "Has our great and formidable leader's untamable heart, finally been tamed?"

Kyla frowned. "You have a woman?"

Laire's expression matched her friend's. "Do we know her?"

Magnus crossed his arms over his chest, assuming an expression of indifference—and he shrugged. "She's just someone I danced with. What are you idiots doing here?"

Tara hurried away, her heart beating fast. She turned, looking back, and could just see Magnus in the darkness, talking to the two young women, and several men, friends by all appearances. Looking at him like that, he seemed so far away—a totally different man than the one she'd danced with just moments before, a man who had belonged only to her, once again.

For that reason, she was grateful for the interruption for her it reminded her . . . he did *not* belong to her.

Nor she to him.

All morning, after discovering Magnus in bed with the two women, she'd wallowed in the lowest depths of heartache. Perhaps, even now, he spoke to the same two women. They hovered close to his side, peering up at him, laughing and smiling flirtatiously.

She'd already all but made herself ill. It wasn't jealousy she'd felt, exactly, although certainly . . . there had been that. Mostly, she'd been disappointed . . . and angry at herself for being so foolish as to entrust her heart and her life to a man whose character she truly did not know. How could she be angry with him? Although he'd sworn to protect her, had he ever really sworn his heart? Perhaps he did intend to leave Burnbryde with her, and even marry her, but what sort of love was that, if he could make love to her with such passion one night, and the next enjoy the pleasures of other women?

And so . . . as the day passed, her mood had shifted from dejection to a new kind of strength, and determination that she would not be defeated by this.

When she'd arrived at Burnbryde a and found herself prisoner in the tower, she'd vowed to escape, and never again be used by any man, and yet what had she done? She had placed herself in a situation where she would suffer exactly that.

Why had she not seen the danger at the time? Why had she not been stronger?

In the end, it didn't really matter if Magnus had made love to those two women last night . . . or five women, or twelve.

Her life was in danger, and she knew now what she'd known before Magnus. If she wanted to escape . . . if she wanted to live, she could only trust herself to make it happen. It was why she must leave him now, and escape, as she had intended to do from the start.

It was why she'd asked him to bring her to Rackamoor, and he had just given her the perfect opportunity to flee, had he not?

So why did she stand here, her feet planted to the ground . . . wavering . . . waiting for him to stop her?

Because what if it wasn't true? What if she had somehow misunderstood and Magnus had not been with those women?

Just then a man and a woman stumbled past, kissing, embracing . . . She briefly glimpsed the man's face in the light of the flames—

And recognized him.

A stab of fear struck through her chest. She had seen him before. At the priory.

It was Robert Stewart, Buchan's younger son.

She stumbled backward, desperate to remain unseen—

Only to collide into something hard . . . and distinctly male.

Two hands grasped her by the shoulders, and roughly set her aside.

"Robert," shouted Duncan, his older brother, striding past her. "The earl is asking to see you. Leave the wench and come."

Tara backed away, nearly stumbling in her haste to escape. She pulled her hood closer, to hide her face, and rushed away from them, only to turn and observe from a distance, and the safety of darkness, as they proceeded away from the bonfire, over a high berm.

Heart pounding, her stomach clenching with dread, she followed at a distance, climbing the incline until she reached the top.

There, she froze, her eyes widening at the sight. Dozens of small fires dotted the night. She perceived the dark outline of countless tents, and men. She gasped, backing away. Panic rose up around her like a dark, consuming wave.

Buchan had arrived.

"Well, my friends, I'm very tired, and believe I shall return to Burnbryde. I will see you there in the morning." Magnus backed away from them.

"Return to Burnbryde, my arse," Quentin responded

with a deep laugh. "You're going to find *her* again, aren't you?"

"I'm so very curious to see who she is," Adam teased. "Perhaps we ought to follow him, and see who she is for ourselves."

"I wouldn't recommend it," Magnus grinned, and broke away, striding into the darkness.

The smile dropped from his lips as they shouted after him, bawdy things he barely heard for the blood pounding in his ears. He had to find Tara and tell her what he'd just learned, that Buchan had arrived and was encamped with an army of gallowglass mercenaries on the other side of that damn hill.

He had to get her safely to Inverhaven now, without delay. Only then could he return to Burnbryde, his mind free of fear for her, and execute the only plan that could ensure their future together.

Only the night was already half gone—he was running out of time. He arrived at the place where the horse had been secured . . . where Tara was to wait for him.

His heart started in bewilderment . . . for neither she nor his animal was there.

He could not call her name, for fear someone would hear.

Instead, apprehension pricked his spine, as he walked in a wide arc, knowing he suffered no confusion about the location. Even in the dark, he knew exactly where he was. *This* was the place.

Even so, he returned to the center of the circle he'd just walked and he dragged his heel over the uneven earth until he found the hole where the stake had been driven. *The Devil in Hell. Where was she*?

Was it possible she been recognized? And taken to Buchan's camp?

He could . . . find a torch and examine the ground for

the horse's tracks, but he knew . . . damn him to hell, he *knew* the ground would be a confusing tumult of indentations and upturned earth created by the prior days of festival.

He pivoted, looking in every direction, stalking to and fro . . . the muscles across his chest feeling drawn, his pulse quickly becoming frantic. All around, he saw nothing but black night and indiscernible shapes and faces. Laughter and music pressed into his ears, the sounds sharp and annoying.

The highlands could be a dangerous place for a woman, and he felt torn between waiting here for her to return, or setting off into the crowd, the tents, the village, the earl's encampment to search for her.

Panic was a reaction foreign to him, but panic tightened his chest and his blood turned to ice.

God help him . . . Tara was gone and he did not know where she was, who had taken her, or how to get her back.

Tara rode north, into absolute darkness, her heart beating so hard she could barely breathe. Tears streamed over her cheeks. Cold wind tore her hood from her hair, and chilled her through.

And she was frightened. She had never been so frightened.

She had never felt so alone.

But she could not go back. The moment she'd realized Buchan was there, just over the hill, panic and fear—and an all-consuming need to be free—had guided her actions.

If she stayed, a wedding to Hugh *would* take place. As strong and certain as Magnus was, how could he save her from that, without getting himself killed? She did not want him to die.

She could only rely on her instincts, and her instincts

compelled her to go forward with her plan to ride away, to assert control over her own future and most of all, to endanger no one but herself. She only prayed the Kincaids were not the savages she'd heard they were, and that they would give her safe haven until she could travel on to the priory. But would she even find the Kincaids? Where did the Alwyn lands end and Kincaid lands begin?

The animal leapt over a berm, delving down a sharp incline. Her stomach turned with the drop in elevation. She had not ridden after being committed to the care of the priory, but she had loved riding before, with her father. She sensed Magnus's horse knew the way, even in the darkness. She told herself that she must trust the animal to get her safely there.

Suddenly—out of nowhere a bright flame appeared, a torch waved in a high arc, just in front of her. The horse screamed and stamped, rearing—dropping her to the ground.

Tara twisted on the earth—reaching for the animal's reins, which dangled, swinging past her, but she wasn't fast enough. The horse raced away in the night, hooves thudding across the earth.

But another sound chilled her blood. Heavy footsteps on the earth, crunching over grass and stone. Footsteps that sounded as if they belonged to a giant. With those footsteps, the torchlight moved closer, until in the night, she saw a face . . . wild-eyed and covered in a mask of tattoos. Glaring fiercely at her.

Tara scrambled away, and screamed.

Chapter 14

Magnus did the only thing he knew to do. He stole Chissolm's horse and he rode north, toward Inverhaven.

Tara was safe. She *had* to be.

No doubt she had been seen by someone who recognized her, and taken straightaway to Buchan. If that was indeed what had occurred, she would have to explain to her guardian how she'd come to be at Rackamoor, alone and in the middle of the night, but he had to believe no harm would come to her.

Tara was smart. There was a reason no one had waited to confront him at the place where they'd agreed to meet. She had not implicated him in any way, and no doubt had taken the entirety of the blame on herself for venturing out unescorted to the festival.

And yet . . . there were other possibilities. *Fearsome* possibilities, the thought of which made him nearly ill.

If a stranger had taken her . . . someone who wished her harm . . .

He couldn't think about it. If he did, he'd go mad.

He would remain at Inverhaven only as long as it took to inform his brother of Buchan's arrival. Afterward, he would immediately return to Rackamoor, and under cover of darkness, go into the camp and confirm whether she was there . . . or returned to Burnbryde.

If she wasn't . . . if she wasn't, he would exhaust himself finding her, and hate himself every moment of every day for the rest of his life if any misfortune had befallen her.

At last, he saw lights shining in the night, the windows and ramparts of the stronghold at Inverhaven.

He'd been followed at a distance by Kincaid border guards, who had not interfered with his progress toward the keep. Still sick at heart, his thoughts clouded full of concern for Tara, he rode straight through rows of encamped mercenaries to the gate, and gave the horse over to a sleepy-eyed, tousle-haired stableboy, asking him to wait for his imminent departure rather than taking the animal away.

At the doors, he spoke to a male servant, giving his name and saying he urgently needed to speak to the Kincaid. It would be after midnight now, and everyone might be abed, but the announcement of Buchan's arrival was worth waking Niall. Indeed, it was worth waking his entire army.

Magnus stood impatiently in the dimly lit entry hall, weighted by guilt over leaving Tara for even a second at the festival. Each moment that passed seemed an eternity that she might be slipping further away, to a place he could not find her. He prayed to God, more fervently than he had ever prayed about anything, that she was safe.

The servant returned. "The Kincaid will see you."

He followed the man to the laird's council chambers. To his surprise, upon entering the room, he spied his brother relaxed in a chair, dressed in tunic and plaid, looking into the fire. On the table beside him were two goblets.

"Magnus." Niall lifted his chin.

"Greeting, brother," Magnus said, striding toward him, his cloak swirling around his calves. "Buchan has arrived, and he's brought hundreds of men with him."

"And I would venture they didn't come just to celebrate a wedding. It is time, then." Niall turned his face to look up at him, eyebrows raised. "Let us discuss the final details of our plan."

Magnus tensed. "You and the men stand ready, and be prepared to come at a moment's notice. I do not know how it will happen or when, but I *will* force the Alwyn's confession," he said with certainty. "And if Buchan was involved, we will know of it. Until then I ask that you wait until I summon you to the border—and I join you there to march against them."

Niall's gaze burned hot. "I look forward to that moment when the Alwyn realizes you are my brother. That he must answer to not only one Kincaid son, but two. Buchan as well."

"As do I." He paced before the fire, agitation running through his blood. Until he found her, he couldn't relax. Hell, he might never sleep again. "Niall . . . I must tell you, there's something else."

Niall leaned forward in his chair, watching him. "What is it?"

"Tara is gone." The words broke from his lips like a confession, and he supposed they were. He felt responsible. Lost. "*Tara Iverach.*"

"From where did she go missing?" Niall asked, with utter calm.

"I had taken her to the festival at Rackamoor, intending to bring her here after, for safety. Niall, it is too dangerous for her there at Burnbryde. Hugh . . . I do not trust him alone with her."

Niall stared at him in silence. *He knew.* Of course he did. Certainly it was written all over his face, that he cared for Tara. That he loved her.

"We were there, together, at the bonfire. She was there one moment, and then she was gone."

Niall nodded. "She escaped."

"Or was abducted, I fear," he blurted, waving a hand. "I don't know . . . I should go, I cannot rest until I find her—"

"No, brother," Niall interrupted. "I'm telling you. She escaped."

Magnus blinked. "Why would you say that?"

Niall leaned back in his chair again, lifting a hand to his chin. "Tara Iverach is here. She's . . . upstairs with El-speth at this very moment."

Magnus's heart seized inside his chest. "She . . . is *here*."

Niall nodded. "My captain, Deargh, stopped her crossing over into Kincaid lands. She came here of her own free will, asking for my protection. She asked to be returned to a priory at Elgin."

Magnus felt as if he'd taken a spear to the chest.

He turned toward the fire, staring at the flames, determined not to let his brother see what those words did to him, that they clawed his insides out.

After the night they had spent together? After the words they'd spoken?

Tara had *escaped* . . . and she had used him to do so? She had asked him to take her to Rackamoor, then she had stolen his horse and fled, leaving him without explanation. Leaving him to believe she'd been abducted or murdered, or worse.

She did not know Niall was his brother. Did not realize he would hear the truth.

Perhaps this had been her plan all along, from the first moment she'd arrived at Burnbryde.

Even in those moments when they'd made love.

To use him so that she could escape, and to never look back. He'd been so blinded by her loveliness. Her *innocence*. He'd never suspected. How could he have been such a fool?

"Well, then," Magnus muttered, turning to face his brother, all emotion struck from his face. "That saves us a bit of trouble and time, then, doesn't it? Let us go over our plans, in more detail. Look here, on this map, and see where even now, we have stationed troops."

Tara dressed herself in the dark gray kirtle the charming Lady Kincaid had left for her. Just moments before, the lady and her servants had departed the chamber, leaving her in a night rail, and cozily tucked into bed.

But she couldn't sleep, or even rest. Not in this unfamiliar place.

When she had spoken to the Kincaid earlier, her cloak covered in mud, he had not agreed to any of her requests. He had promised no sanctuary or to provide her safe passage to Elgin. He had only regarded her in a quietly terrifying manner that somehow reminded her of Magnus, although the two were enemies, and most certainly nothing at all alike, Magnus being so muscular and fair-haired, and the Kincaid, so dark and stalwart. But she could not sleep until she knew he would provide her with an escort, at dawn's first light, so that she could safely get far away from here.

She moved silently down the corridor and approached the room where the Kincaid had met her, but heard voices talking quietly. She couldn't quite understand what they said, but she thought she heard the words *Buchan* and *Burnbryde*.

That voice . . . it made her body go alert, and compelled her to move closer. Magnus?

Every muscle in her body seized tight as she stepped closer, and peered inward. The two men stood side by side at the table, looking at something—the map she'd seen when she'd been in the room earlier.

Why was Magnus here, standing there beside the Kincaid, speaking with such easy familiarity?

"I would place men here . . . and here," said Magnus. "With couriers on horses, ready to bring word to you on any changes they observe in the positioning of the earl's men."

"What about here?" asked the Kincaid, pointing.

Magnus shrugged, but nodded. "If you've the men to spare."

"We do have men to spare. They are your forces as well, to command at your will. I will make the announcement today to my captains, so there will be no question of our support for you."

The words Tara heard made no sense, but the two men weren't enemies, that much was clear. They plotted something together. Something that involved warriors, and borders, against not only the Alwyn—but Buchan as well. Magnus had told her *something* was underway, and she'd instinctively known he meant something dangerous but never in her life had she imagined that he plotted a rebellion against his father with another laird.

"What does *that* mean?" she said from the door.

They turned to look at her.

She stepped forward, moving toward them. "What does it mean, Magnus, that the Kincaid's forces are yours to command as well?"

And then she saw it. That while the two men were

indeed very different, one dark, the other fair . . . they looked very much the same.

"You are—" She covered her mouth with her hands.

Magnus stared at her, his lips unsmiling.

"Brothers." He moved toward her, wearing the eyes of a stranger. "I am the second son of the murdered Kincaid. The Alwyn, through his treachery, is responsible for the deaths of our mother and father, our younger brother, and many of our kinsmen. The loss of our lands. And soon, he will know our vengeance. Buchan as well, for it is almost certain he was involved."

Brothers. He was not the bastard son of the Laird Alwyn, but a Kincaid. For a moment, her spirit rose up in support of him, this man she loved. Or . . . had loved.

"You were going to bring me here," she concluded. "These are the people of whom you spoke. The people you trusted."

Was that why he'd made love to her? *Seduced her?* Pretended to want and protect her, so he could *control* her and in that way, keeping her from truly escaping. Ensuring that Buchan would come—if not to Burnbryde, then here, to Inverhaven? Had she been nothing but bait? A lure, to draw his enemy forth?

She didn't want to believe he could be that calculating, but even now he stared at her without any trace of warmth, as if she meant nothing to him. As if he did not even know her. It broke her heart, even more than it was already broken after finding him with the two women in his bed.

She would not allow herself to be drawn into this. She would not be destroyed, in some battle to the death between men filled with hate.

She straightened her shoulders. "I don't much care what the two of you are plotting. All I ask is that I be conveyed away from here, as soon as possible. Indeed, I would leave at first light if you can spare just a few horses and men to accompany me. I am willing to pay well for them."

"With what?" Magnus demanded tersely.

She pulled her mother's necklace from her throat.

"You came prepared, I see," he said in a softly taunting voice. He stepped closer, so close she felt the heat of his flame-hot blue gaze. "Do ye know, I was . . . very concerned for your safety tonight, after you disappeared. I . . . did not know if you had been abducted, or something worse. But now . . . seeing you here, I don't see that you and I have anything more to say to each other." He backed away and turned to the Kincaid. "If my brother agrees to your terms, I won't stop you."

The Kincaid looked between the two of them and laughed. "That is not how this story will unfold. Now that Buchan is here, I'm reluctant to stray from our plan. There is only one course of action, and we shall hold to it."

"A plan?" Tara asked. "What is that plan, and what could I possibly have to do with it now that Buchan is here, exactly where you wish him to be?"

She bristled, knowing she had been part of the plot all along, without her knowledge. The fire crackled.

The Kincaid looked at her. "You will return to Burnbryde."

Her stomach clenched at the idea of returning to that smothering place. "I can't. I *won't*. Why would you even ask it of me? He is here, now. Encamped outside Rackamoor, practically at Burnbryde's front steps. You have no need of me anymore."

Tara kept her eyes focused on the laird, but felt Magnus's gaze on her, darkly accusing.

"I'm very sorry, Mistress Iverach." The Kincaid looked at her with what appeared to be sincere sympathy. "I have no wish to distress you, or make you feel endangered in any way. But understand that I and my brother are singular in our desire to exact justice on behalf of our murdered parents, and our kinsmen. I know Buchan better than you do, I vow." The Kincaid walked slowly, between them both, in measured steps. "He's a mercurial bastard, and if he learns you are gone, and that there will be no wedding, I would not be surprised if he severs his alliance with the Alwyn, and takes all his men and leaves, just like that. We can't let that happen. I promise you will have safe passage to the priory at Elgin. After you help us."

"But I cannot marry Hugh," she choked out.

"You won't have to marry him. I promise you that."

"You won't be there," she exclaimed. "How can you say I won't be forced? How could you stop it?"

"I offer a solution. A very good one, if I must say."

"I'm listening."

"You will marry Magnus instead. Here, tonight. Before you return to Burnbryde."

Magnus's head snapped up.

"What?" he thundered, scowling.

"Marry Magnus!" Tara exclaimed. "Why would I do that?"

"You cannot marry Hugh if you are already married to another man. If a wedding takes place, the vows will not bind you, once the truth is known."

"But Hugh won't know the wedding is invalid. He will expect a wedding night." She closed her eyes. "I *can't*."

"And you won't. Again, if a wedding is indeed to take place, Magnus will send word, and our army will demand the immediate and full attention of the laird and his son, and your guardian, before night falls. I promise you that. There will be no wedding night. To further assure you, once the armies amass at the borderlands, and Burnbryde's castle is left to the care of lesser warriors, I will send a company of men to escort you straightaway to freedom."

"How do you expect to do that?" she demanded, doubting his words. Doubting everything. "Do you think the Alwyns will just let me leave?"

Niall scowled, and held silent for a long moment. "I have one of Buchan's banners, from my years spent in his service, which will be flown by my men when they approach Burnbryde, and I know how to write a very official, command, which will appear to come from Buchan to release you to his protection."

His plan would work, she believed. She hoped. The Alywns would do anything to please the earl.

Still, she scowled. "I don't want to marry Magnus."

"And I don't want to marry you," Magnus retorted, his eyes aflame.

The Kincaid spoke in a tone of patience. "The marriage won't be binding. Once it is all done, you will be delivered safe and unharmed to the priory, as you have requested, and both of you can request that the marriage then be annulled. We can all swear that you were wed under duress, and that no consummation took place."

Tara felt warmth diffusing through her cheeks, remembering otherwise.

"I won't do it," she whispered.

The Kincaid smiled at her. "Mistress Iverach . . . think about it. I'm afraid you don't have any choice. What say you, Magnus? Are you ready to take a bride in the name of our cause?"

"Fine," Magnus hissed, clearly annoyed. "Let it be done, and quickly. If we are to return to Burnbryde before morning reveals us, we must depart posthaste."

"It is true what you said," Tara declared. "I do this under duress."

A priest was summoned, and a sleepy-eyed Lady Kincaid, who stood in her night rail and shawl beside Tara through the brief ceremony, during which Magnus impassively held her limp hand.

After, the Laird and Lady Kincaid accompanied them into the courtyard where the horses waited, as well as a small company of men—led by the tattooed warrior who had apologized so profusely for startling her horse earlier, causing her to be unseated.

To her surprise, she saw Gilroy there among them.

"Gilroy!" she exclaimed.

Magnus's hand went to his sword, but Niall lifted a staying hand. "With everything that has happened tonight, I forgot about Gilroy. He had renounced his loyalty to the Alwyn, and is now a sworn and loyal Kincaid."

"He is not to be trusted," Magnus growled. "He attacked Tara and thieved from her."

"Nay, I tried tae frighten her away," said the old man.

"Why?" demanded Magnus.

"I did not wish to see the same fate befall her as befell her poor sister."

Her heart pounding, she moved close to him. "What fate is that?"

"I dinna know. I canna say. I can only tell ye that she wasn't ill that morning when she left the tower. The fever was a story the lady made up, because the girl never returned. Somethin' happened to her, I fear. Something terrible. The lie they told, it burdened my heart to be part of it, and when I heard her sister was to come, I did what I could to make her want to turn around and flee. Only you arrived and thwarted me plan." He looked at Magnus then.

At last. At last she knew her sister had not died in that tower fever, as everyone had told her.

"Her sister died there. Was possibly murdered. By

whom, we do not know for certain, though I suspect I know." Magnus looked at his brother, his expression stern. "No, Niall. She stays here, where it is safe. I will return to Burnbryde and when she is discovered missing, I will—"

Tara strode past them both, and took the reins of a horse. "Nay, Magnus. I must have my confession. Just as you must have yours."

"You could be harmed, Tara," he called to her, angry now.

"So could you. I make my choice to return, just as you make yours."

There was silence all around, as she climbed into the saddle.

Magnus clenched his jaw, clearly turned to his brother. "When it happens, it will happen quickly."

"We will be ready," Niall answered.

Magnus looked at Tara, his eyes reflecting the torchlight—making him seem distant and inhuman. Certainly not the man she had known.

"Come," he said brusquely. "We haven't much time."

Despite the vows they'd just spoken, she could not think of him as her husband. Not when they had both clearly indicated their intention to nullify the union as soon as possible. She felt just as alone as before.

They rode out of the gates, into the pitch darkness of the night. She gathered her cloak around her, shivering from the cold, fearing she'd be frozen by the time they arrived at Burnbryde. Suddenly he was there, circling back to ride beside her, his face stark in the night, and his breath puffing from his mouth and nostrils.

"I know these lands as well in the dark as in the light of day," he said gruffly. "Give me the reins, and I will lead the animal along the proper path."

"I can ride well enough without your help," she retorted.

"Just give me the reins," he demanded, in a tone of impatience.

When she did not give them over, he reached and seized them from her hands.

"Magnus!" she cried, looking at him. "Have you nothing at all to say to me?"

She wanted him to say something meaningful. Something sincere. She wanted an apology for having been used. For having been seduced and kept in a place of danger to further the Kincaid cause.

He circled around once more, drawing up beside her again, so close their legs brushed.

"Aye, I have something t' say," he gritted out between clenched teeth, his burr thick and laden with fury. "Those words I said to you when we were alone together . . . the things we did in your bed. . . ." His eyes glittered in the night. "They *meant* something to me. What in the *hell* did they mean to you?"

In that moment she knew the truth. That until she'd run away from Rackamoor, his heart had belonged to her completely, just as he'd sworn that night when they first made love. She was given no opportunity to respond. He jabbed his heels into his horse's side, had sped forward, leading her horse by the reins, at such a speed she could only hold fast to the pommel, and clench her thighs so as not to be thrown off.

They continued at the same hard pace until they arrived at Burnbryde, stopping once they reached the cemetery. Already, the sky lightened to lavender with early dawn, which only heightened the anxiety Tara felt, that they might be discovered together, that everything would fall apart. They left their horses and Tara followed Magnus on foot, her feet crunching over the frosted ground. At his lead, they stealthily darted into the shadow of the castle wall when the watchmen above made his paces in the opposite direction.

They stole into the shadowed crevice and approached the secret passageway, which would lead to her room.

He hoisted the ladder, and lowered it into place. In doing so he pushed back his cloak, and she saw the gleam of his dagger at his waist—and she knew, without a doubt, that no matter how angry he was with her, he would kill to protect her.

But not because he cared for her, not anymore. Frozen and exhausted, she could only watch him, her heart aching at the sight of his height and his strength—and his stark, drawn features. Despite everything, she wanted nothing more than his arms around her, to feel his warmth, and his kiss. And yet his gaze did not so much as touch upon her.

"Magnus," she said. "I ran away from you at Rackamoor because I saw Buchan's army, and I was afraid. But also . . . also because I came to your window to see you, the morning after the hunting party returned, and I knocked . . . but it wasn't you who answered, though I know you were there."

At first, his countenance did not change. Then . . . the meaning of her words registered. He closed his eyes and his lips pressed thin.

"Kyla and Laire." His eyes opened, ablaze. "Tara, no. It wasn't like that. Hugh's man Ferchar attacked them during the evening feast, and I only gave them a safe place to stay for the night, where they would not be harmed. I've known them both since we were children."

Did she believe him? She thought so, and it pained her heart that she'd misunderstood and come to the wrong conclusion, but at the same time, certainly he had to concede how it had looked to her, and how any reasonable explanation would be hard to surmise.

"What else was I to believe?" she said, pressing her hands to her lips. Tears flooded her eyes.

"Not that."

"I discovered you with two women in your bed."

"You should have told me, instead of thinking the worst of me."

"Told you? And risked my one remaining chance for escape? No, Magnus. Not knowing if I could trust you, I chose to keep silent and protect myself."

"We've no time to argue over this. Not now. You first," he said brusquely, guiding her onto the first rung. "Wait for me there, after you unlock the gate. I want to be certain no one is there waiting. That no one has discovered your absence in the night."

She climbed, and pulled the key, worn at her throat with her mother's necklace. A moment later and they were both inside, climbing the narrow passage to her room.

Holding her aside, Magnus went first, crouching and pushing open the door and the tapestry, guiding her with his hand, as she followed.

And yet Tara gasped at the first thing she saw upon entering the room.

Anna stood beside the hearth, in a heavy woolen night robe, her pale night rail peeking out, staring wide-eyed back at them.

Chapter 15

"Where have you been?" Anna hissed. "Oh, it doesn't matter. I won't tell. I won't tell *anyone*, but *you* must leave—" She rushed toward them, waving her hands, *shooing* Magnus away. "Before someone sees you."

Magnus turned to her, his expression grave, speaking words only she would hear. "I won't ask you to trust me again, Tara. I think we can both agree that's been lost between us. Just be careful, Tara, and know that I'll do my best to protect you."

She remained silent, supposing that to be true.

He crouched, and disappeared into the passageway.

Anna rushed behind him to close the secret door. Turning back, she approached Tara.

"Quick. We must get ye into bed, before Mary comes in with the water for the basin and sees. I had come in to light the fire, and found you gone. Look at you, you are freezing." Her hands touched Tara's face, her frozen cheeks. "Where have you been?"

"The bonfire at Rackamoor." She was suddenly too

tired to think. To talk anymore. "Yes, the bed. I need to sleep, if just for a little while."

She pulled her clothing, and Anna helped her remove it.

"Where did you get these clothes? They aren't yours."

"You don't want to know."

Anna's eyes widened. "I think I do."

"I can't tell you." She sat on the edge of the bed, as Anna pulled her boots off her feet.

Still kneeling, the maid peered straight into her eyes. "Mistress, is Magnus your lover?"

"No, Anna. I assure you, he is not." Not anymore.

"Oh . . . ," the maid answered, her voice softening with disappointment. "I was going to say how thrilling, if you had answered yes."

Magnus slept for a brief time, but awakened to summons from the laird. After quickly washing and dressing, he made his way to the Alwyn's council chamber. As he did so, he thought of Tara. His secret, untrusting wife.

Their "wedding" had been nothing but empty words spoken, without meaning or emotion. But binding still, by law, if they so wished it.

The memory of it all—*everything* that had taken place the night before, ate at his insides, leaving him agitated and dissatisfied. Aye, he had wanted Tara, and even though he was married to her, he'd certainly lost her.

He entered a room already filled with the clan's council members. They clustered near the far window, taking turns approaching the laird who stood smiling, along with Buchan, who looked very much the same as when Magnus had seen him last, when he'd been just a boy of fourteen. Imperious, self-important, and completely indifferent to those who fawned over him.

Dim morning light filtered through the open window,

along with a bracing cold, casting the men in gray. The Alwyn wore splendid garments, a dark green tunic and saffron robe, while Buchan wore dark gray wool and leather, his boots daubed with mud. His sons were also there, watching from the corner as their father accepted the salutations of each man. It was they who had changed since he had seen them last, grown into men, just as Magnus had.

He made his way toward them, at the end of the line of men.

The Alwyn's face warmed with pleasure at the sight of him—something that still surprised him each time it occurred. "And this is Magnus."

At this, the earl did straighten, his eyes narrowing with keen interest. "The war-captain I have heard so much about."

His two sons moved closer, peering over their father's shoulder, assessing him. Yes—he wanted them all to see his face. To know the man who would hold them accountable for the crimes of the past.

"Welcome to Burnbryde, my lord." He bent his head.

"Hmm, thank you," he answered. "Unfortunately, my visit must be brief, as duty demands my presence in Edinburgh."

His statement appeared to startle the laird, for his brows gathered and he frowned. "How brief?"

Magnus boldly dared to speak then. "We will accommodate your schedule, my lord, whatever it is. But I would request a private meeting with you and the laird, to discuss this conflict with the Kincaids, as we request your counsel over what can be done."

The earl did not answer. Instead he looked out over the crowded room with annoyance. "Yes. I agree. The three of us alone, without all of these ears, hovering about."

And yet his sons also remained. Together they stood at the window, looking out at the distant ocean. Only after the room cleared did Magnus see Hugh, sitting by the fire, his eyes closed and jaw slack as he dozed, unaware of the activity around him. Buchan's gaze flitted over him, dismissively. The laird strode toward him and kicked his leg, jolting him awake. His expression dazed and sour, he stood.

When the door was shut, Buchan lifted his hands. "I am an important man, with little time to spare. My ward—"

"You wish to see her?" asked the laird, stepping toward the door. "I will summon her."

"What for?" Buchan squinted, as if the laird's suggestion were utterly pointless. "No. Let us simply call the priest and get the wedding done." He glanced at Hugh. "Are you not ready to be wed?"

"Oh, I am ready. Ready and eager," Hugh answered with a gravelly chuckle. "Mistress Iverach is . . . lovely. I thank you for providing her to me."

Magnus's blood turned to ice. His fingers curled tight, his hands forming fists. The words were a grievous offense to his ears, and more affecting than he had ever expected them to be.

The earl let out a huff of breath. "I regretted the decision as soon as it was done. She is a lovely girl, in possession of quite a fortune now that her sister is dead, and I'm certain I could have made a much better match for her, but I do not rescind promises. It is why I am here. To finish this thing with the Kincaid imposter. Because of a promise I made long ago."

Magnus's stomach muscles clenched at the speaking of his clan name.

"Do you believe the man claiming to be the Kincaid is truly an imposter?" he dared ask, with the intention of eliciting more words. The confession he needed. "Or could he be the Kincaid son he claims to be?"

"It doesn't really matter," answered the earl, flashing a cold grin. "The Beast, as I knew him when he served as my guard, will forfeit the lands, as I have promised them elsewhere. Let no one say I do not reward those who have been loyal to me. Have I not always?"

It wasn't the confession Magnus needed.

The Alwyn nodded. "Aye, and we are grateful. Please say you will allow us to celebrate your presence here tonight with a feast?"

"Yes, yes. I will agree to that. But the wedding must take place tomorrow morning, and immediately after . . . we take back your lands."

Magnus's pulse increased. Tara . . .

It had been so simple to swear to protect her. He had meant the words. Now, for the first time, doubt crept into his soul. What if, in the turmoil of the coming days, he could not keep Hugh from her? What if . . . what if he were killed, and she were left behind?

The earl spoke again. "It must all be done quickly. I can spare no more time than that, and really, it is to your benefit as my mercenaries can sometimes be . . . undisciplined, at best. I fear Rackamoor will not survive them."

The Alwyn shrugged. "Rackamoor is a sacrifice we are willing to make."

Magnus struggled not to flinch at the callous words. There were people involved. Homes. Farms. Families and children—not to mention the women who would no doubt be preyed upon . . . and the Alwyn so weak a leader he did not even attempt to assert command.

If he could get the confession he needed. Magnus pressed, knowing he risked the displeasure . . . the suspicion of the powerful man he wished to implicate. "So many highlanders of the time spoke out against that king." The king who had been in power before Buchan's father. "What crime did the Kincaid commit, so beyond the others of his day, to bring about the end of his clan?"

The earl exhaled through his nose, as if the request for his time tried his patience. Buchan leveled a look on him. "He displeased the wrong person.

"Now . . ." continued the earl, "I wish to review your forces, so that all weaknesses can be ascertained. Afterward, discuss our plan of confrontation and attack."

"Of course," Magnus answered, before the Alwyn could speak. "We have made many preparations, in anticipation of your arrival, and I do believe you will be pleased."

The earl clapped a hand to his shoulder, and looked at the Alwyn. "This one . . . I like him. If you don't watch out, I may take him from you. He would do well in my service."

Buchan's sons nodded in agreement, while Hugh glowered.

The Alwyn murmured, "Magnus has proven himself most valuable to the clan—and to me."

Hugh, his expression clouded with darkness, pushed past. "Forgive me. I just remembered somewhere I need to be."

Magnus, in that moment, understood that he was not the only son who had been judged and humiliated for every flaw. Unhappiness affected different men in different ways . . . some striving to overcome their life's challenges, while others fell into darkness.

For that reason, he could not take the chance Hugh would seek out Tara.

Magnus's hand shot out, grabbing hold of his arm. "I forbid it."

"*You* forbid *me*?" Hugh's eyes widened, sparking with rage.

Magnus feigned a respect he did not feel. "Who else knows more about the new stock of horses that have been added to our war stable?"

It was an exaggeration at best. Hugh rarely set foot in the stables, but at hearing himself praised, he stood taller, and his scowl turned into a self-pleased smile. "Let us go there now, then."

The rest of the day passed all too quickly out of doors, at the armory, the stable, on the practice grounds. Repeatedly, Magnus directed conversation in the direction of the past, and it became frustratingly clear neither Buchan nor the Alwyn wished to speak of those fateful days, leaving Magnus more certain that ever, that the reasons for killing his father and attacking the Kincaid clan had been wholly unsubstantiated.

Last, they rode with a large guard, along the border, where from overlooking hills, large companies of the Kincaid's mercenaries could be seen looking back at them. No one knew the surge of pride Magnus felt at seeing them . . . or the impatient clamor of his blood in his veins, to see the next day done so that he could join them.

"It appears our enemy is aware of your arrival," the Alwyn declared, his words a boast. "Let them watch. Let them gaze, wide-eyed upon their impending doom."

But the Kincaids would be the Alwyn's doom—and very possibly the earl's as well.

The same boasts continued into the night, during the promised feast. But Magnus sensed an underlying foreboding in the room that always came before a battle, as the warriors knew that some who sat among them tonight, would not return tomorrow. Ale flowed, and inebriation and gluttony ensued.

Normally Magnus sat with the men of the Pit, but his presence had been requested at the laird's table—though frustratingly, he had been placed too far from the laird and the earl to overhear what they said, for the clamor of the room. Instead he had been subjected to the coarse talk of Hugh and his few loyal hangers-on.

Pensive, he ate and drank little, waiting for Tara to appear—but hours passed and she did not, and neither did the Lady Alwyn. While he was thankful she would not be submitted to his present company, he wanted nothing more than to see her. How could she have believed that after the words he'd spoken to her . . . the promises he'd made . . . that he would fall into bed with not one, but two women? He had never given a woman his heart. Never imagined a future beyond the next battle. She'd given him a reason that he must survive—and in a moment, stripped that reason away.

Certainly she had cause to fear betrayal. That she'd only been used. And wasn't that what he and his brother had done to her, once again?

"Where is your bride-to-be?" he asked Hugh, who sat across the table.

"I have been told she prefers to *rest* tonight." He laughed coarsely. "Rest, indeed." He swigged a deep gulp of his ale, which left his lips shining, and he belched. "She will need all the rest she can get, for I will rut between her legs for days on end when she is mine. So ferociously she won't be able to walk for weeks."

His companions laughed and slapped his back.

Magnus stood, unable to conceal his disgust, and left the room.

Late in the night, Tara paced the floor in her night rail, avoiding looking at the pale ivory kirtle and embroidered *lèine* that hung on the far wall. Her wedding garments, that she feared she would indeed have to wear as she suffered through a false wedding to Hugh. But those were not the thoughts that consumed her.

The reality of what he intended to do . . . the danger he placed himself in, had slowly settled over her, and she realized . . . Magnus could die.

Just the thought made her frantic to speak to him—to tell him she was sorry for her part in their disagreement. But she had slept little in the previous two days and at last, weariness sent her to bed.

She dozed. . . . slept . . . until some sound or . . . movement awakened her. Opening her eyes, she saw the dark outline of man sitting near the center of the room, the fire to his back, the shadows masking his face . . .

She pushed up with a gasp, and left the bed, afraid—

Only to realize.

"Magnus!"

He sat, broad-shouldered and proud, in a tunic and plaid, his long legs encased in leather boots. In response, emotions tore through her soul, more powerful than anything she'd ever felt.

"I did not intend to wake you," he answered, not moving. Only . . . watching her, his expression too shadowed to see. "I just . . . wanted to see you one more time, before tomorrow."

She stood with her arms at her sides, her heart pounding, her body begging . . . *aching* to return to his arms. "I wanted to see you too. It's why I left the window unlocked."

He bit his lower lip and shook his head. "When I found that window unlocked, I . . . I thought you'd made the decision that you should have made, days ago. I thought you were gone. Escaped, at last. That I'd never see you again. Tara . . . *why* are you still here?"

"I never thought of leaving. Not without seeing you.

Not without making things right between us. No, Magnus. If it is revenge you want, and I can help, then I will stay. Even if I never learn what truly happened to Arabel, I will see this thing through for you."

"Tara . . . I am so sorry—" he rasped, his expression solemn.

She lifted her hands. "I should have demanded to speak to you at the window, instead of believing the worst."

"But I understand now, why you didn't. You had to protect yourself. You had to survive. I should have been more understanding, in knowing how difficult it is for you to trust."

She went to him then, unable to keep from touching him. His legs flexed powerfully, as he rose up, seizing her against his chest, only to fall back again onto the stool, his hands closing onto her hips, bunching her linen gown, his face pressed against her neck.

"I do trust you. I won't ever question that trust again."

"I should not have brought you back here."

"There is no place I would rather be," she answered. "I couldn't be there, wondering what was happening to you. No matter what, I wish to be here with you."

"Be with me, one last time," he murmured, his voice thick with desire, his lips pressed against her temple.

"One last time . . . ?" she whispered. "No, never the last."

His arms, his hands tightened on her, with such ferocity it stole her breath, and he kissed her with breathtaking passion. The muscles of his shoulders roiled under her hands . . . as he gripped her thighs . . . lifting her, bringing her legs to either side of his hips . . . bunching her gown at her waist—

Beneath her, his legs flexed and with a sudden, upward thrust—

His sex stabbed into her—

"Yes," she cried.

—shocking her through with pleasure.

"One last time before it is done, and we can be free of this place."

Her head fell back. She glimpsed stars on the ceiling, as he groaned her name, and thrust into her again, deeper now, at the same time pulling her hips hard against him, stretching her, filling her, proving again that she belonged to no one but him.

"I want to see *my wife*." He tore her gown over her head and cast it to the floor, smoothing his hands upward over her waist, her ribs, and with his hands and mouth, devoured her breasts and nipples. "You *are* my wife, Tara, and if I survive tomorrow, I have no intention of ever letting you go."

She smiled, loving the words he spoke—the promise in them.

His body . . . the ways of lovemaking were still so new. She knew little about what to do . . . how to please him. But passion overtook her, and she could only respond and move as her body commanded.

"I want to see my *husband*, making love to me," she answered, daring to rise up, her knees braced on the stool on either side of his hips, enough to see between their bodies. He held her by the waist as she stared down at the erotic sight of his gleaming, thick sex disappearing inside her.

"Beautiful," he growled, looking too, lifting her to the crown, only to plunge deep again. "*Ah*. I can't see enough of you. I can't get enough."

He kissed her deeply, his tongue delving into her mouth, pulling her down, off her knees—and to their mutual satisfaction, he filled her completely.

As he kissed her . . . caressed her . . . Tara rocked

against him, hovering sweetly, perfectly on the verge of climax, her legs hanging down, her toes grazing the floor, but she needed him closer, deeper, something he needed too, because with a growl, he wrapped her legs around his waist and gently pushed . . . guided her backward . . . backward, her body falling downward, until her hair fell across his boots, and her hands touched the floor.

She fell into a delirium at the sensation of this new pleasure—a pleasure that only intensified when he stood, and pumped his sex deep inside her. Suspended by his hips on her hands, she climaxed—biting down on a scream, only vaguely aware now that he lifted her against his body—still clothed, and carried her to the shadowed bed.

He left her for only a moment, before returning, as naked as she. Sinking down on top her, his hips between her thighs, he banded one arm beneath her body, the other under her shoulders, his hand in her hair.

"I'm not finished," he said with a chuckle, the sound emanating from deep in his chest.

"How fortunate for me," she whispered, laughing too.

Their hips moved in tandem, she inviting him, welcoming him inside, knowing he had not yet spent himself.

"You feel like paradise." He moved slowly, coaxing her to return to the same edge of pleasure she'd just experienced. Amazingly, she did. Soon, she was moving . . . moaning . . . sighing, meeting each movement of his hips, eager to take the pleasure he gave her.

Suddenly, braced above her on his elbows, his flexed arms, he stilled, looking down at her, his eyes dark in the night. Her hands rested against the taut sides of his torso.

"What is it?" she asked, savoring the feeling of him deep inside her.

"I love you, Tara," he said intensely, his nostrils flaring. "Remember that. I'll die to protect you."

Tara's heart clenched. The words felt like a good-bye—

But he moved again, urgently now, his eyes going glassy. He rolled, holding her . . . bringing her astraddle his hips, dazing her with a rush of sensation and pressure between her legs, and deep in her womb. Cold hair bathed . . . teased . . . her heated skin. Her breasts swelled and her nipples hardened. She gasped as his hands cupped and caressed them. His body felt so good, his touch so magical. She never wanted the night to end.

"I love you, too, Magnus." Instinct told her to move. She rocked against him, once . . . twice . . . her palms planted against his chest, then harder . . . *and harder.* "I love you too."

His eyes glittered in the darkness, his gaze fixed on hers. He pushed up onto his elbows, then . . . his hands. The sound of their pleasure—their moans, and the sound of their skin shifting . . . thrashing, against the linens filled the curtained space. His hips jerked off the bed, and she let out a throaty gasp, her womb . . . her body . . . exploding with joy.

"My love." His head fell back, and he groaned. "Always, my love."

Magnus left her sleeping. Before, because of the forced circumstances, he had not felt as if they were married, but now . . . now she was not only his wife, but a sacred part of his soul. For that reason he would fight tomorrow—not only as a Kincaid, but for him and Tara. Tomorrow, he vowed, he would join her as a victor. Never again would he creep away in secret from her bed, a shadow in the night.

He left the tower, and in darkness, continued to the village, to a small cottage perched on the far hillside. There, he quietly opened the door, and passed inside. He did not want to frighten Robina by waking her from her sleep, but neither did he wish to waken her entire household, and all the children therein. A small fire still burned on the hearth, providing some warmth to the room, and faint light by which to see. He carefully stepped over one boy, and then a little girl. They were everywhere—at least seven of them—sleeping on their pallets. In the far corner, he saw her sleeping, and beside her, turned away, the hulking back of her new husband, the widower and father of all the children she'd come to love so dearly.

He touched her shoulder gently. "Mother."

Her eyes opened . . . and focused on him.

"Magnus!" she exclaimed.

"Shhhh," he shushed. "Quiet now. We don't want to wake them all. Can I talk to you?"

"Yes." She sat up, with her long dark braid falling over her shoulder. "Is something wrong?"

"No."

"But you haven't come to visit me for so long. And now, here you are, in the middle of the night."

She led him to the small kitchen, where she pulled the door closed behind them, and gestured for him to take a chair.

"No, mother. I will stand."

"What is it?" she asked. "I see it on your face. Something has happened. Something has changed."

He nodded. "I know who I am."

She went utterly still. "What do you mean."

"I know that I am Faelan Kincaid, and not the Alwyn's bastard son."

She exhaled shakily. "Oh . . . oh, Magnus. How did you find out?"

"From Niall. The mark on my arm. He recognized it as matching the one on his."

"You must hate me." Her voice grew thick, and she spoke through tears.

"I don't." His chest flooded with emotion. He did not want to hurt her. "No. You saved my life. I have no doubt of that."

She reached for his hand, and peered up at him in the darkness.

"Tell me what happened that night," he urged.

"I still don't know, exactly. I only know that the Mac-Claren and the Alwyn betrayed your father's trust, and turned against him. When they attacked, I and many others who serve your family as servants, fled the castle, into the hills. It was there I found you . . . and the warrior who had gave his life to protect you." She wrapped her arms around herself and shivered. "He was dead. Horribly slain, and you, grievously injured by a blow to your head, and barely breathing. I do believe he gave his last breath to save you. To get you away from danger."

"Did you see my younger brother? Cullen?"

"No. I do not know what happened to him."

Magnus clenched his teeth on his disappointment. "What then?"

"I was so fearful that you would die. Your poor mother. Your father. They loved you and your brothers so much. I knew I had to keep you alive. So I carried you as far as I could, until I could carry you no more, and then I slept. But I awakened to soldiers. Alwyn men. Though your mother never knew . . . no one did, I had fled Burnbryde years before, cast out of the village here by the Lady Alwyn, when she found out about me."

"You were the Alwyn's mistress then," he said.

"Aye," she murmured. "That much of the story is true. I did what I had to, to ensure that you survived. I demanded that the soldiers take us to him, and I told him that you were his son, that I'd kept secret from him. He wasn't a good father. No, but he gave me a cottage, and we were safe. I . . . gave you a new name, and over time I filled your fragile, healing mind with false memories, like the old Celts used to do when they wanted to make someone forget. My old grandmother had the skill, and I learned it from her."

She peered up at him through the darkness—and reached for him, pulling him into her embrace.

"Oh, Magnus. Faelan. You aren't my son, but I love you just as much as if you were."

He held her tight, against his chest. "And I love you too. Which is why tomorrow, I want you to take your new husband there, and those children, to the festival in Rackamoor. Camp there for several days, until it is safe to return."

"What are you planning to do?" she asked worriedly.

"What I must do. I'm going to avenge my father . . . my mother, and my clan."

"I'm afraid for you," she whispered.

"Don't be," he answered, thinking of Tara. Envisioning her face in his mind. "I have every reason, now, to want to live."

After they talked a while longer, he returned to the front doors of the castle, where he entered to find the great hall still filled with revelers. He passed unnoticed, continuing on to the chapel, where he said a brief, silent prayer for strength and for Tara's safety. At last, he descended to the Pit, and entered to find most of the men there, asleep or talking beside the fire.

Chissolm stood when he entered and followed him to his chamber, where in a low voice he said, "This thing we do tomorrow, against the Kincaid . . ."

"Yes?" he answered.

"Do you agree with it?"

The question startled him. He did not know, exactly, how to answer. Was it merely a question posed by Chissolm? Or was someone questioning his loyalty to the cause?

"We are Alwyn warriors, are we not?" He answered, deciding on caution. "We are paid to fight for our laird . . . not to make decisions for him. Why do you ask?"

Chissolm backed toward the door. "It's just that . . . if you were not leading us tomorrow, I, and the others, might not feel so easy about it all. We have been told for so long that the Kincaids are our enemies, but no one seems to know the truth of why. Something feels wrong."

The words teased his tongue. The truth of his birth, his hatred for the Alwyn—

—and his plan for tomorrow.

In the end, he met his friend's gaze directly, and spoke a different sort of truth.

"Battle has a way of revealing the absolute truth about men—and tomorrow you'll learn that truth about me. It's up to you and the others to decide whether to follow me, or go your own way."

Chissolm looked back at him, his expression grave. "I don't understand what you're trying to tell me. I feel like I've been given a riddle, and no way to solve it."

"You'll know the answer tomorrow. I promise you that. For now, just know that I will always lead you and the others, in a way I know to be right and honorable."

Chissolm nodded. "Ye always have. And I know that tomorrow, you will."

Chapter 16

Early the next morning, Tara followed the Lady Alwyn—
who leaned heavily on the laird's arm—to the chapel,
telling herself that as the wife of Faelan Kincaid, she
must be brave, despite her regret that she still had no answer as to what had happened to Arabel.

When they reached the chapel, she peered inside, and
saw a room crowded with warriors and women and
familiar—and unfamiliar—faces.

But where was Magnus? As she entered, the room went
silent. She glanced around, and her heart beat harder,
in fear. He was nowhere. Not even in the dark shadows
at the back of the room.

The Alwyn turned to her, and bent to kiss her cheek.
"God bless you on this special day."

The lady peered at her from beneath a sparkling veil.
"I pray you will be happy."

Suddenly Hugh was there, taking her roughly by the
hand and leading her forward toward the waiting priest.

And suddenly, Magnus *was* there, in front of them—
tall and masterful, his expression like stone.

He glanced at Hugh, but it was Tara's gaze he held. "That which God has joined together, let no man separate."

"Mmmfff," Hugh responded, his lip drawing back into a snarl.

Tara's pulse thrummed in her veins, hearing his words. Words that reminded her she was already married. That she would never belong to Hugh, because she already belonged to him.

Hugh led her, brushing past Magnus, and continuing on toward the priest.

And yet despite Magnus's meaningful words, standing here, at the sacred altar, she felt as if she were not inside her own body. As if she were trapped inside a terrible dream. The Laird and Lady Alwyn stood to one side, and Buchan and his sons to the other.

She reminded herself for the thousandth time, that even if she went through the motions of the wedding, she wouldn't be married to Hugh because she was already married to Magnus. She closed his eyes, and in an instant, remembered the touch of his hands. The scent of his body.

Always, my love.

The ceremony began, and it seemed only a moment before the priest looked at her expectantly. She breathed heavily, as everyone looked at her. The walls closed in. She couldn't. She could not speak the words.

It felt like sacrilege to speak the vows with Hugh. With *any* other man.

"I can't breathe," she gasped, and pushed past the bodies and faces surrounding her, hearing their collective murmurings of dismay in her ears.

"Come now, child!" Buchan called out behind her. "I command you to return."

She only ran faster, her rich kirtle hissing against the

stones, out through the back of the chapel, into the dim light of the day. Away . . . away, running down a well-trodden path, and through a narrow gate and into the open air—

Until the ground ended at her feet. Gasping, she filled her lungs with air.

Trembling, she peered down from the cliff, to the black, jagged stones below. An immense wave crashed, bathing her skin with frigid spray.

"Don't," said a voice behind her. "*Don't jump.*"

She spun around to see Hugh standing behind her, his arm extended. His eyes wide and fearful . . . as if the edge of the cliff filled him with terror.

"Why would you think I was going to jump?" she asked, eyes wide.

"It's so dangerous there," he said, his countenance gone ashen. "Don't make me suffer the sight again. I command you to come away."

"The sight of what? Do you mean Arabel? Did my sister jump? Or did she fall? Was it an accident, Hugh, or did you *push* her? Did she fall down there? Is that why she isn't in the graveyard? Oh, please just tell me so I can know the truth. She was my sister and I deserve to know."

His eyes went from sharp and black . . . to cloudy. He squinted. Lifted a hand to his head. "I . . . don't know. I can't remember. I just . . . recall her running from me, and standing . . . like you are now . . . saying how much she wished me well, but that she carried another man's child, and that she loved him, and because of that she could never love me . . ."

His expression transformed to one of fury then. "I was so angry. She was to be *my* wife. I would have cared for her. Been loyal to her. But already, she'd been disloyal to me? And a child, who I'd be expected to raise as my own."

He let out a low growl, and made a sharp, shoving motion with his hands, the palms flattened toward the sea.

"I *must* have pushed her," he hissed, shaking his head. "She wanted to be free. She wanted to go back to him. She wouldn't have jumped."

A sudden gust of wind tore at Tara's heavy garments, rendering her unsteady . . .

Suddenly, out of the corner of her eye she saw a dark shadow move forward—

"God, get away from that ledge."

Strong arms seized her, crushing the air from her lungs, pulling her back. Lifting her high and safe, against a solid chest.

Magnus. Just as another blur of movement drew her eye.

Robert Stewart stormed forward, his face a mask of hatred.

His booted leg came up, its heel landing at the center of Hugh's back. With a shout, he *shoved*, pushing Hugh over—

Tara screamed, her eyes fixed on Hugh's wide-eyed, open-mouthed face as he twisted, falling, his arms and legs flailing.

And then, there was nothing but the sea and the clouded sky.

Someone wailed—the Lady Alwyn, who stood white faced with shock beside her husband, who stood frozen in place.

"Oh, my God," Magnus uttered, turning her face against his chest, where Tara closed her eyes, trying to forget what she'd just seen.

"Why did he do that?" she cried. "Hugh did not try to push me. I was safe."

The Alwyn approached the empty ledge, his face a

mask of shock. Lady Alwyn continued to cry, grief-stricken, and staggered toward the ocean, arms out-stretched as if she could bring back her son.

Buchan glared at Robert, who glared at everyone. Duncan stood, arms crossed over his chest, looking unaffected.

"You murdered him!" Lady Alwyn screamed, tearing her veil from her head.

" 'Twas not murder," Robert growled. " 'Twas retribution, and as rightful as God's justice. Hugh was the murderer."

Magnus lowered Tara so that she stood on the ground, but he held her close to his side, a steadying hand at her back.

Robert stalked past, his jaw clenched, his hair blowing wild in the wind. "Don't chastise me, father. It was my child she carried—you know that."

"As if she were the only woman you've seduced," Buchan replied, staring back into his son's eyes. "The only child you would have sired. You're like your father in that way."

"Not with her. She . . . *Arabel* was different, and you took her from me. *You* sent her here, because you didn't want me to have what you couldn't have . . . happiness . . . love . . . forever . . . and he murdered them both. And I'll never forgive you for allowing it to happen. She should have been mine, father. She should have been mine."

Tara watched . . . listened in shock.

Buchan peered back at Robert. "Well, it's too late to do anything about it now, isn't it? So let's get on with our day. With our lives. All of us."

Robert cursed loudly, and turning on his heel, strode toward the ledge, and there, looked down. Duncan strode forward, joining him there.

Buchan turned his attention to the Alwyn. A look of

sympathy came over his features, and he sighed. "I'm very sorry, but . . ." He squinted, and shrugged. "There was *always* something *wrong* with that boy. You know it. I know it. You're better off without him. You've a much finer son there, to put forth as your heir."

He pointed at Magnus.

The Alwyn gestured to Anna and Mary, who had come forward to support the lady, who had fallen to her knees, and appeared insensible in her grief. "Take her away from here. Put her to bed."

He then turned to look at them all. He appeared pale . . . shocked. His eyes, bright with grief. But the words that came from his lips were deferent.

"You're right of course, my lord."

The wind still blew, and the ocean still crashed, and an air of shock still hung everywhere. There was nothing right in any of this. Tara felt numb, inside and out, feeling as if she were surrounded by madmen. Her only comfort came from Magnus, who remained at her side, silent and strong. Watching and waiting.

Still, she did not know how to feel. Yes, Hugh had killed her sister, but she wasn't convinced he'd intended to. Clearly his thinking had been twisted . . . and he, perhaps ill of the mind. She could not believe he deserved to die in so terrible a way.

Anna and Mary helped Lady Alwyn to stand. The lady heaved out deep, broken sobs . . . clearly heartbroken. Overcome with grief. Of course she was! Her son, her only child, had just been executed in a most cruel and unexpected way. No matter how deeply Tara had disliked him, his mother had loved him as any mother with a heart would love her children, even with their faults, unconditionally. She broke away from Magnus and put her arms around her, only to have the woman sag against her, weeping in in her arms.

The Alwyn joined her, but only for a moment.

"I'm so sorry, my love," he said to his wife rigidly, without touching her. "Remember him fondly."

It was a horrible, unfeeling thing to say! Tara could only think to get Lady Alwyn away from here.

"Anna. Mary. Help me, please. Let us get the lady to her chamber."

Just then a warrior wearing Buchan's colors appeared from the castle. "My lord. We have received word from the border guards that the Kincaids and their army have crossed over into Alwyn territory, but have stopped. They appear to await our response."

The women left the men, entering the castle, where Magnus intercepted Tara and drew her back and away, out of hearing of the two maids, into deeper shadows against the stairs.

He watched over her shoulder for any intrusion, his hand on her arm. "Be ready, for the carriage bearing Buchan's standard will come for you—"

She shook her head, her heart seizing in fear because she knew why he insisted on her leaving, on getting to safety. Because he believed there was a chance he wouldn't come back. "I won't go. You will triumph. You will come back for me."

"Tara, *listen* to me," he said, his voice rough—his gaze pleading. "Let the riders take you, as planned, to the priory. It is far away from here. You'll be safe. Wait for me there, with Elspeth. Do you understand?"

She finally knew what he was doing, sending her as far away as possible. Because the Kincaids might not triumph. Because he might die.

She nodded, tears filling her eyes. "I will wait for you there."

He kissed her once, hard and passionately—and in the next moment, was gone.

* * *

Magnus returned with the others to the laird's chamber, in armor, his weapon sheathed at his side. There, the earl and the laird donned their armor, along with his lordship's sons.

"There he is." Buchan raised his hands in greeting. "The future laird of this clan."

The Alwyn nodded, seemingly recovered from the shock of his son's death. "Aye, Magnus will serve the clan well."

Magnus flinched inwardly.

He turned to the Alwyn. "If I am now your heir, then I must understand what I'm fighting for. Why I will confront and kill my good friend, Elspeth MacClaren's husband." He held his stance, proud and tall. "I have asked questions, and been denied the answers, time and time again. Like an outsider. But I am an outsider no more. Arm me with the answers. I deserve to know why I am to hate this enemy. We were once allied to the Kincaids. Why did we rise up against the laird and his clan?"

The laird leaned forward. "Because like the marriage agreement with Mistress Iverach, both of them . . . it benefitted me and this entire clan, to do so."

"I heard he was a traitor. But there were many so-called traitors in that day, who did not agree with King David's policies with the English. What made this traitor so grievous?"

"He simply was," answered the Alwyn darkly.

Buchan nodded. "Indeed. He simply was."

The two men quit the room, one after the other. Frustrated by his failure to extract a true explanation, Magnus looked down at the ground for a moment, but looked up as Duncan passed by, then Robert.

And yet Robert paused, his eyes reflecting deep inner torment. "Welcome to my world. You're son enough to do his bidding. To kill and betray as he commands, in the name of blood and loyalty. But what loyalty is shown to me? To you? As you said, the Kincaid was no more a traitor than any other highlander."

"What was it about?" asked Magnus, his blood throbbing in his veins, feeling he might be close to the answer.

"What's it *always* about?" Robert teased, his tone and manner elusive.

"Land. Power. Influence."

Robert wrinkled his nose, and squinted. "All the boring old answers. They apply, of course, but here . . . here there was something else."

"You tell me," said Magnus.

"Hate," he answered bluntly. A smile turned the corner of his lip. "*Envy.*"

"Envy." Magnus's eyes narrowed. "Over what?"

"What else?" Robert chuckled. "My father's greatest weakness. It was over a woman."

Magnus blinked, startled. It wasn't the answer he'd expected to hear.

Robert muttered, walking further into the corridor, but turning to speak as he continued to back away. "Supposedly, the only woman my father ever truly loved." He stopped. "Only if you know my father, and his way with women . . . *many* women, you'll conclude, as I have, that he only *loved her*—" He spoke these words with obvious sarcasm. "—because he couldn't have her. But what does it matter now? The Lady Kincaid is dead."

An hour later, Lady Alwyn lay on her bed, staring out at nothing. Tara held her hand, feeling only sympathy for her now.

In the next room, Robert Stewart stood at the window, from which he observed the gathering forces in the distance, his expression sullen and mutinous. Despite his objections, he had been left by his father to oversee the defense of the castle. She feared that any escape now would be impossible, with him as her keeper.

"I will go to the kitchen and bring you some broth," Tara said. "Mary says you haven't eaten for days."

"I don't want broth," the lady responded, listlessly. "I don't want anything."

"Don't say that. I know you are grieving, but there are many who care about you. You know that, don't you? You must keep your health."

"My health," she said in a resigned voice. "It means nothing to me. I do not deserve to live."

"Because your son killed my sister? Don't say such things."

The woman pressed a hand against her heart, and closed her eyes. "Hugh . . . did not kill your sister. No, my son paid the price for my sin."

Tara started with surprise. "What do you mean, he did not?"

The lady gaze fixed directly on hers. "I . . . killed Arabel."

Tara stared at her, slowly removing her hand. A coldness spread through limbs.

"You?"

"It was . . . an accident, but I killed her just the same, in anger. They were on the cliffs. . . . just as you were with Hugh today. I came upon them, and he was . . . trying to woo her, but she refused his efforts. She avoided him . . . his embrace, and when he asked what he could do to make her happy, she told him nothing. Because she was in love with someone else . . . and that she carried that man's child."

Hearing it again made Tara want to weep for her sister. Tears filled her eyes.

"What did Hugh do?" she asked.

"Hugh said he would tell Buchan, and end the betrothal, but the girl told him Buchan already knew."

Tara's heartbeat thundered inside her chest, making it difficult to breathe. "And then . . ."

The lady's eyes widened in horror at the memory.

"Hugh was very angry. Hurt. Betrayed. As was I. She was to be my son's bride, and for her to be sent here by Buchan in such a condition, with child, with the expectation that we would simply accept her, just because of who he was, just as we have always done his bidding . . ."

"Tell me what happened then," Tara insisted softly.

"He . . . stormed away, but I did not. I . . . decided to confront her. I . . . grabbed her arm but I surprised her—and she pulled away . . ."

"She fell," said Tara, tears spilling down her cheek.

The lady nodded. "She stumbled. She fell. Trying to get away from me." The woman gasped, and covered her hands with her face. "Oh, I still remember the look on her face. Just as I will always remember Hugh's. It will torment me until I die. We could not even get her body back."

Tara closed her eyes, horrified by the idea of her sister's body laying broken at the bottom of the cliffs, until the rising tide carried her away. Just as Hugh's would be. And as much as she despised this place, and its secrets, she could not bring herself to hate the Lady Alwyn, who was clearly tormented by the guilt she still carried, and grief for her son.

Lady Alwyn let out another small sob. "Now that Hugh is gone, I intend to leave this place, once and for all, and commit myself to a convent, to spend the rest of my days seeking penance in peace. Perhaps I shall even go to the cloisture from which you came. If you can see it in your heart to forgive me, come with me." She reached for Tara's hand, seizing it. "Don't stay here. Your mother and father would not have wanted this for you."

Once, all she'd wanted was to leave this place. But now . . . she only wanted Magnus. Her heart beat louder with each moment that passed, knowing she might never see him again.

"Don't think of me now," she answered softly, pulling her hand away. "Try to sleep."

Tara sat beside the bed, her back rigid, her chest tight with anxiety and fear for Magnus and Niall, and all the other Kincaids. It wasn't long until the lady slept.

Suddenly, Robert appeared in the doorway. "I've received word that a carriage has arrived for you, sent by my father." He held a missive in his hand.

"Oh?" she replied, avoiding his gaze.

"Yes . . . instructing that you be sent to be placed under his protection, at the encampment at Rackamoor. Come, gather your things. Quickly now. I'll escort you down."

Her pulse racing, she gathered only a few items that she could carry. Her cloak. Her sister's jewelry box. She already wore her mother's necklace.

In silence, she followed Robert downstairs, and out of the tower, and down the front steps of the castle, where a carriage waited, a rider positioned off to the side, holding the standard of the Earl of Buchan. Robert brushed aside the efforts of an old warrior to open the carriage door, and offering his hand, assisted her up himself.

And yet instead of saying good-bye and closing the door, he looked inward, staring at her in silence.

"What is it?" she asked, anxiety pooling in her stomach. What if he realized the ruse . . . what if he did not allow her to leave?

He held up the missive, crumpled in his hand. "I know

this did not come from my father. And I know this carriage will not take you to him. But I loved Arabel, and I failed her unforgivably. You are her sister. Flee far, Tara Iverach, and live free."

Chapter 17

As war-captain, Magnus chose the men of the Pit to ride with him into battle. If he were to turn sides, he wished for them to be closest to him, and bear the clearest witness. These men, his friends for so long, provided an impressive escort to him, along with Buchan and the Alwyn.

Though Hugh had counted few true friends among the warriors of the clan, word of his shocking death had spread through the ranks, and hung like a cloud above the men. It wasn't that they grieved for him, but at a time of conflict, the perceived instability of leadership could cause cracks in any army's foundation—their unity—which was not a bad thing, considering Magnus intended to shatter it all to hell.

They rode to the forefront of the Alwyn forces, which were thickly flanked on either side by Buchan's men. They presented a fearsome sight, but across the field, a solid line of warriors, no less formidable, faced them.

Line upon line of Kincaid clansmen and mercenaries alike gripped weapons, and at their forefront sat Niall atop his dark horse. Magnus's brother and his kin. His pulse swelled with a pride such as he had never felt in all his life, and he knew if he died here today, it would be well with his soul as long as the Kincaids prevailed. His only regret would be leaving Tara, and the life they could have lived, and knowing the children they could have had. But he was willing to sacrifice himself for her too.

Several men accompanied the Kincaid laird, also on horses—among them his tattooed captain, Deargh. Magnus also saw Elspeth's father, the MacClaren. Though gaunt-faced and diminished from his previous stature because of his recent illness, Elspeth's father—the laird Niall had defeated only a fortnight before—had summoned enough strength to ride and face the man who had once been his co-conspirator against the Kincaids. No doubt he fought to clear his conscience.

Magnus knew, without a doubt, the Alwyn himself would never seek that sort of redemption.

His heart beating like a war drum, Magnus watched as the Alwyn rode forward, alone, setting himself forth as leader of the Alwyn's gathered force.

The laird shouted, so that all could hear. "I will not address you as the Kincaid, because I don't believe that's who you are. But know this . . . when you are defeated . . . when you are run out of this place—or *slain*—you, and the MacClaren *coward* there at your side, will relinquish your lands to me."

Only the sound of wind sweeping across the plain, joined his voice. All else was silent.

He continued, bellowing. "The Earl of Buchan himself"—he pointed his gloved hand toward the earl—"is here to bear witness to my claim, and to support me in defending what is mine. What has *always* been mine. Know that you can't win."

His horse snorted, and shifted. "But I am not an unreasonable man, imposter. Save your life. The lives of your men. Your women and children. Surrender now. You'll be taken prisoner, peacefully, and the king will decide your fate."

Across the line, Niall stared at the Alwyn. "I imagine that you told our father something very much like that, on the night you betrayed him. No, thank you. We decline. I and my brother, and all these men."

A cheer rose up from the men behind him.

With their voices, Magnus's Kincaid blood warmed in his veins . . . thundered in his heart. He sat taller and ready in his saddle, his hand on the pommel of his sword, and exhaled through his nose.

The Alwyn shouted. "Your . . . *brother?*"

Magnus kicked his heels into his mount's side, and rode forward.

The sound of his horse's hooves upon the earth drew the Alwyn's notice, and his head snapped to the side. Magnus's gaze locked onto his.

Their gazes held as Magnus crossed the unseen line dividing their two clans.

A low murmuring moved through the Alwyn ranks, men's voices speaking in low tones, broken by more than one exclamation of shock.

He turned round to face the Alwyn, and all the men who stood behind him. Buchan and his men. His companions from the Pit. And all the rest.

"My brother speaks of me," he thundered, wanting all to hear. "I am *Faelan Braewick, son of the murdered Kincaid.* Avenger . . . of my father's wrongful and murderous death."

The Alwyn's face turned white . . . his eyes flashed with rage. Silence held the meadow, and all seemed frozen in place.

Until . . . movement drew his eye, on the Alwyn side, among the men on horseback. His muscles, already tense,

tightened in response, and he gripped his sword . . . ready
to meet an attack—

But it was Chissolm. He rode forward, circling round,
and stopping his mount behind him.

"I stand with you," he said. "I am an Alwyn warrior
to my bones . . . and in this, I stand with the Kincaids."

Another long moment of silence passed. Then . . .
Adam and Quentin did the same, followed by all the
others of the Pit. They rode forward, and turned their
mounts in a line behind him.

"We stand with you," said Quentin, in a calm, loud
voice. "We, as Alwyn warriors, stand with the Kincaids."

Heat rose up through Magnus's chest. Satisfaction and
pride, such as he had never known, warmed him against
the cold, and gave him strength.

And yet in the next moment . . . other warriors followed, on horseback and on foot—a steady flow of Alwyn
men—crossing over the same invisible line he had
crossed, to stand with the Kincaids. Even some mercenaries from the earl's army.

"We stand with the Kincaids," many shouted as they
crossed, repeating the same words.

Magnus heard the distant sound of hooves, thudding
over the earth. It was then he saw a rider approaching at
some speed. Voices murmured all around, and the me-
tallic sound of swords being unsheathed filled the air.

He saw the carriage then, in the far distance, passing
quickly along the outer edges of the gathered forces. An
outrider carried Buchan's banner, but as the carriage
crossed over, passing behind the Kincaid lines, the man
threw down the standard—and circled round to trample
his horse over it.

Magnus looked at the Alwyn then . . . and grinned.
"What do y' say ta that?"

"Who is that in the carriage?" his foe demanded of the

men seated on horseback behind him. "Who just passed through the lines?"

"The former Mistress Iverach," Magnus announced.

The Alwyn's head snapped back to him.

"Former?" he growled.

"Aye, we were wed two nights ago. She is my wife."

The Alwyn, his face now red with rage, opened his mouth, but it was Buchan who rode forward and spoke.

"All of this is . . . very impressive," said Buchan, with a wave of his hand. But condescension underscored his tone. "But no matter. You dig your own graves. All that matters is my decision. It is I, as Justiciar of the North, who speak for the king."

"Nay, brother," answered a loud voice. A hooded rider rode forward from the line behind Magnus, to stop at his side. His gloved hand came up, to push back his helmet.

"It is I, John, Earl of Carrick, who speaks for the ruling council."

Magnus started in surprise. The Earl of Carrick. The king's eldest son.

"Brother. Truly?" Buchan answered in a chiding tone. "You hold no authority here, in the North. Nor do you hold authority over me."

"I do hold authority over you," Carrick replied in a clear voice. "It is I who holds the title of Guardian of the Realm, and in that capacity, I command you to come with me now to Edinburgh, to answer to the Council not only for your actions here at Burnbryde and Inverhaven, but elsewhere."

"You intend to take me prisoner?" Buchan exclaimed, his brows raised in disbelief.

"Aye, brother. You and that man there at your side, who has done your unlawful bidding."

"My lord," Magnus said, raised a gloved hand.

"Yes?" Carrick said, turning his head to look at him.

"I'd much prefer to fight him."

"I'm sorry to deny you, but I can't allow it. Not today at least. Not while my father lives. In this, you must accept my judgment."

"Yes, my lord," answered Magnus, his chest weighted by disappointment—but exhilaration, all the same. For the Kincaids had prevailed.

"Who shall govern the Alwyn clan?" said Niall, walking his horse closer. "Who shall possess these lands, and the castle at Burnbryde?"

A man's voice interjected, loud and clear. "The Alwyn council will meet—and I vow, they will accept, Magnus, now known as Faelan Braewich of the Clan Kincaid, who was declared the Alwyn's *ceann-cath*, just this morning." Magnus recognized him as a member of the laird's council.

"Who am I to question that choice?" Carrick answered. Looking at Magnus, he announced. "Have your vote, and I will see that the will of the clan is formalized. This Kincaid will henceforth be known as Laird of the Clan Alwyn."

A cheer surged up from the men, rising up to fill the air. The men of the Pit, raised their swords into the air.

"No!" the Alwyn shouted, in the moment before soldiers seized him from his horse.

Buchan's nostrils flared, as he too, was led away. Turning to look over his shoulder, he glared at Niall and Magnus, but said nothing.

Magnus heard his threat all the same. That he would return. That their conflict wasn't over.

He shouted after him. "Aye, and we'll be here waiting for you."

At Burnbryde, the celebration lasted long into the night.

They had returned from the border, to find the Lady

Alwyn in her carriage, emotional, but seemingly at peace with her husband's defeat, prepared to depart for the priory, and no amount of persuasion would change her mind. She left with a small company of men who remained loyal to her husband. The Earl of Carrick remained as a guest, along with a goodly number of his men, to support Faelan Braewick's assumption of power, but they encountered no resistance.

Niall leaned forward on the bench, holding Elspeth in the crook of his arm. "Buchan . . . in love with our mother? I still can't believe it."

Tara held Faelan's arm close, her cheek resting against his shoulder. "Most certainly, she did not love him back. After all, it was he who caused her death."

"Intentionally?" Faelan murmured. "Or did he think to kill our father and claim her?"

Niall frowned. "Perhaps we will never know."

Faelan looked into his brother's eyes. "I can't suffer the thought that he and the Alwyn will escape punishment for it. I have to believe we will meet again."

"You're right, brother," Niall said. "I know Buchan. I know this isn't the last we will see of him."

Elspeth stood. "Let's not talk of that now. Let us just be happy tonight. Come, my love. Will you dance with me?"

When it was nearly dawn, Faelan drew Tara into his arms, and kissed her again, long and sweet, and best of all, in full view of everyone around them.

"It is late, my lady, my *Bain-tigheanachd*," he murmured. "Come with me."

She sighed, exhausted . . . and more happy than she could ever have imagined. She did not know where he took her—where their new chambers together, as man and woman, would be—but they did not go to the tower, which suited her very well.

It was not a private chamber where he led her. Instead, he paused at the door of the chapel, and drew her inside.

To her surprise . . . a priest waited there, at the altar, dressed in his vestments.

He wasn't alone. Waiting there with him, their faces illuminated by candlelight, were Niall and Elspeth, Carrick, and all of the warriors of the Pit. Anna and Mary, too. Deargh. And the two young women she had already, in the hours before, claimed as friends: Laire and Kyla. Everyone smiled back at her. Some, with tears in their eyes.

"What is this?" she asked, her heart filled with love for all of them. Her new family.

"Will y' marry me, Tara?" He looked at her, his blue eyes vivid with adoration and love.

She looked at him, her eyes filling with happy tears. "We are *already* married."

He grinned. "But will y' marry me again?" He took both her hands in his. "This time with love in your eyes? A smile on your lips? And a kiss after speaking the vows?"

"Aye," she answered softly. "Aye, Faelan, my Kincaid rebel. That I will."

Stay tuned for more Kincaid romance
from Lily Blackwood with the

WARRIOR
OF CLAN
KINKAID

Coming soon from St. Martin's Paperbacks